THE KEEGAN TRAIL

Kurt James

DEDICATION:
I would like to dedicate this book to my brother
Craig Dale Reifschneider:
End of the darkness, there will be a light as your steps
are one after another,
Sometimes you were my hero, sometimes my foe - but
always my Brother.
Your life, our lives as brothers - what a twisting
whirlwind as time flew,
Good bye Big Brother, just know that I always honored
and loved you.

ACKNOWLEDGMENTS:
Once again I want to thank my lifelong friend Kurt "Wally" Wollenweber who without his continuing support I could not fulfill my dream of being a storyteller.
I would also like to thank my co-worker and friend Rick Paulson for his efforts in helping me fine tune my work of fiction.

Disclaimer:
This is a work of fiction. Names, characters, businesses,
places, events and incidents are either the products of
the author's imagination or used in a fictitious manner.
Any resemblance to actual persons, living or dead, or
actual events is purely coincidental.

KURT JAMES

KURT JAMES

TABLE OF CONTENTS

CHAPTER 1

We were pushing the horses hard trying to stay ahead of those Redlegs, but they were tiring fast and there was not much left in them. We were going to have to find a place suitable to make a stand before both horses gave up. I had never run a horse to death, and I was not about to start now. My three year old mare "Sammy," which was short for Samantha was just about done for. Sandy's horse named "Horse" was just as bad as mine.

Looking back over my shoulder, I could see the former Union soldier named Captain John Merna and two of the other five lift their Winchesters to their shoulders to fire even more 44 slugs in our direction. Even though more than ten years had passed since the end of the Civil War, these bastards were still hunting down anyone with a Missouri accent. No wonder it was called Bloody Kansas before and during the war. I hate Kansas.

Feeling the heat and hearing the air sing as one of those 44 slugs split the air by my head, I was thankful that those Union boys could never hit anything firing from horseback. That being said, that last one was a tad close for comfort. Way too close.

Sandy started to cross at a full gallop in front of me, forcing Sammy and myself to make the turn with him. Just as I was about to give him the ole' stink eye, he pointed to an old farm house - a wooden one instead of a sod house. I would have preferred a sod house because they stop bullets better and not much to burn except maybe part of the roof.

Feeling Sammy stumble and almost go down told me that the old wooden farm house just in front of us and a couple of miles east of Dighton Kansas would have to do.

Glancing at Sandy, I shook my head up and down in a "yes" motion indicating to my best friend that I understood, and he took point as we headed to the old abandoned house.

With Captain Merna and the other five Redlegs not more than a 100 yards behind us, I glanced at Sandy, knowing he knew the drill and would grab all of his weapons and what ammo he had as soon as we dismounted. Near death experiences and fighting Union Redlegs were not new to us seeing how we had fought on the southern side of the War Between the States.

Both Sandy and I pulled hard back on our reins and dismounted on the run with a practiced maneuver. Almost with the same motion of pulling my Winchester from its scabbard and slapping Sammy on her left hindquarters to send her galloping away, I made fast tracks toward the door of the old house hoping that the door was not locked or barred in some way.

Sandy has always been a tad faster than me on his feet and got to the door before me. With no time to see if it was indeed locked, he gave it a heavy kick with his boot, and the door sprung open as we both piled in as three 44 slugs splintered the door frame. I quickly moved to my left and slammed the door shut as two more slugs hit the door, the last one ricocheting off to parts unknown.

Using my lever action, I jacked a 44 shell into the firing breech of my rifle and found an open window and let loose two rounds in quick succession in the general direction of those Kansas Redleg boys to keep them honest and ducking their heads.

The midsummer dust was still swirling in the air as John Merna and his boys dismounted in a hurry, slapping their horses to scatter them so they would not get accidentally shot. Sandy fired a couple of shots in their direction as well before he said, "Do you believe it Mac? It has been over ten years and those boys still wear them damn red leggings. I still cannot imagine being that mad about the little ole' Civil War. Remind me again my friend - who won the war?"

Firing and missing once at an exposed leg stuck out from behind an old wagon about seventy feet out, I started to laugh at Sandy, "They won Sandy, and we lost."

Looking at me with a smile stretched from ear to ear, he replied, "I just don't get it why they are still mad! You and I have not worn any gray except trail dust since before Robert E. Lee gave up his saber."

Sitting down with my back against the front wall, I was thankful for whoever had built this house; it must have been a fine carpenter because none of those 44 slugs seemed to make any holes in the wood siding.

Since Captain Merna and his Redleg boys quit firing at the house realizing it was not doing any good, I took the time to ponder a few things. The house, as I had already determined, was abandoned but well built. Not one piece of furniture was left, and the one room house was completely empty except for Sandy and myself. The broad glass windows had long ago succumbed to the Kansas summer heat and the winter cold and were cracked and broken. We could defend this place for a long spell if Merna and his boys didn't set it afire. Of course, those Redlegs were always setting things on fire during the war. I guess it was not a question of if, just a question of when. Just a matter of timing is all.

Sandy was taking this lull in the action to eat some venison jerky as he glanced out the window from time to time to keep tabs on Captain Merna and his band of misfits. He of course had a huge smile on his face.

Ron "Sandy" Sands had always been my best friend growing up. Women seemed to find him handsome with a 6'2" solidly built frame. He was built like his father and could move like the wind. His hair was dark and most of the time he let it grow long until it was lying on his shoulders. He tried to keep his face clean shaven when we had adequate water available to shave, thinking the ladies liked him better that way. He was a dead shot with any rifle and a fair shot with his Colt pistol. Then there was his constant smile.

Even in the heat of battle, he was always smiling and never seemed to be bothered much by the bullets being flung around him. He was one of a kind that's for sure. He was a good and decent man, and I could not have asked for a better best friend.

Sandy always called me "Mac" even though my name was McCall Patton. Sandy and I were roughly the same build except I had larger hands, which is what Sandy always said was the reason I was such a fast draw with my Colt pistol. My hair was dark like Sandy's hair, but I liked to keep it short and tidy like my Ma always liked it. Most folks that we ran across just assumed we were brothers since we looked so much alike.

We both grew up in Clay County in Western Missouri; some folks called Clay County "Little Dixie," and it was also home of Frank and Jesse James who were my second or third cousins. I could never remember which.

Missouri back during the Civil War was a border state and some fought for the Union, but most fought for the south. Coming from an area called "Little Dixie," Sandy and I ended up on the southern side of the conflict. It was in our blood and most of our kin fought for the "Missouri Bushwhackers" as did we. The Kansas and Missouri border became a battlefield all on its own that most of the time had nothing to do with the real reasons which brought about the Civil War. We fought the Kansas "Jayhawkers" and of course the "Redlegs" which were Union forces even if they were never recognized by the U.S. Government. Captain John Merna and this bunch were the worst of the worst.

Sandy and I were not part of the raid on Lawrence, Kansas that massacred more than 200 people by Quantrill's Raiders, whose band consisted of a lot of the same folks we fought alongside. Sandy and I were disgusted at what transpired that day and left the fighting behind and went home to work our farms with our families. It was back home where I had my first run in with Captain Merna.

At the end of the Civil War, Captain Merna and his brother Bob and a bunch of renegade Redlegs raided into Clay County hoping to find Frank and Jesse James. Of course they never found Frank or Jesse, but they burned the home I grew up in to the ground after killing my folks in an all-out pitched battle. I was able to escape and the very next day with the help of my best friend Sandy was able to track down and kill Bob Merna and two other Redlegs in a shoot-out in the back woods. I considered the score even and settled. Captain Merna had a different thought and had always hated me for killing his brother that day.

Even though I had never forgotten what John Merna looked like, I never again saw him until yesterday in Alamota, Kansas which was southeast of Dighton - a station and shipping point for a division of the Atchison, Topeka, and Santa Fe Railway. He was alone at the time, and we had a few words as Sandy and I bought some supplies for the trail heading to Colorado. At the time I saw no harm in letting him go about his business since the war had long been over. I had no idea he had five other former Redlegs traveling with him. Merna and his outlaw Redlegs jumped us this morning hoping to kill us on the plains where there would be no witness to their act of murder.

Sandy lifted his Winchester and said, "Heads up Mac! We got a brave soul heading this way on his horse with a flaming torch. They mean to set us afire!"

CHAPTER 2

Reaching over and taking a piece of venison jerky out of Sandy's vest pocket to chew on, I waited for the eventual report of his rifle. Anyone riding within 200 yards of Sandy and his Winchester was as good as dead.

It was not more than a couple of seconds when I heard the crack of Sandy's rifle, and he turned to me with that Sandy smile and happily reported, "Scratch one Redleg scum leaving five left including Captain Merna."

Looking out my window, I saw the rider down and not moving with his flaming torch lying harmlessly on the ground. "I reckon that will give them boy's second thoughts about trying to set the place on fire."

Sandy got sort of excited and pointed toward the west side of the barn and said, "Hey Mac, I think I see Horse."

I smiled to myself because this was an opening to a conversation that Sandy and I had at least once a week. "You mean a horse? Or do you mean your horse named Horse?"

Turning to look at me with no smile this time, Sandy said in a serious tone, "Why do you always have to do that? My horse - Horse - you dipshit."

Trying not to smile, but failing - since this was a sore subject with my friend - I started in again enjoying the banter, "What idiot names a horse - Horse?"

Using the same old argument once again Sandy replied, "Well, your mare is named Sammy and that's a boy's name. Now, how stupid is that?"

Still smiling I said with half a chuckle, "Sammy is short for Samantha. How many times do I have to tell you that?"

The smile broke out again on my friend's face. "Your Ma and Pa must have been brother and sister since in the part of Clay County that I grew up in Sammy is a boy's name and not short for anything."

I shook my head because that was a different response than Sandy had ever used before and he seemed mighty proud of it by the shit eating grin on his face. "That may be so my friend, but naming a horse - Horse - is about as senseless as naming a dog - Dog."

That famous Sandy smile evaporated and in all seriousness said, "You know when I was seven, I had a dog named - Dog. My Pa named him."

Shaking my head and smiling once again, "Oh my, that statement alone proves my point that idiots run amuck in your family."

Laughing out loud this time Sandy replied, "That may be true because my Pa was none too smart, but he could sure throw rocks. He could hit a two pound squirrel on a dead run in the head almost every time."

We both started laughing so hard the tears started to roll down our faces. A good friend knows all your best stories and your best friend has lived them right alongside of you. Sandy has been alongside me since I was six. Doing the deciphering in my head, that sum total came to a total of forty-two years. We were inseparable back then and the same was true today.

We were still laughing at our corny jokes when Captain Merna and the Redlegs started firing a volley from their Winchesters at the windows taking out any of the remaining broad glass, reminding the both of us this was one of those near death experiences we seem to have all the time. Ducking our heads and keeping low, we made a smaller target hoping that a ricochet didn't find one of us. After a full two minutes of blasting away with their Winchesters, they suddenly stopped.

Sandy started smiling once again when the barrage of bullets ceased. "You think they ran out of ammo or just stopped to take a leak?"

Most times Sandy was the joker and I was the serious one. "More likely testing our defenses while they think of a plan to burn us out."

Several minutes went by and the silence was thick as molasses as we both were staying low. Sandy slowly moved his way back to the window and inched his way up to take a peek. Soon as his eyes lifted above the window sill, one report from a rifle sang out and Sandy grabbed his head and fell back with a thump onto the wooden floor. "Son of a bitch, they shot me in the head!"

I moved quickly crawling across the floor toward Sandy, not wanting to stand and give the sniper who they now had in position a shot at me. Sandy was thrashing about on the floor still holding his head cussing up a storm. Finally getting along side of him, I could see a substantial amount blood flowing through his fingers as he held his hand to the side of his head. Grabbing his wrist gently, I said, "Quit hollering and let me take a look."

As I slowly pulled his hand to expose the bloody wound, I looked him square in the eyes and I saw no fear whatsoever, but boy howdy he sure did look pissed off. Once the wound was exposed, I brushed some of the flowing blood away to get a better look, and I started to laugh. "Hell son, that bullet didn't pierce your noggin, just took half your ear off. I think you will live."

With a confused look Sandy said, "MY EAR!"

Still laughing, "Not your whole ear, just half of it."

The smile once again appeared on my friend's face. "This is not funny, Mac. You would not think it was so funny if it was your ear that got shot off."

A tear started to form again from laughing so hard. "Quit your whining; it is just half your ear. You're acting as if your whole damn head got shot off. Besides that if they had shot at me, they would have missed because my head is too skinny."

Sandy, still holding his bleeding ear, crunched up his face and said, "Too Skinny? What is that supposed to mean?"

Holding back the laughter that wanted to come out, I said as seriously as I could, "Yes, my head is skinny and not fat like yours. If your head had been as skinny as mine, that bullet would have missed by a good two inches is what I am saying."

Sandy's face went blank as he was studying my face, and then his smile broke out again. "Oh, bullshit, your head is just as fat as mine."

We both started to laugh again as only friends can do when just outside there were men that wanted to harm us both. If that is not the meaning of true friendship, I don't know what is.

Sandy pulled his hand away and leaned closer to give me a better look. "Seriously, how bad is it?"

Taking a long gander at the wound on my friend's face, I tilted my head as if I was in some sort of deep thought before I replied, "Actually Sandy, I think they might have done you a favor by shooting off half your ear?"

Sandy scrunched up his face once again and responded, "A favor? Have you lost your mind, Mac?"

Trying to sound serious, "All I am saying is that when a man has elephant like ears and someone shoots half of it off, they might have done him a favor. Makes you more handsome I believe."

Sandy had his smile again when he said, "You are always digging at me Mac, always jabbing me with your "observations" and talking out of your ass. Besides, you have never even seen an elephant."

Looking as if his comment had hurt my feelings, "I have too seen an elephant. Well, sort of anyway. I saw one in a picture book that ole' Miss Eldridge had in second grade. I even remarked to her at the time how its ears resembled yours. We just never told you because she said it would hurt your feelings, so I kept quiet all these years watching them things flap in the wind. I got used to them, I guess, because I hardly notice them anymore."

Before Sandy could reply, another round of 44 slugs started hitting the siding on the old farm house and the walls inside as the slugs found their way through the broken windows. The air was full of wood chips from the barrage that was not letting up. Having to keep low to make a smaller target, I knew this round of fire was cover for someone sneaking up with a flaming torch. It was how those dirty Redlegs went about doing their murderous work. Just as that thought crossed my mind, I heard not one thump, but two thumps on the roof, which I was sure were torches landing up there.

Sandy heard the thumps also. Still down on the floor and holding his bleeding ear, he looked at me, "That didn't sound good, my friend."

The situation went from bad to worse as the flames from the torches caught hold of the wooden roof and smoke started to fill the old house. It started to look as if Sandy and I had two choices, and both it would seem would get us killed.

Either choke on smoke and burn to death or take our chances on the outside where a hail of bullets from those Kansas Redlegs would fill us full of holes.

As the flames on the roof started to lick underneath at the support timbers, I could see hot orange and yellow flames rolling like waves in an ocean across the wooden timber. I could taste the burning ash that was dancing in the heat as dark rolling smoke filled the house as I looked to my friend. If I was to die today, I could not think of a better send off than to die with my best friend. Being lifelong friends was no accident; it had been our fate, our destiny. It seemed only fitting I guess that we should die together.

Sandy had scooted up with his back against the wall next to me, and his bleeding shot to hell ear had been forgotten with the more pressing matter as the house was burning down around us. The starving and hungry flames had now taken hold of all four walls, and the smoke was abundant.

I started pulling cartridges out of the loops on my holster and quickly started to reload first my Colt and then my Winchester as I was choking on burning ash and smoke. Sandy saw what I was doing and that famous "Sandy" smile crossed his face as he quickly followed suit and started loading his weapons.

Still sitting on the floor, we both looked at each other with shit eating grins as we jacked a live round into the firing chambers of our Winchesters and pulled back the hammers on our Colts. Sandy spoke first, "Hell yes, let's do this!"

We stood as if we were one person and started our surge for the door.

CHAPTER 3

S andy has always been a smidgen faster than I, and he made the door slightly ahead of me. The fast spreading fire had already weakened the wood surrounding the hinges when Sandy heaved his shoulder into it. The door didn't spring open - it just fell down as Sandy ran out on top of it.

That was as far as he made it; just outside the door frame a volley of gunfire erupted and stopped him dead in his tracks without his firing a shot. Sandy stood for what seemed several seconds as Captain Merna and his Redlegs pumped even more 44 slugs into him.

Sandy was catching all the lead until one caught me alongside my head and spun me backwards into the burning farmhouse. It stunned me so that I didn't even realize I had dropped to my knees. I tried to stand, but my legs were not responding as they should. I looked back towards my best friend and saw his body had fallen in such a manner as to block the door.

Hell, we were both going to die without getting even one last shot off; I am sure Sandy, if he was still alive, might have seen some humor in that.

My head wound was seeping enough blood into my eyes that it clouded my vision; of course, at this moment in time all I would be able to see was smoke and fire anyway.

I lowered my head to the floor so I could breathe just a little better as the last of the remaining air had not been consumed by the ravenous fire yet. The heat on my back was building to the point of being painful as my body started succumbing to the raging inferno. I then felt the floor move slightly, and then it suddenly buckled downward as it caved into a crawl space beneath the house.

The four foot drop into the crawl space under the farmhouse gave me some new non-tainted air to breathe which cleared my mind for a couple of seconds. Rolling onto my back, I could see the floor had given way before the roof and the whole house was now totally engulfed in flames. From my new vantage point, I could no longer see Sandy up above in the door frame, and I could only imagine that his body was already being consumed by hellfire and flames.

The heat of the fire found new air to feed it as it rushed over me. The clean air hastening over my body brought some moments of clarity to my mind. In the few seconds of dropping into the crawl space, the new air that was nourishing the inferno raging above me also cooled my smoking clothes and body. Looking across the crawlspace to what would have been the rear of the house, I saw daylight at the end of a tunnel. A tunnel? My mind took a second to ponder that thought. Then it snapped into my mind - of course a tunnel! An escape route that was probably built for an Indian attack. Willing my body to move toward the funnel of air, I crawled and scampered as fast as I could until I was fully into the passageway. Just after gaining some safety in the three foot round shaft, I heard a loud snap above the roar of the flames as the main support of the roof had finally failed and collapsed into the crawl space, plugging the house side of the burrow with blackened timber and wood planks. With the escape passageway now plugged at one end, the tunnel started to fill quickly with smoke and ash as I hurriedly moved toward the open end of daylight and fresh air.

Gaining the exit and the life-giving fresh air, I was hesitant to breach the opening giving Captain Merna and his cohorts a chance to finish the job of murdering me just as they had murdered Sandy.

Reaching downwards, I realized that my holster was now empty. I had lost not only my Winchester but also my Colt pistol sometime during the house burning and my sudden plunge into the crawlspace. I took a few seconds in this new relatively safe end of the tunnel to see how badly I was injured. My head wound was still seeping blood from the bullet graze that at first had dumbfounded me. I realized my head was not as skinny as I led poor ole' Sandy to believe. My hair and clothes were singed, and it felt as if I had a few burn blisters forming on my back. All in all I came out of the shoot-out and the house burning pretty well intact as I stretched my arms and legs, and they seemed to be functioning now as expected.

The smoke was still heavy in the escape tunnel but had lessened some as the fire had almost consumed all of the wood and had nothing else to feed it. I could still hear the snap crackle of tree sap as it sizzled on the collapsed burnt timber and planks.

Wondering now if Captain Merna and his renegade Redlegs were still outside admiring their handiwork, I heard a couple of horses snort and paw the earth with their hooves from outside the exit from the tunnel. Looking down the burrow of light, I could not see them, so they must be directly on top of me.

They were close though because I heard Merna's distinctive gravelly voice as he chuckled as he spoke, "Jesus, that old farmhouse went up fast. Nothing is as fun as shooting and burning up a couple of lowlife rebels such as McCall Patton and Ron Sands. I guess the score is now settled for those sons of a bitches killing my brother. A good roasting seems only fitting to me. "

The next voice I recognized also was that of John Loveless, Captain Merna's second in command, "What now boss?"

Merna took several seconds before replying, "After gathering Patton's and Sands' horses, we keep heading west as planned."

Loveless cleared his throat and was hesitant to answer, "Well - about those horses, we can't get anywhere near them. They are way too skittish of us and keep bolting away."

Captain Merna, making a command battlefield decision, "I guess leave them be. We can't waste any more time before the smoke draws people and maybe the law this way to investigate and we can't be anywhere near this place if and when they get here. Leave Burt's body where he got killed and gather up Allen, Randy, and LB and let's make tracks toward Colorado."

Having said that, the Captain and Loveless started moving their horses toward the west. The only good news on this murderous day was that they were not taking Sammy and Horse with them. Little did Captain Merna know that he and his remaining Redlegs would pay the price in blood for what they did today. It was not a matter of if - it was only a matter of when!

Deciding to wait in the escape passageway until I was sure that the Captain and his Redleg renegades were long gone, I thought about the five men I now was going to have to track down and kill. You don't get away with trying to kill me and slaying my best friend without some payback.

Captain John Merna was of course the leader of the Redleg renegades and was a Jayhawker through and through. He was a tough and tumble man known to have killed a few men with just his fist, but during the war, it was rumored that the Captain took a sadistic pleasure in finishing off those that were dying and helpless with his command saber that he wore with pride. The Captain would just ride up to the fallen soldiers and dismount and coldly look in their eyes as he pierced them with his gleaming saber. The Captain was shorter than I and about six feet tall and weighing about 200 pounds. The Captain's hair was short and dark and he always seemed to have a week's worth of brown stubble on his face. I saw yesterday and today that he still carried that command Civil War saber that he loved to use on the helpless, and it was obvious he could not let go of the war that ended more than ten years ago. Even with all that burning hate for the Confederacy and especially any rebels from Missouri, he still was a man that commanded respect and loyalty from those that followed him.

John Loveless was Merna's second in command and was loyal to his leader like some old hound dog. Loveless was older than Merna and had shoulder length white as snow hair that matched his goatee that he liked to wear. He was a small man and if I had to put a number on it, I would say he topped out at about 150 pounds. I heard tales that he had been a great sharpshooter during the war and had shot numerous Missouri Bushwhackers out of their saddles in his day. He seemed to be just as ruthless as his commander.

Allen Wells was a skinny no-good no-account that carried two Colt pistols and fancied himself as a quick draw. He carried his pistols with the grips pointed forward. He had short blonde hair with a short matching beard. He of course was from Eastern Kansas, and the story was that his father was killed fighting some Missouri Bushwhackers near the border and had an ax to grind against any and all rebels from Missouri.

Randy Vaughn was sort of a mystery to me. I had never heard from what part of the country he hailed. He was small with short dark hair and was clean shaven and looked like a school boy even though he was in his late forties or early fifties. He was hell on wheels it was said with his Colt 44 that he had tied down on his right side.

Larry Brown, known only as LB, was probably next to Merna the most dangerous man of the bunch. He was about 5'10" tall and weighed in about a buck eighty, clean-shaven with dark brown hair. His family was massacred in Lawrence, Kansas by those that rode with Quantrill's Raiders and it would seem he had not forgotten it. He was by all accounts the fastest draw of all the Redleg renegades with deadly accuracy when it came to standing up fights.

I had earned a reputation since the war as a man to be reckoned with my Colt pistol as well. It was a reputation that I never wanted or needed, but nevertheless I still had. Some said LB was just as fast as Lucas Eldridge, Johnny Ringo, Chance Bondurant, and myself.

Feeling that enough time had passed, I crawled out of the escape tunnel and stood and stretched the kinks out of my muscles and gave my "come to" whistle so Sammy and Horse could find me.

CHAPTER 4

The escape tunnel exit was sandwiched in between what was left of the house and a small brook that was a couple of feet wide. Walking to the brook, I looked at my hands and arms which were completely covered with soot and ash from the fire. As I looked back toward the house, I was thankful that the person who had built such a solid structured home had the foresight to dig the escape tunnel.

My only wish was that Sandy or I would have thought to look prior to the house being set afire. A sense of guilt was starting to set in with the realization that Sandy was dead.

Sammy and Horse in no time had located me and with plenty of snorting, tossing of their heads, and pawing the ground with their hooves, they seemed plumb happy to see me. Horse, even though she was happy, kept looking over her shoulder back toward the smoldering burnt out relic of the farm house looking for Sandy. Seeing this brought a tear to my eye. Sandy and Horse had a special connection that most people never even have with other folks. Sandy's death was going to be hard on her when she realizes he is not coming back.

After my initial cleanup I was able to get most of the soot and ash free from my arms, hands and face. My hair was singed in several places and had a couple of burns starting to pus up on my back. I would have to keep them clean so they did not get infected.

First things first, I stripped the saddles off of both horses and started to rub them down, giving each a good brushing with my wooden curry comb from my saddlebag. After the rub down and brushing, I fed them both what little grain I had and each got some sugar for a treat. I left them both un-hobbled so they could graze on the tall summer grass that was growing abundantly after recent rains here in the Western Kansas plains.

The day was growing late and the sun within the hour would drop below the western horizon. Looking skywards, I could see what looked like rain clouds gathering in the north, probably too far away to give Sandy and me any trouble this evening. Wow! I can't even believe I just had that thought. It still had not really sunk in that my best friend was no longer here. Sandy was dead and I was just going to have to deal with it. I really should look after his remains but could not bring myself to do it right now. Our friendship down through the years I didn't take lightly, and I will miss him so. We were both capable men, but we were stronger together. Sometimes he was my hero, but he was always my brother.

I needed to clean my bones that were the results of the fire and put on clean clothes. Reaching into my saddlebag, I produced a somewhat clean pair of Levi denim trousers, a clean pair of wool socks, and a new flannel shirt that I had purchased several days ago in Larned, Kansas. I had lost my hat along with the Winchester and one of my Colt pistols in the fire. A new hat was going to have to wait until I made it into the town of Dighton.

I stripped off my blackened clothes, and I washed my body and my clothes the best I could in the small brook. After cleaning my scorches, I gathered up my tin of chokecherry poultice that I had brought all the way from Missouri. Chokecherry had been and still was the Plains Indians' cure-all for all types of ailments such as a cough, colds, the shits, wounds, sores, pains, and severe burns. They swore by it, as did I, and always had a tin of the poultice.

After smoothing some on all my burns that I could reach, I started to even feel better.

After dressing and stamping my feet back into my boots once again, I gathered up my saddlebags and located my backup Colt and loaded it from shells from the loops on my holster. It felt like growing a new arm just having a Colt back in my holster. After palming my pistol several times, I felt just as fast as I was before and ready to take on Captain Merna and his renegade Redlegs.

Once I was well heeled with my pistol, I walked over to Sandy's and my saddles and flipped them over. Years ago we got into the habit of stashing money in a hidden pouch that we had stitched in between the skirt and the back jockey on our saddles. Counting the money that was still in my pocket with the $500 from my saddle and $300 from Sandy's saddle, I had a total of $857. That was more than enough money for what I needed to do.

The grumblings in my stomach reminded me that I had not eaten all day and since no trees or wood were to be had, I gathered enough dried buffalo chips for a decent cooking fire. I fried up a warm meal of fried beans and fatback bacon, and the chore of cooking was keeping my mind occupied for the time being.

I kept looking toward the burnt out farmhouse with smoke tendrils still rising above what remained of the charred wood, hoping it was all a dream. As the minutes turned into hours, it was really starting to sink in that Sandy was dead to this world. No more of those famous Sandy smiles or jokes about his horse and his family. No more having my best pal having my back. Never thought about going through life without him; it never crossed my mind. It was driving me crazy having Sandy there one minute and still being a big part of my life, and just like that he would never be again.

Darkness had fallen and there would be no sleep for me until I went and looked at what was left of Sandy. The clouds had stayed in the north for now, and the sky above my head was filled with a half moon and more stars than I could count. The wind had picked up some, and the tall Kansas plains grass was swaying to the tune of the midnight wind. Sandy had always said there was magic in the wind at night, and he reveled in the sound of what he called the "Midnight Wind." I always thought when he spoke of such things that it was silly and childlike. Now I am not so sure that maybe

Sandy was more in touch with nature than I would ever be. I made a promise to myself right here, right now that I would pay more attention to all those things that made Sandy happy like the tune and the magic of the midnight wind.

Although a half-moon, it was plenty bright tonight to see by as I made my way back to the skeleton of the burnt out farmhouse. I walked slowly as more than a few thoughts of my friend filled my head.

Sammy and Horse decided to join and followed behind me. I think they both knew that my mind was troubled and that Sandy was gone. Sammy was smarter than most people that I had come across, and Horse was second only to her.

Standing where the front door of the old farm house used to be, I saw exactly what I thought there would be. The hellfire had been so intense that Sandy's body had all been consumed and there was not much left to bury. My friend, my compadre was nothing but bone fragments and scattered ashes.

Almost falling over with grief, I squatted Indian style as the tears started to flow. My Mama use to say grief is really love, it is all about trying to give that love and you no longer can. Looking at the ashes that remained of Sandy, I realized sometimes your heart needs to catch up with what your mind already knows.

Lying down on my side, I reached out with my right hand and grabbed a few ashes, not knowing if they were wood or the remains of my friend, but it seemed like the right thing to do. I slowly rubbed them in my fingers for reasons I cannot explain. I cried; I didn't sob for Sandy, for he would have thought sobbing was not manly. I cannot tell you of the sense of loneliness I felt at this moment. I was empty on the inside. I had known Sandy for more than forty years and not once had I ever told him I loved him. Men from Missouri especially from "Little Dixie" never said those words to another man. It was how we were raised. Pulling my fingers and the ashes closer to my face with emotion in my voice, "I wished I had said it when you were alive, but I know you knew it in your heart. I loved you Sandy and you will be missed."

Exhausted, I rolled over onto my back tuckered out after the fight with the Captain Merna and the Redlegs. Closing my eyes to try and stop the tears did not work; it only slowed them down some. After losing track of the time in my sadness and in the dark of the night, I fell asleep next to the ashes of my best friend.

CHAPTER 5

Waking about an hour before dawn, I was stiff and sore from the events of yesterday and sleeping on the ground probably did not help. Walking back to the brook behind the house, I cleaned up once again.

With no desire to start a fire and cook some breakfast, I ate a cold meal of elk jerky and hard biscuits left over from a couple of days ago.

With practiced ease, I saddled and packed Sammy and Horse and they seemed sullen this morning. My thoughts were that the new day drove home the fact to both of the mares that Sandy was no longer with us.

As I stepped into the stirrup and squared myself into the saddle, out of habit I reached up to tug down my now non-existent hat. It was going to be a long hot day without a hat. Sandy would have had a field day with that and would have kidded me nonstop for days. I am going to miss my old partner that's for sure.

With Horse tied behind Sammy, I gave her some rein and her head and walked both horses back up to the front of the burned out farmhouse. Dismounting, I took an old sugar sack and fed the last of the sugar to the horses and walked back to the very spot that Sandy had died.

Bending at my knees and with a couple of tears in my eyes, I scooped up five handfuls of bone fragment and ashes of my recently departed friend and carefully placed them in the sugar sack. Sandy and I had made plans on doing some gold prospecting in the mountains of Colorado and by golly Sandy was still going to make the trip even if he was just a couple of handfuls of soot. Other folks might not understand this, but Sandy would have still wanted to go. So go - he shall.

Tying Sandy's sugar sack tightly so he would not spill out, I then cautiously placed him in the saddlebag on Horse. As I started the horses west towards Dighton, Kansas, both horses looked back several times as if to say goodbye. Sandy's death was going to take some time to sink in for the horses and myself.

I had never been this far west in my lifetime; everything in front of me, every step was new territory that I had never seen before. Sandy and I had gotten a wild hair to travel to Colorado and see the Rocky Mountains for ourselves and do a little gold prospecting.

Now that Sandy was dead, nothing as far as the adventure ahead had changed except the fact I had five renegade Redlegs that had to be dealt with first and foremost. I heard Merna telling Loveless that they were heading west to Colorado as well. I can't wait to see the look on Captain Merna's face when he sees the one and only Mac Patton ride up. There would be blood, of course. Not mine, theirs; they just had their chance.

About midday I spotted what must be Dighton, Kansas just ahead. Dighton was a brand new town that sprang up on these windswept Kansas grasslands. A couple of years before the Civil War, they had that Homestead Act where the government gave you 160 acres of land which used to belong to the railroads. To gain full ownership, all you had to do was improve the land and live on it for a full five years. Dighton and towns just like it scattered across the west became supply depots for all those hard working homesteaders for the surrounding countryside.

Today was warm, but not too hot with a slight wind out of the north, keeping the horses and I cooled down some. My head was starting to burn though from not having a hat to keep the sun at bay from cooking my brains in my noggin.

I had not seen one tree close or far since leaving the farmhouse that Captain Merna and his boys burned down. Come to think of it, I don't recall seeing one yesterday as we hot footed it when we got jumped just right outside of Alamota. Men like myself have to have trees. I could only guess how brutal the winter could get here with no trees for shelter and to slow the drifting snow.

I rode down the dusty road that was the main street of Dighton…which wasn't much to write home about. If I wanted to give Sammy some spur, I would be on the other side and heading out of town in less than a minute. There were five houses, Moomaw Dry Goods store, Maughlin Saloon, which doubled as an eatery, and of course a jail house that had a wooden sign attached to the front proclaiming Gary Lewis as the town Marshal and Bruce Lewis as the Deputy Marshal. Carpenters were busy hammering away and building two new buildings; one looked like a post office and the other was a two-story affair that was more than likely some sort of hotel.

A new hat, ammo, Winchester rifle, and a new Colt pistol were my priorities so I dismounted and hitched Horse and Sammy to the hitching post just outside of the Moomaw Dry Goods store. Once inside the proprietor named Dan was a likable fellow and eager to make a sale. After coming to terms on a brand new Winchester 73 rifle, a used Colt pistol, 100 rounds of ammo, three pounds of beef jerky, two pounds of fatback bacon, a sack of beans, salt, sugar, flour, and three cans of peaches, I had just about everything I needed except a new hat. Dan explained that there was not a new hat to be found in all of Dighton at this time, but he had a used one that he took in on trade if I wanted to take a gander at it. What he showed me was a sorry looking affair that had seen better days. It was misshaped and sweat stains made up most of the coloring on what use to be a white hat. Holding this hat in my hands and turning it over a couple of times thinking it would just fall apart, I said, "The previous owner must have been in dire straits to have to negotiate a settlement on a bill to give up such a fine looking hat."

Dan Moomaw's face went blank and he stared at me with some bewilderment, which I thought was just about the funniest thing I had seen in a long while and a huge grin broke out on my face.

Seeing me smile, Dan lightened up and smiled also as he replied, "I was pondering if you were actually impressed with the hat or not."

Hearing Dan's words started us both laughing. After thirty seconds or so of some good ole' boy laughter Dan said, "Seeing how I have been trying to sell this hat for two months now without any takers, I will just throw it in with the rest of your purchases, Mister?"

Tugging down my sorry looking new hat on my head, I said, "Patton, McCall Patton. Most folks just call me Mac."

Now you would have thought I had just shot Dan Moomaw because his demeanor went south and his smile evaporated. He stumbled his words as he spoke, "Mac Patton? As in Rebel Mac Patton? The gunfighter from Missouri? That Mac Patton?"

My hand instinctively went to the top of my Colt as I looked at Dan in the eye trying to decipher where this conversation was headed. "Some call me Rebel Mac, mostly those that were and are my enemies. I prefer just plain ole' Mac. As for a being a gunfighter Mr. Moomaw, that is a reputation I never wanted nor do I deserve. That would imply that I enjoy the act of a gunfight. I assure you that I am scared shitless every time it has come down to them or me. I just have been given enough talent to be faster than those that wanted to see me dead."

CHAPTER 6

Dan the proprietor said in a level voice, "I understand Mr. Patton that sometimes the road that life gives us is not of our own choosing. Now standing here with you, I can see that you are a man of integrity and wisdom. I should also add you also carry yourself as a man that I would not want to cross. I think that is a good thing."

Reaching out to shake Dan's hand, I stated, "In my younger days Mr. Moomaw, I would have killed a man for trying to sell me such a shitty hat!"

Dan's face once again went blank as my joke seemed to be a little too real for someone I had just met. His hand was extended but did not grasp mine until I laughed and smiled. Now laughing with the tension eased, Dan grasped my hand in a hardy handshake and pumped it up and down as a little kid would do. "All I could think of I just sold a Colt pistol to you, Mr. Patton."

The absurdity of that statement got us both laughing as I settled up on my bill with the storekeeper.

After packing my purchases on Sammy and Horse, I took off my new used hat and once again saw how sorry looking it truly was. Snapping it back on my head, I thought to myself it would keep the sun from cooking my brain pan until I found a better hat on down the trail. As I led the horses to the hitching post in front of the Maughlin Saloon, a new thought crossed my mind, and I voiced it out loud, "As crappy as this hat may look, it is mighty comfortable." The advantage of a beat to hell hat is that it was all broken in and rode my head like a fine horseman.

Tying the horses off at the hitching rail, I took my new Winchester 73 from the scabbard and took the rawhide thong that held my pistol safely in my holster off. I had learned in my advanced years that danger and death were everywhere and presented itself when you least expected it. It paid to be cautious and to be aware of your surroundings at all times.

Looking west under the cloudless forever blue sky, I was not close enough yet to see the far mountains of the Colorado gold camps. The Kansas plains beyond Dighton were flat as far as my eyes could see. The summer grass was tall and seemed plentiful as it swayed back and forth in the slight breeze of the day. Being new to the country, I had no way of knowing if the tall grass was normal for this time of year or if it was just a banner year for moisture. I was leaning more towards it was an unusual year; I had a feeling that most years brought hot and dusty days to this part of the country during the summer months.

Using the tip of my Winchester, I opened the bat wing doors to enter the saloon. I stood just inside the door for a minute, letting my eyes adjust to the darkness of the room. Once adjusted I was able to see four folks in the Maughlin Saloon, and two of the men wore badges; I could only assume that they were the law here in Dighton - Marshal Gary Lewis and his Deputy Bruce Lewis. They had been having a drink at the bar being served by an attractive middle aged woman, and they turned to look at me. Being cautious men themselves, they set down their drinks on the bar to free up their gun hands as they turned to study the new well-heeled stranger in their town.

By the look of the Lewis pair, they had to be brothers. The one wearing the Marshal badge was taller with almost blonde hair that was cut short, and his manner was of one that was a capable man for any type of trouble that might find itself in Dighton. He stood 6' 2" and had the narrow hips of a prize fighter. He wore his gun tied down with the handle pointed backwards for a standard draw. I assumed by the badge this was Gary Lewis.

The Deputy Marshal whom I assumed was Bruce Lewis was a shorter version by at least a half of a foot than his brother. These were two gents that I did want any type of confrontation with today. With what happened yesterday to Sandy, I guess I just about had my belly full of anger, hatred and death for a spell.

The third man was seated at the far right at a table far from the broad glass windows so deep in the shadows that I could not make out his face very well. He looked harmless enough as he was nursing a bottle of whiskey that was half full sitting in front of him, but my gut instinct told me differently.

Walking slowly and non-aggressively toward the bar, I placed my Winchester on top of the bar with the barrel facing away from the brothers as I asked the woman bartender if there was a chance of getting a bite to eat in this fine establishment.

She smiled and it split her face in two that went from ear to ear as she reached across the bar to shake my hand. "My name is Donnis Maughlin, and my husband Bill and I are the proud owners of this saloon. And these two sour looking gentlemen with the badges are my brothers Gary and Bruce. To answer your question, I do have some roasted turkey and fried taters. For two bits I could fix you up a plate."

Liking Donnis immediately I said, "That would be the highlight of my day, Mrs. Maughlin."

Donnis looked at me a few seconds as if she was holding something back. As her eyes drifted upward to my newly acquired used hat, her smile returned once again and she said, stifling a laugh, "It would seem that Mr. Moomaw has found a new home for a certain hat that he has been trying to peddle for several months."

Taking off my hat and carefully examining it as if it was a diamond or a fine piece of china, "I assure you Mrs. Maughlin that I paid nothing for this elegant head warmer after Mr. Moomaw saw that my head was hat starved and threw it on top of my other purchases. I would also like to state that though it may lack the looks of fine and manlier frontier hats, it is by far the most comfortable hat I have ever worn."

Donnis and the Lewis brothers were smiling and looking as if they were trying to decipher if I was touched in the head somewhat. Donnis broke the spell as she turned toward her brothers and said, "Now for you two, you need to head over to the Heaths and help them with those cows."

Now the Lewis brothers may have been the law in Dighton, Kansas, but it seemed that their sister Donnis was the boss. I chuckled quietly to myself as the brothers Gary and Bruce finished their drinks and skedaddled off through the bat wing doors to the Heaths with their marching orders.

Watching Donnis as she ramrodded her brothers, I was taken not only by her good looks, but also by her personality. Just in the few moments that I have known her, my gut told me she was more woman than most men could handle. She was my age or just a tad younger with dark hair with a streak of well-deserved gray in it. She had a few pounds added to her frame that somehow made her more striking. She was a woman that knew what she wanted in life and didn't back down. Her husband was a mighty lucky fellow.

After the Lewis brothers had made their quick exit from the saloon, Donnis turned back toward me and said, "Turkey and taters coming up, Mister."

Still smiling after our banter over my hat and watching Donnis run off her brothers like some trail boss, "McCall. McCall Patton is my name, but feel free to call me Mac."

If the name "Mac Patton" meant anything to her, she didn't show it; her smile still remained. "Patton? We have some homesteaders in Lane County named Guy and Audrey Patton. Are you any relation to those folks?"

Shaking my head "no," I replied in a pleasant voice, "I don't recollect any of my clan of Pattons making it this far west, so I do not believe so, Mrs. Maughlin."

As she headed through a door behind the bar, she said, "They seemed to be hardworking and pleasant folks much like yourself, Mr. Patton. Go grab a seat and a table while I rustle up your grub."

Finding a table with a seat with my back against the wall and facing the man in the shadows, I could still not see his face, but he seemed content to drink his whiskey from a shot glass at a slow pace. My gut was telling me that the shadow man was not what he seemed to be, and my senses were on high alert. Laying my Winchester on the table with the barrel pointed in the direction of the man in the shadow, I firmly planted my behind in the wooden chair and waited for Mrs. Maughlin and my turkey and taters.

The food as it turned out was surprisingly very good for saloon fare, and my belly was thankful as I made my way to the bar to pay my tab. Once at the bar I handed Donnis enough money to pay for the meal and the one beer I drank plus a generous tip for the fine service she had provided.

I kept my eye on the shadow man the whole time whilst I was eating and now that I was standing at the bar, the shadow man stood slowly and finished what whiskey he had left in his shot glass and placed it quietly upside down on the table in front of him.

There was something familiar about the shadow man in the way he moved. I turned to face him as he stepped out of the shadows into the light as he spoke in a deep voice, "Rebel Mac Patton! It would seem sir, that you are indestructible and immortal. I watched you die just yesterday, but here you are eating a plate of turkey and taters. I ask myself how that could be."

Once out of the shadows, I could see the red leggings of the renegade Randy Vaughn, one of those that rode with Captain John Merna…one of the men that had murdered Sandy and had tried to murder me.

CHAPTER 7

O nce I realized who the shadow man was, everything at
that moment became crystal clear. My awareness was
so focused I could hear the tick, tock of the clock
behind the bar, and the smell of whiskey and sweat became acute
to my nose. Out of the corner of my eye, I saw that the owner and
bartender Donnis had moved to a much safer position as she
realized the danger that now was presenting itself in her place of
business.

As I turned without speaking to Vaughn, he moved non-
aggressively toward the bar and stopped about forty feet away.
Randy Vaughn had always been the mystery man that rode with
Captain Merna and his misfits. He spoke with no accent, and I had
never heard what part of the country he was from. Even though he
was a small man that looked younger than his years, I knew
enough about him to know he was better than most with his Colt
44 and was a dangerous adversary.

Vaughn raised his hands slowly and placed them on the bar
showing me that he was not looking for a fight. "I just want you to

know Patton that I quit Captain Merna and his bunch after what happened yesterday."

In a calm and even voice I finally spoke, "You quit? But it would seem you forgot to take off those red leggings after you quit, Vaughn."

Vaughn looked down at his legs and the red that encircled them and chuckled, "Hell Patton, been wearing them during and after the war, and it has just become a habit I guess. It is true, though, I have quit. The Captain and the others have decided to go their way and I have decided to go another way."

Out of curiosity and with no emotion at all, I asked, "Why?"

Responding as if his mind was troubled, "Captain Merna's mind has snapped. We used to fight for a righteous cause, but somehow that has gotten twisted since the end of the war, Patton. All he cares about are things that happened in the past that no longer matter anymore. We were heading to Colorado to the South Park region around the town of Fairplay to find the Reynolds gang's buried loot. Even though I never saw it, the Captain said he had a map taken off a dead former Confederate officer that showed the exact location of the treasure. A treasure hunt is one thing and hunting down and killing former confederate rebels along the way is another thing altogether. No offense Patton, but what happened to you and Sands yesterday seemed like the righteous thing to do since you both had killed the Captain's brother in Missouri. But the Captain heard of another former Johnny Reb living out west of Dighton pounding dirt for a living. Captain Merna wants to make an example of all of you rebels and headed out that way. This farmer, the sod buster by all accounts, is a good, God-fearing family man. I just can't be a part of that anymore, Patton. So I quit."

The history and the legend of the Reynolds gang flashed quickly through my mind.

I had heard the story about the James and John Reynolds gang before and was intrigued by it as well. The gang was large and had about fifteen Confederate cavalrymen who conducted raids and robberies in Colorado near the end of the Civil War. Not many thought there was a Confederate presence in Colorado, but the fact of the matter - there was.

Some newspapers thought the Reynolds gang were just bandits that plunder towns, stagecoaches, and gold miners in the high mountains. The truth was they were Confederates out of Texas from Company "A" of the Well's Battalion with orders to disrupt Union supply trains and gather Confederate recruits from the Colorado mining camps. After the gang's first few stagecoach robberies - near Kenosha Pass, Como, and Fairplay - local papers not knowing their real mission called the group the "Reynolds gang." It was never known if the jars of gold dust, paper money, coin, and jewelry were supposed to be funneled back to help support the Confederacy or the gang was going to keep the treasure and loot for themselves.

As the story and the legend go about the Reynolds gang, it was not long before a posse was formed to track down the Confederate gang. Of course, once confronted there was a running shootout with the posse with one of the gang being shot and killed. The rest of the gang had split up and disappeared into the surrounding mountains, hastily burying their ill-gotten gains. Several days later, five gang members had been located and captured. Several others, including John Reynolds, made their escape into New Mexico Territory with a supposed map of the buried loot. The five captured members of the gang were beaten, interrogated, and put on trial in Denver. Accused of rape, murder, and robbery, the men were found guilty only on the charge of robbery and ordered to Fort Lyon for sentencing. They never made it to Fort Lyon because they were shot trying to escape or were just executed along the trail as some believed. It would be interesting if Captain Merna had actually ended up with the map of the Reynolds gang's loot.

After I had heard and run it through my mind the story of why Randy Vaughn quit Captain John Merna and the rest of the Redlegs, it didn't mean squat to me. Sandy, my one and only true friend, was still dead and his ashes were sitting in a saddlebag just out in the street not 100 feet away. Speaking still with an even and non-emotional voice, "I am happy for you Vaughn that you finally came to your senses more than ten years after the war, but I don't think that gets you a pass on helping kill my friend and trying to kill me just yesterday."

Vaughn turned his body and faced me fully and squared up his feet directly under his shoulders in the classic gun fight stance. "I was afraid you would feel that way; I was hoping we could come to an understanding without my having to kill you now. I am curious how you escaped that burning house? I saw with my own eyes as you went down."

Squaring my own body for what was to come, "Homesteader had built an escape tunnel from Indians. Just found it after Sandy had gotten shot full of holes by you Redleg scum."

Randy Vaughn's face was smug as he started for his Colt. Vaughn had confidence in his ability with his sidearm, but that confidence vanished as I cleared my holster before he even touched his Colt. My first bullet caught him at the top of his ribcage dead center, which caused his legs to buckle and he started to go down. My second bullet was a little off center as Vaughn's body had begun to tilt to the left causing me to shoot him in his shoulder instead of his head.

Walking over to the dying ex-Redleg, I pulled his Colt 44 out of his holster and placed it on the bar and slid it down the length of it toward Mrs. Maughlin who was at the end of the bar. Reloading the two spent shells in my Colt, I watched Vaughn as his eyes fluttered some before he spoke, "Mac Patton you are the fastest gun I have ever seen. Should have known it when I saw you wearing that crappy hat that you were one tough son of a bitch."

Bending down to look into Vaughn's eyes, "Nobody gets a pass for killing my friend - nobody! As for the hat, it is the most mighty comfortable head warmer I have ever worn."

Vaughn's eyes drifted upward toward my hat, and a smile crossed his face just before he died.

Just like all gun battles that I had been in on the battlefield or in stand ups just like this one, I did not feel the victor or even happiness. Killing someone and taking everything that they will ever be away for eternity is nothing to be proud of. In most cases it was them or me is all. It was really that simple and not hard to understand.

Standing and putting my Colt back in my holster, I turned toward the owner of the saloon Mrs. Maughlin and said, "I apologize for this happening in your place of business and I wish it could have been avoided here especially."

Donnis poured two shots of whiskey, one for herself and she slid the other one down in front of me. "I heard everything Mr.

Patton, and I can assure you that you will not have any trouble from my brothers over this shooting."

Reaching down into Vaughn's vest pocket, I found a twenty dollar gold piece and put that on the bar. "It looks as if he had enough money to cover expenses for the cleanup and burial."

Donnis slowly worked her way down to retrieve the gold piece and said, "Please have a seat, Mr. Patton; my brothers will be back soon so we can put this matter in the eyes of the law to rest."

CHAPTER 8

After several hours the Lewis brothers finally returned to their sister and brother-in-law's saloon. Donnis had already hired a man to take care of the body of Randy Vaughn and to make him ready for a two dollar burial with no headstone in the cemetery east of town. As far as I was concerned, that was a fitting end for a man that took a hand in the death of my best friend.

Marshal Gary Lewis and his brother Bruce were more interested in getting some supper than taking a statement from me about the shooting since their sister had been a witness to the whole deadly affair. As far as the law in Dighton saw the death of Randy Vaughn - with a plate of warm turkey and taters sitting in front of the law officers - it was a closed affair five minutes after they had returned back to town.

While I was waiting for the eventual return of the Lewis brothers, I could not stop thinking about the conversation with Vaughn that we had prior to our gunfight in the saloon.

First thing in my mind was wondering if Captain Merna actually had a map showing the location of the Reynolds gang's buried loot or that was just a carrot on a stick for his men to keep them moving across the state of Kansas as he tried to find ex-confederate rebels to inflict his unlawful brand of justice.

The second thing on my mind was that Vaughn said the Captain's mind had snapped. Of course Vaughn would have been a good person to judge that because he had spent close to fifteen years with the man. What Captain Merna was doing now running down and killing former rebels more than ten years after the war had ended did not seem to be the doings of a sane and rational man.

The third thing was Merna went looking for a homesteader west of Dighton, who was not only a former confederate but a family man. I feared the worse for this rebel brother.

Seeing how I was free to go after my shooting with Vaughn, I spoke with Donnis about what the now dead Redleg had said about the homesteader out west of town.

Donnis rolled it around some and pondered what Vaughn had said, and she thought he must have been talking about the Irish family O'Rourke. Ardan and Bree O'Rourke were homesteading out in that direction and were hard working folks and had made good on the improvements required to own the land. She had heard one time that Ardan had fought in the war, but she was not sure on what side. They also had a young daughter about ten or eleven though she could not recall the young girl's name.

The Lewis brothers had not put much stock in the fact that Merna may be heading in that direction to harm the family O'Rourke. After a few choice words from their sister, they did however agree to head in that direction in the morning.

Thinking that time was of the essence and the sun still had not disappeared into the western horizon, I had Donnis sketch me a crude rendering of the trail to the O'Rourkes. I had only about an hour left of daylight by the time I rode the four miles west and one mile north.

After saying goodbye to my new friend Donnis and a couple of grunts from her almost mute brothers, I stepped into the stirrup and reined Sammy and Horse west into the dying sun.

THE KEEGAN TRAIL

Riding west, I started to think about the name O'Rourke. I had not known any Irish personally that had fought for the confederacy, but the southern side did have its fill of a few Irish generals such as General Thomas Reade Rootes Cobb out of Georgia. Of course, being how Missouri was my home, I knew of the Missouri Volunteer Militia that was commanded by an Irishman Colonel Joseph Kelly. I even remember some of the words of their battle hymn "Kelly's Irish Brigade."

Looking at the sugar sack riding with Horse carrying the ashes of Sandy, I knew my best friend would have wanted me to sing it - to give him ammunition to make fun of me. Smiling at the thought, I started to sing "Kelly's Irish Brigade."

Listen all ye that hold communion
With southern Confederates bold
While I tell you of some men who for the Union
In the northern ranks were enrolled;
They came to Missouri in their "glory,"
And thought, at their might, we'd be dismayed;
But they soon made them tell a different story

When they met Kelly's Irish Brigade, me boys
When they met Kelly's Irish Brigade
Didn't those cowardly Lincoln-ites tremble?
When they met with the Irish brigade?

They have called us rebels and traitors
But they have thrown off the name of late
They were called it by the English invaders
At home in the Eve of ninety-eight
The name to us is not a new one though
Tis' one that shall never degrade
And each blue-hearted Irishman
In the ranks of Kelly's Irish Brigade

When they met with the Irish Brigade, me boys
When they met with the Irish Brigade
Didn't those cowardly Lincoln-ites tremble?
When they met with the Irish brigade?

After singing the Confederate Irish battle hymn in a laughable baritone, I looked back toward the sack carrying Sandy's ashes and bone fragments for some sort of needling rapport. I was suddenly struck and overwhelmed by grief and sadness - so much, in fact, I almost fell out of the saddle and had to pull back on Sammy's reins to bring her and Horse to a sudden halt.

The storm that was deep inside of me that held my angst and sorrow of losing my one and only best friend suddenly came forth like a windswept dust devil on the western plains of Kansas. Whatever door that had been holding back the tears collapsed as my memories of my friendship and life with Ron "Sandy" Sands flooded my mind and spirit. Every moment, every wonderful moment we spent barefooted along the banks of Crockett Creek fishing for catfish or fumbling for the affection of the young pigtail girls of Clay County raced through my mind. All those reminiscences of everything that was good and decent in our lives and of our friendship spun out of control through my thinker. Even the horror of our time together in the war fighting for the Confederacy against Union Jayhawkers and those damn Redlegs clouded my mind. In good times and in bad times, my friend never lost that famous "Sandy" smile; his humor and wit was far and above anyone else I had ever encountered in my life. Sandy was sometimes my hero, sometimes he was downright irritating, but he was always my best friend.

The darkness of the western horizon overcame me as I finally was able to get my emotions under some sort of wrap and was able to stop the tears. I was just thankful I was not in some sort of room with folks and had to deal with the looks and questions about something that I didn't even know how to explain. It would have made me look weak in front of others and that would not have been tolerable. Men from "Little Dixie" especially from Clay County, Missouri didn't fret, and they most certainly didn't cry.

Sammy had turned her head and was looking at me as if I was not right in the head. Horse with Sandy riding sugar sack had also moved up beside me and was staring at me with what looked like concern. Shaking my head, realizing how foolish I must have been for the horses to take notice, I spoke to both of them in a clear, confident and loud voice, "You two need to knock it off; I just got a little blown sand and grit in my eye and was trying to clear it out. So you both can stop being my Mama and go back to what you know best and that is being horses."

After having said my piece, I could tell Horse and especially Sammy still acted as if I was still somewhat touched in the head, but they both now seemed to accept that fact and they pointed their noses due west. Having once again fooled them into thinking I was the ramrod of this outfit, I gave Sammy her head and a slight jab of my left spur as we headed west again in search of the Irish family O'Rourke.

The slight summer wind this evening was filled with the pleasing smell of wheatgrass and prairie dust. The sky was full of more stars than I would care to count, and the clouds had decided to stay away this night and let the sparkle and twinkle of the heavens rain down on me. The moon, although cut in half, gave off plenty of light to travel by, and it was not difficult to locate the crossroad that would take me north one mile to the former Confederate's homestead.

CHAPTER 9

After finding the crossroad, I turned from my westerly direction to the north. I was hoping to find the O'Rourke family safe and that Captain Merna and his Redleg cutthroats had bypassed this homestead on their way to Colorado.

Knowing that we were close, I notched up the sixth sense that was my gut feeling. Stopping once, I spoke to Sammy and Horse about the possibility of danger ahead and they seemed to understand the importance of stealth in this regard. I most certainly did not want to get shot by Ardan O'Rourke protecting his family from those that suddenly appear out of the darkness. I also did not want to ride into an ambush by Merna's men. Getting shot and killed so early in my pursuit of those that killed Sandy would only feed the humorous tongue lashing that I would receive from Sandy as soon as I walked past the Pearly Gates. Laughing somewhat to myself, I thought, "Letting Sandy one-up me even in heaven would not be desirable."

My night vision was excellent in the cloudless and the half-moonlight this evening, and it was not long before I could see the outline of two buildings not far in the distance.

The good news was the wooden house and barn were still standing and had not been set afire. No light, sound or movement was detected as I dismounted Sammy, which in this case was a good thing. Even in the darkest shadows, nothing seemed out of place or amiss. For in the darkness and of this hour of this Kansas night, all seemed as it should be.

Seeing nothing that would indicate that Captain Merna's Redlegs were even close, I decided to bed down and get some sleep. In the morning once seeing that the O'Rourkes were up from the smoke from their cook fire, maybe I would ride down and see if the O'Rourkes would be willing to feed a hungry former confederate some breakfast.

I stripped the saddles and gave both horses a quick brushing and rub down and of course a small treat of sugar. I left Sammy and Horse un-hobbled so they could graze on the plentiful Kansas summer grass as I rolled out my bedroll. After a quick doctoring of my burns with some more chokecherry poultice, I quickly found sleep knowing the horses would alert me if something gets out of kilter.

After waking up before the sun peaked above the eastern horizon, I sat up and could feel the cool early morning breeze as it came out of the north. The air felt refreshing and smooth as it parted around me as if I was not even in its way.

Sammy and Horse were close by and were grazing to the south of me. As the sky started to lighten, the sun finally crested the far eastern vista. I took out my field binoculars left over from the war and started to study the house not 300 yards away. All was quiet at the O'Rourke homestead.

Problem was it was too quiet. The O'Rourkes being homesteaders made their living when the sun shone, and folks like this were normally up by this time. I should have at least seen the smoke coming from their chimney as they prepared their breakfast. The other troubling aspect was that no horses - be it riding or work - could be seen or heard.

As the minutes wore on and the sun had finally risen in full view, I decided to approach the house. I feared the worse for the O'Rourke family.

After saddling Sammy and Horse, I stepped in the stirrup and firmly planted my behind in the saddle and turned Sammy toward the homesteader's house, giving her rein and a slight jab with my right spur as we moved north. I took the rawhide thong off the hammer of my Colt that held it in its holster while riding since I was not sure if I was riding into harm's way or not.

Slowly and cautiously the horses and I made our way to the front door, and still there was no movement of any type in or around the house, and the surrounding countryside was quiet. I dismounted, keeping an eye on the barn as well as the house in case I just rode into an ambush.

Still, there was no sound other than the slight wind out of the north. Stepping within ten feet of the front door, I called out, "Hello! Anyone home? I am looking for Arden O'Rourke."

Still nothing. "I mean you no harm, I am going to try the door, so don't shoot me."

Stepping up, I gently pushed on the door and it moved faintly toward the indoors. The door was not locked in any way. Raising my Colt pistol waist high, I used the tip of my boot to open the door all the way. Once the door was fully open, the stench of death flooded my nostrils, and if I had not seen as much death as I had in my war experience, I would have been overcome with the reek and would have had to empty my stomach.

Ardan O'Rourke it seems had made an attempt to save his family as he lay on the floor beneath an old lever action repeating Henry rifle that had seen better days hung in its support on the wall next to the front door. Ardan looked to be about the same size and my age with reddish hair that you see on most of the Irish. The bullet wound that would have ended his life was small and just above his right eye. The bullet wound was ragged around the edges and had bled very little on the entrance. The exit wound must be on his back somewhere and not visible from his position of lying on his back. If it weren't for that hole and that he was ice cold, bluish even, looking at Arden's face, you would have thought he could be asleep. There was a wound in the center of his chest as well that looked to be that of a large knife or if my gut instinct was right - a saber. The gunshot to the head would have killed him and what I thought to be a saber wound was to finish him off as he lay helpless on the floor. Captain Merna once again proved he was a bloodthirsty bastard.

Bree O'Rourke had been a very attractive dark haired woman, and it would seem had been killed after her husband; her now lifeless body lay on the bed in the bedroom. Her dress had been torn and shredded and the skirt was lifted above her waist as those that had killed her had also taken her dignity. Pulling a blanket off the floor where it had been flung during her rape and assault, I covered her. The renegade Redlegs had not even wasted a bullet on Mrs. O'Rourke - they simply had cut her throat.

After seeing the carnage of the remains of Ardan and Bree O'Rourke, I thought about what Randy Vaughn had said about Captain Merna. "Captain John Merna's mind has snapped. We used to fight for a righteous cause, but somehow that has gotten twisted since the end of the war, Patton."

There was no doubt left in my mind that the Redleg Captain and the men that followed him had stepped off the edge of madness with the killing of these innocent folks. They were nothing to them except that the husband had fought for the gray during the war. Captain Merna and his men went out of their way to hunt them down and kill them.

Walking back to the kitchen table, I pulled out a sturdy hand hewn log chair and sat down to ponder my next move. If the Lewis brothers, the local law in Dighton, lived up to their word to their sister Donnis, then they would be on the trail sometime this morning heading out here. Remembering the looks on their faces not believing that Merna and his men would be on the trail to harm the O'Rourkes, I decided it was a long shot at best that they would actually take the time to ride out here.

I thought it would be best to give these decent folks a Christian burial and then leave a note of what happened and what I found here. Then I would keep heading west toward those that killed not only my best friend Sandy but also the O'Rourkes.

Standing up to hopefully locate a decent enough digging shovel to dig a couple of graves, I was suddenly hit with another notion and I spoke it out loud, "Didn't Donnis say the O'Rourkes had a daughter about ten or eleven years old? If so, where was her body? Could they have left her alive and kidnapped her?"

Just as that atrocious thought had meandered through my mind, I heard a dog bark, not outside as I would have expected, but below my feet. Looking to the floor beneath the table, I could now see the faint outline of a trap door to some cellar or hideout below the floor. The O'Rourkes had a backup plan in case of trouble just like the fellow that had built the house that Sandy died in.

Moving the table to the side and off the trap door, I once again heard the dog bark and a very faint young girl's voice say, "Hush Hugo."

Now knowing that the young girl O'Rourke had not been kidnapped and seemed to be hiding below with apparently a dog, I said to the floor and the girl hiding beneath it, "I am not here to harm you, and I do not want you to harm me. Do you have any type of weapon like a knife or gun in there with you?"

There was no answer and I could only imagine the young girl running what I said through her mind, trying to decipher if I was a good guy or a bad guy. "My name is McCall Patton, but my friends call me Mac. I am thinking we can be friends so you can call me Mac. What is your name, little sister?"

With a wavering voice, but full of defiance the girl replied, "I am not your little sister! And you can leave Hugo and me alone now! Before you go, please take the table off of the trap door if you would."

I will be damned; the girl had not only been in hiding but trapped under the kitchen table with no way out. That would explain why she had not come out before while I was watching the place from afar. Trying to ease her fears, "So your dog is named Hugo? What type of dog is he litt…? I am assuming you are the child O'Rourke?"

There was a moment of silence before she spoke again with more confidence and still with rebelliousness. "Yes, his name is Hugo and he is just a mutt, but he is a man killer I assure you, Mr. Patton."

I almost laughed at her boldness because the dog's bark I heard was one from a young pup. "I am sure he is a man killer and a good companion and also a great protector. Missus?"

Another several moments of silence passed as she was still trying to decide about the truthfulness of a man she could not see and had arrived so soon after the deadly tragedy of what had befallen her family.

Still with that strong, confident young voice, "Okay Mr. Patton, I am going to trust you; for now just remember all I have to do is sic Hugo on you and he will have you for supper. My name is Keegan Doreen O'Rourke."

CHAPTER 10

Knowing full well the young girl probably knew her folks were dead from what she had heard from her hidey hole when Captain Merna and his men were here in the O'Rourke home, she had not as yet seen the bodies.

Making sure that Keegan's mother was covered once again and taking another blanket from the bedroom, I covered her father as he lay on the floor.

As I reached down to grasp the almost hidden handle of the trap door, I spoke with a calm and reassuring voice, "Glad to meet you Keegan Doreen."

Pulling up the heavy wooden door, I set it aside and looked down into the compartment below the floor that had saved young Keegan and her pup. What I saw brought a tear to my eye but also a smile as the young girl who looked frightened, but with an air of boldness, looked up at me with her beautiful brown eyes. She held Hugo, the man killer pup, tight to her side; he also looked scared shitless but also had his owner's air of rebelliousness as he looked up at me and started to growl.

Trying to reassure the young girl that I meant her no harm, I said with a serious tone, "That Hugo does indeed look like a man killer. Now Keegan, before I help you out of there, I want to ask you a question. Do you know what happened to your folks?"

The tears welled in young Keegan's eyes, but she held her own as she spoke without a tremor in her voice. "I know they are both dead, Mr. Patton. I didn't see it, but I heard it all. Those men that came here had hate for my Pa because he fought for the Confederacy and they killed both my parents. I wanted to come out and help, but Pa had placed the table on the trap door so I could not sic Hugo on them."

Keegan was a pretty girl with long brown hair with a reddish tint and probably was a tad over four feet tall and looked to weigh about seventy pounds. Her eyes were the telling part of her essence, and they told me she was smarter than most, and they had the shining glint of defiance that I had heard earlier in her voice. Keegan Doreen O'Rourke was small in stature only; her personality, I would wager, was big as all the outdoors. I liked her immediately.

Hugo, the defiant one, made me smile as he snarled at me, proving he was more than ready to defend his owner. He was a mutt all right and somewhat resembled the breed of dog that I know as a rat terrier, but he was a mix of other breeds as well. I would guess he was only five or six weeks old and weighed in at about five pounds. He was black with tan markings around the eyes that reminded me of a mask a bandit might wear. I liked Hugo immediately as well.

Keegan, holding the man killer Hugo tightly to her side, was still not sure of me and kept her eyes on me with a look of concern as she made her way up the six wooden steps. Hugo had not given up his snarl and grimace as of yet as he watched me.

Once out of the hidey hole that had kept she and Hugo safe from the likes of Captain John Merna and his men, the coppery scent of blood that was mixed with the scent of decaying death had an effect on the young girl and pup.

Keegan stole a glance at the blankets that covered both of her folks, and the tears formed and started to flow. She didn't scream or start to bawl as most girls of her age would have. Her tears spoke of the love in her heart she felt at the death of her parents.

After the initial glance, she turned toward the wall away from looking at those that had loved and brought her into this world. I could only imagine what was going through her mind at this very moment. Still looking at the exterior wall of her home, Keegan spoke with her voice cracking, "I thank you Mr. Patton for letting us out of the cellar. Hugo has not had any water for two days. Do you have any water?"

My heart skipped a beat on how brave this little girl was at this very moment in time. She also had been without water for a long spell, but her first concern was that of her young pup. "I do indeed, Miss Keegan. Let's step outside so we can get both of you some fresh water and air."

Keegan was still holding on tight to Hugo, and she led the way as I followed them outdoors. The air outside no longer had that stench of death, and Keegan, Hugo, and I took in a huge lungful of the Kansas mid-morning air.

Having grabbed a wooden bowl from the kitchen for Hugo, I filled it to the brim with water from my canteen and then handed the canteen over to Keegan, who drank as if there was no tomorrow until she finished what was left of the water.

Once Hugo and Keegan finished drinking the much needed water, the young Irish girl sat down and latched on to Hugo the man killer - the only thing left in her world - and buried her face into his side as the silent tears once again flowed like raindrops.

Leaving the young girl with her memories of what was and her grief of what is, I located a shovel from the nearby barn to start to dig the graves for the O'Rourke's. As I looked for a suitable place for the two graves, Keegan pointed to the west and with sadness in her voice said, "They need to be buried on the west side of the house Mr. Patton. My folks liked to watch the sunset in the western horizon, and I think it would be really nice that they could still see it in the evenings."

Heading toward the west side of the house, "Then it shall be Keegan, so they can forever watch the distant horizon as the sun settles. Please call me Mac; Mr. Patton was my pappy and now that I think of it, he didn't like being called Mister either."

Keegan looked at me with those big brown eyes and I saw just a smidgen of a smile as she replied, "I think I like you Mac, and thank you for all that you have done."

Before getting to the task of burying Keegan's parents, I saw that Sammy and Horse were unsaddled and I put them in the O'Rourkes' corral and pitched them enough hay to get them through until morning. There still was no sign of the law dogs from Dighton - the Lewis brothers.

By mid-afternoon I was sweat drenched from the arduous task of burying Ardan and Bree O'Rourke. Keegan helped as much as her small seventy pound frame could, and she was also sopping with sweat. We made crosses from some barn wood that Ardan had stored for future repair work. Keegan carved her folks' names into the wooden crosses with some help from me, and I was much impressed how she was handling this whole wretched affair. Keegan was stronger than most women I knew of any age, and I knew no matter what she would go far in life. She had sand; she had gumption - she was one to ride the river with even at her tender age of eleven years old.

Hugo the man killer no longer snarled or growled at me and had accepted the fact that I was not a threat to his beloved owner, and he even wagged his tail at me a few times.

Keegan said the "Lord's Prayer" over her folks' graves without shedding a tear. Then she started to sing "Amazing Grace" in the most wondrous and angelic voice. My mind was a whirlwind of emotions as I was still grieving myself for Sandy. Knowing the words, I pitched in with my off-key voice. Halfway through the song, Keegan and Hugo both leaned into me seeking that human comfort that only comes from touching another and by the end of the song, Keegan and I were both a mess. The tears flowed easily from Keegan and myself. Most folks that knew me would have laughed at the sight of my shedding a tear, and I would have been embarrassed to show my emotions on my sleeve, but with this young girl standing by my side, it seemed like the right and natural thing to do.

After the graveside service, Keegan and I cleaned up the best we could with a bucket of water from a hand dug well that Keegan proudly announced that her Pa had dug all by himself. After I asked her about relatives that may be close, she told me the only one she knew of was her Aunt Larisa Devin O'Rourke, who she called Aunt Risa, whom she had not seen since she was seven.

Aunt Risa it would seem lived in the Colorado mountain town of Blackhawk west of Denver.

Not wanting Keegan to eat her supper this evening in the very house that still smelled of the death of her parents, I was able to rustle up some of the O'Rourkes' chicken eggs and fatback bacon with a fresh loaf of Dutch oven bread and cooked us some mighty fine grub over a campfire as Keegan, Hugo, and I watched the distant sun fade into the western horizon as this day of death came to an end.

CHAPTER 11

I rolled out my bedroll next to the campfire and gathered up enough bedding from inside the home to make Keegan and Hugo a bed next to the fire also. During the night I was awakened several times to hear the almost silent sobs of the young Irish girl, and my heart went out to her in such a manner that I wasn't used to. With the life that I had lived with so much violence and death, I had almost forgotten how to feel for those that had to rely on others for their safekeeping and strength. I was never good at giving comfort - not that I didn't want to - I just didn't know how.

Just before full sunup, I was awakened by Hugo the man killer pup who yesterday afternoon had finally taken a liking to me and had decided I had slept enough and was licking my face. Startled somewhat, I shoved him a little harder than I probably should have before stating the obvious, "Damnit dog - quit that!"

Once my eyes adjusted to the half-light of the encroaching morning, I could see both Hugo and Keegan with eyebrows raised, giving me the evil eye. A rebuffed Hugo went over and plopped down by his owner's side as they both were still giving me the ole' stink eye. This was starting out to be a pain in the ass kind of day. Looking back at them both, I tried to match their stink eye to try for a mean stare to match their own and after I realized I was acting like a kid, I said, "Give me a break, I am not used to having a kid and a dog to look after. Besides that Hugo's breath smells a tad rank!"

Keegan had pulled herself to a standing position with her hands on her hips with Hugo hunkered up next to her leg before she replied with more than a little enthusiasm, "Well Mr. Patton, you are a tad rank smelling yourself!"

Standing myself and facing the young Irish girl looking all defiant and holding her own defending the man killer pup, I was struck by the idea she was somehow my Ma reincarnated into this little Irish lass. Lifting my right arm then my left arm and after taking a quick whiff, I decided that there was nothing wrong with the kid's sniffer that was for sure. Thinking I should give her a chore to do so this smelly standoff would come to an end, "Keegan would you please gather us up a pail of water so Hugo and I both can clean up while I rustle up some breakfast?"

Keegan stood for several more seconds before a slight smile crossed her face as she went about finding a pail. Yes sir, that little girl had sand and she had brass, and I was afraid for her future husband. Smiling, I thought to myself, "That little shit thinks she won."

Frying up the last of the O'Rourkes' chicken eggs and fatback bacon, I was pondering what to do next. It was now clear the Lewis brothers from Dighton were not going to make an appearance anytime soon or maybe never. I didn't blame them really. I am not so sure given the same circumstances that I would have believed that Keegan's family was in harm's way either. For all I know the Lewis brothers were hunting quail or fishing in some remote pond. The fact of the matter was I still had Keegan's well-being to consider for now until I could once again hit the trail looking to track down and end the lives of Captain Merna and his renegade Redlegs.

After a filling breakfast and during some well needed armpit cleaning, I thought of my options for the young Irish girl. I could back track to Dighton and leave the girl, but she had no relatives there. Scott City, the next big settlement, was due west twenty or so miles and I could take Keegan there. I could then send a telegram to Blackhawk, Colorado and her Aunt Risa, put the young Irish girl on a train, and then be done with this business. I was never much on backtracking so I decided it was going to be forward and westward toward Scott City.

The sun was already higher in the sky than I liked, and it was taking more time than I wanted to get ready for the trail toward Scott City. The first order of business was to write down what happened here with the death of the O'Rourkes and what my plans are in regards to Keegan. I mentioned the fact in the note that the young Irish girl's final destination would be in Blackhawk, Colorado and her Aunt Risa. Having never owned any land anywhere, I was baffled on how it worked with the O'Rourkes' homestead, so I left instructions that if any money was to come about from the sale of the land and the possessions, it should be sent to Keegan Doreen O'Rourke in the care of Larisa O'Rourke - Aunt Risa - in Blackhawk, Colorado.

After finding suitable clothes for Keegan to ride with - a pair of leather riding breeches, flannel shirt, boots and a hat to protect her noggin from the sun - I walked away so she could get dressed.

Once dressed, she brought out her father's hat and handed it to me. "I noticed Mac that your hat is dirty and falling apart, and I think my father would have liked for you to have his hat. It is almost brand new; he bought it a year ago in Dighton from Mr. Moomaw at the general store. He traded in his old beat up hat for it."

Keegan's gesture of offering her Pa's hat was so genuinely sweet that I took it without even trying to say no. It got me to pondering if the beat to hell hat I was wearing could possibly be her Pa's old hat. It was a small world indeed.

After saddling Sammy and Horse, I introduced Keegan to Sandy's old horse and helped her into the saddle and handed her the reins. "Keegan, you can ride Horse and she is a fine mare and gentle. Just don't pull too hard back on her reins because she will go to bucking; other than that she will let you tell her what you want her to do."

Keegan patted her neck gently and said, "She is pretty, but her name is kind of dumb. Who names a horse - Horse?"

A grin broke out on my face, and I looked at my saddlebag still carrying the sugar sack and the ashes of Sandy. "Believe me Keegan, that is a conversation that I had at least a thousand times with my best friend Sandy, but that is a tale for another time."

Once I got Keegan settled in her saddle came the part that I dreaded the most. Clearing my voice, "Keegan, I want you to know that we have to leave Hugo here. He will be fine and I am sure there is plenty of grub and water out in the tall grass for him to eat and drink."

The tears started to form and Keegan in a pleading voice said, "Why Mac? Why?"

Her tears were making my eyes cloud. "Hugo has the heart, but he does not have the legs. He will not be able to keep up and it is best he stays here."

Hugo, without a care in the world and not knowing that our conversation was deciding his future and fate, started to playfully attack my boot. There was a minute of total silence as Keegan tried to regain her composure. I looked at her and then at Hugo, who had finally gotten the tip of my boot in his mouth and was trying to gnaw a hole in it, and my heart melted, "Dammit kid, give me a minute so I can figure out how to make this work, but Hugo can go to."

Keegan's face went from sadness to almost giddy as she almost spit out the words, "Oh thanks Mac! Thank you so much! You are a good person, Mac!"

Leaving Sandy's sugar sack with his ashes in the bottom of my saddlebag for a cushion of sorts, I then added a couple of rolled socks for more of a cushion. I then picked up Hugo with his tail wagging so much that any fly caught in the cross wag would have died an instant death, and I placed him gently on top of the socks and Sandy. Knowing Sandy would have seen the humor in this, I felt somehow it was the right thing to do.

As we headed westward, I heard Hugo bark twice, and I looked back at him with his head and two front paws hanging over the top of the saddlebag, and I swear that dog had a shit eating grin and seemed ready and willing for the adventure that was awaiting him on the trail.

Looking at Keegan as she looked at Hugo with pure love and a smile that matched the man killing dog, all I could think of was, "Mac Patton, what the hell did you get yourself into now?"

CHAPTER 12

T he trip toward Scott City was uneventful, except more times than I cared to count Hugo would go to barking, and I learned that this was his signal that he needed to relieve himself on the Kansas prairie. During one of Hugo's breaks about midday, Keegan and I drank from the canteen and ate some deer jerky I had purchased in Dighton from Mr. Moomaw.

As we watched the man killing pup circle as dogs do before finding the right spot to relieve some water on some Kansas dirt, I realized that the man killing fur bag had a pee bag about the size of a kernel of corn and traveling with a dog the age of Hugo was one big pain in the butt. Sammy and Horse seemed a bit peeved as well of all the constant stops and distractions. As soon as the horses and I would get annoyed at the little bundle of man killing fur, Hugo would finish his business and start barking and wagging his tail and playfully attacking my boot as if it was some critter meant on the destruction of his owner. Trying not to smile but failing, I would give Hugo enough water to fill his now empty pee bag and then pick up the strange little dog under the watchful eye of the Irish lass and gently tuck him back in the saddlebag on Horse.

Sammy now had a routine after I had finished securing Hugo; she would stick her long nose close enough for the mutt to give her a couple of licks. Somehow, in less than a day, I went from being the ramrod of this traveling circus to just being a hired hand to the new boss Hugo. One thing about the new boss - though he was only just a little shit - he had a personality that matched Keegan's.

The warm, but not too hot day moved swiftly like the fat clouds in the lazy blue sky overhead; I realized with Keegan and Hugo under my care and along for the ride, for the time being I didn't have time to think about Sandy and those that had murdered him. Pondering that thought as it rolled across my brain pan, I have been yet undecided if that was a good thing or not.

Even with all the stops and distractions today, Hugo's traveling circus made the outskirts of Scott City an hour before sundown. Deciding to make camp about a half mile from Scott City, I took out my binoculars and studied the town.

Stopping and surveying a town before entering was what I thought of as a must do chore that I had picked up in the Civil War. Reconnaissance and gathering information of unknown lands and towns was what had kept me alive up until now.

The "City" part of Scott City seemed overblown from what I saw westward and before me. Scott City like Dighton was not even an official town. Scott City was even smaller than Dighton with just a train depot and what I took to be a general supply store. The telegraph poles and wires that led up to the train depot told me that I would be able to send Aunt Risa in Blackhawk, Colorado a telegram with the news of her brother and sister in-law's deaths and the impending arrival of Keegan and Hugo.

Although Scott City was not an official town, it did happen to sit in Scott County and after reading a newspaper as I awaited the Lewis brother's arrival in Dighton after killing the Redleg Randy Vaughn, I knew some more about the person it was named after, Winfield Scott.

The Confederacy called Winfield Scott, "Old Fuss and Feathers." At the start of the Civil War the old warhorse was the Union's senior general, and it was his war strategy called the Anaconda Plan that served to defeat the southern states. Before the

Civil War, Scott commanded forces in the War of 1812, the Black Hawk War, the Mexican-American War, and the Second Seminole War. Although at the time he was my enemy during the war, I had high respect for General Scott. How a county in western Kansas had gotten named after him somewhat baffled me though. The US government and its workings were a puzzle I have been yet to decipher.

I watched Keegan as she pitched in like a real trooper without much talk or fanfare doing the chores of the campsite without asking her. I could sense her rising fretfulness of the unknown - knowing that tomorrow she and her pup would be sent on a train to live with an aunt that she had not seen in several years. With her folks just within the last day being buried, I was sure it was a scary situation for her just being eleven years old. With never being married and with no kids or grandkids that I knew of, it would be my hope that if I did, they would be just like Keegan. The Irish girl was as tough as they come that was for sure. A soft spot had grown in my heart in just the short time I had known the Irish girl and her man killing dog.

After seeing that Sammy and Horse had been rubbed down and fed some grain and of course a tad bit of sugar, Keegan, Hugo and I feasted on a rabbit I had shot earlier in the day. For dessert we opened a can of peaches that I had purchased in Dighton.

There was very little banter this evening between Keegan and myself other than what was needed. I caught her wiping a tear a time or two as she tried to hide her sadness from me. It broke my heart watching her trying so hard to be strong in the aftermath of losing so much. Not knowing what to say or what to do with this young girl to make her feel better - I did nothing - which made me feel guilty. Guilty of what I was not completely sure, but it was pulling on the strings of my thoughts and heart. I pondered as I watched the night sky and the stars' light raining down on me how in this tiny amount of time I had come to care about the girl that was neither blood nor kin to me and that damn dog. I thought, "Mac, you are acting like you are addled and have gone soft in the head since Sandy had been killed."

I awoke just before dawn and it must have been a tad cool during the night because Keegan had moved her bedroll so she was sleeping just in front of me and Hugo was sleeping all curled up above Keegan's head and just below my chin. I was able to move slowly enough to be able to stand as to not disturb their slumber.

Stirring the ashes from last night's cook fire, I was able to find enough heat to set another couple of buffalo chips on the fire so I could fry up some bacon and beans for our breakfast. The one advantage I discovered with cooking with buffalo chips was that you didn't have the snap, crackle, and pop that would send a hot ember flying into your lap or bedroll.

After breakfast, I made Sammy and Horse ready for the trail as Keegan cleaned up the campsite and made sure our fire was completely out. Hugo seemed to be torn to which one to follow behind during the morning chores; having decided to follow on Keegan's heels, he would stop and look in my direction from time to time and bark and wag his tail.

The last week or so had been difficult for sure. First Sandy had been murdered, and I barely escaped with my life and still had the burns on my back which seemed to be hurting more today than yesterday. Then coming upon the murder of the O'Rourkes and the rescue of Keegan and her pup from a cellar they could not get out of. Now I was dropping off the Irish girl and her pup to an unknown future by sending her off to a distant aunt that lived in Colorado and not knowing if she still lived there or for that matter was even still alive. I kept telling myself it was not my problem and I had already done more than most folks would have done. Rolling it around some, I was bothered by it and it did not feel right, but it was of no concern of mine.

Once in Scott City at the train depot and after finding a suitable bench for Keegan while holding Hugo to wait on, I spoke with a white haired older gentleman who sold the tickets for the railroad and doubled as the telegraph operator.

I learned that the train would not go the 340 miles or so to Blackhawk, Colorado, but instead it would travel 300 miles to Denver. That would mean that Aunt Risa O'Rourke would have to make the trip of forty miles from Blackhawk to Denver to be able to fetch Keegan and Hugo from the train. I didn't like that at all. Keegan was tough as nails, but she and the dog would be at the mercy of anyone with ill manners or intentions along the way. The second thing was I would never know if Larisa O'Rourke would even get my telegraph. I shook my head thinking, "It is no concern of yours, Mac!"

Once that thought crossed my mind, I slapped down the money on the counter hard enough to startle the old man who sold the tickets. I was feeling angry and I was not sure why.

Now with the railroad ticket in my hand for Keegan and her dog, I asked the operator to send a telegraph to Blackhawk, Colorado. As the white haired man switched gears from selling tickets to telegraph operator, I looked at the very young Keegan Doreen O'Rourke sitting on the bench with Hugo sitting on her lap with his front paws on her chest licking the silent tears off of her face. I stood transfixed for a couple of minutes with the telegraph operator now waiting on me as I watched Hugo give what comfort he could to the young Irish girl. Turning back with a heavy sigh and a tear in my eye, I told the operator, "The girl is no longer taking the train. I would like to return the ticket for my money back."

The old man must have felt the intense moral struggle I just went through and with a smile of concern, he reached out and patted my hand while replying, "Not a problem young man. Do you still want to send the telegraph?"

Looking him in the eye and a slight nod of my head to acknowledge his kindness, "I do indeed, sir."

After sending the telegraph to Aunt Risa, I read my copy once again. "Message - intended for Larisa O'Rourke. This is to inform you that Ardan O'Rourke and his wife Bree had been killed by renegade Redlegs. I will be delivering Keegan and her dog as soon as time permits. I will send updates along the trail. Signed McCall "Mac" Patton"

Walking back to Keegan's bench, I tried to speak in a disgusted voice, "Damn our luck, it would seem that this train and all the rest down the line have been sold out for the foreseeable future. I guess I will have to see to it myself that you and Hugo get safely to your Aunt Risa."

At first I thought Keegan was going to faint when she was trying to take in what I just said. Then her face lighted up like a full moon on a cloudless night. She then jumped up and almost tackled me in a hug as Hugo decided to attack my boot again. She looked up into my eyes as her tears started to flow, "Really Mac? Really?"

Trying not to let the tears cloud my eyes, I turned my head so Keegan wouldn't see them, "Yes, I guess you are stuck with me until we get to Blackhawk, Colorado. We better get on the move since we are burning daylight moping around here."

As Hugo was safely tucked away in the saddlebag riding shotgun with my best friend Sandy, Keegan and I both got settled in our saddles and headed westward toward the far blue mountains of Colorado.

After about a mile, Keegan smiling and with more happiness than I could ever muster pushed Horse up alongside me and said, "Mac, what is the name of this trail?"

Looking and sounding confused, "I guess I don't follow what you are getting at, Keegan."

Keegan was still all smiles. "I read a lot, and most trails heading west have a name like the Oregon Trail, the Santa Fe Trail, or the Mormon Trail. I was wondering what this trail was called."

Stopping Sammy to ponder her question for a spell, "I reckon I don't recollect this trail having any name at all. I don't suspect many folks traveled this way westward."

Keegan, with a smile turning slowly into a frown, "That is sort of sad, I was hoping it had a name is all."

Still pondering the trail ahead I said, "All them trails you spoke of were just dirt and grass until someone gave them a name. Seeing how this trail does not have a proper or an official name, I don't see the harm in us naming this trail."

Keegan's smile returned with my suggestion, "Oh, how wonderful; you pick a name, Mac."

Watching the sun make its arc across the sky, knowing we were wasting time with this jabber about trail naming, I said the first thing that floated into my thinker, "I think we should call it the Keegan Trail."

Keegan looked westward as far as she could see before she turned once again in my direction and responded with, "I would like that, Mac! I would really like that!"

Giving Sammy a slight jab of my right spur, I headed her toward the west and said, "Henceforth from this day forward this will forever be called the Keegan Trail."

CHAPTER 13

After leaving the Scott City train depot, Hugo's traveling band of misfits fell into the routine of the trail now known as the Keegan trail. Sammy, Horse, Hugo, Keegan and I learned the fastest and quickest way to stop and let Hugo do his outhouse duties without too much loss of time.

The day was not nearly as hot as yesterday with the sky filled with dark clouds that were full of rain yet to be released. By midday I was feeling sickly and hot and my back felt as if it was on fire. It would seem that my burns that I received during the farmhouse fire had gotten infected. I pulled back on Sammy's reins to bring her to a halt and grabbed my canteen to drink some warm water; my arms felt weak as they trembled tilting the canteen to get a drink.

Looking back at Keegan, I realized that my vision had become blurry and she and the horses were difficult to focus in on. A steady rainfall of sweat burned my eyes and dripped from my chin even though the day was cool. Keegan said with apprehension in her voice, "Are you okay, Mac?"

Trying to ease any concern of the young Irish girl and speaking in a level tone, "I think I caught a fever. I have some burns on my back that I could not reach to do any proper doctoring and it would seem they may have become infected. As soon as we find us a water hole or creek, I am going to need your help Keegan to doctor the burns I cannot reach."

Keegan rode Horse up alongside me and reached out and touched my arm just as a splattering of raindrops fell from the sky. "You are burning up, Mac!"

Looking around for any type of protection from the rain that was just getting started and seeing none, I pointed Sammy's nose westward, giving her a slight jab of the spur as we moved out with Keegan, Horse, and Hugo right behind me. The rain was not constant yet, but looking toward the darkening clouds plump with water, I knew that it was just a matter of time before the Lord opened up the heavens for a real gully washer.

My head started to ache to the point that I felt that my brain was trying to pound a hole through my thick skull. I could not recall ever having a headache that made my vision as blurry as this one.

About a half hour later looking to the south, I saw a stand of trees and some cattails about 100 yards off the trail, and where there are trees and cattails there would be water of some sort. I tried to lift my arm to point to indicate to Keegan, but I failed miserably. The fever in just this short of time had sapped my strength, and it was almost impossible to even stay in the saddle. I must have blanked out for a few seconds. I did not recall Keegan moving up and grabbing Sammy's reins, but there she was taking Sammy and myself to the trees. As she spurred Horse into a trot, the rain started in earnest and between the now pouring rain, sweat, and the raging fever, my eyesight was damn near gone and my welfare was now in the hands of the Lord and an eleven year old Irish girl. Through the haze I saw Keegan looking back at me with rain soaked, plastered hair and she had to shout in the now quickening wind, "Stay in the saddle, Mac! If you fall, I will never be able to get you back up again!"

Opening my eyes, I could barely see that we had made the stand of trees. The cattails circled a small watering hole that was maybe twenty-five feet across. The trees were close and tight and should provide some shelter from the storm that was now raging from the north.

With a flash of lightning and a crack of roaring thunder, Keegan let loose of Sammy's reins and was able to locate a suitable rock in height to help her dismount Horse, which she did in a quick fashion. She then hurried back and grabbed Sammy's reins and led her to the same rock she used to dismount so I could use it to help me dismount. I shook my head "no" thinking I don't need a damn rock to dismount my horse. Taking some extreme effort, I was able to kick my right leg over the saddle, but in my weakened condition I missed grabbing the saddle horn and face planted the ground and the rock with a jarring thud. Rolling onto my back, I could now taste the coppery taste of blood mixed with the sweat and rain just as the thought crossed my mind, "Mac that was dumb!"

Keegan bent over me and yelled louder than the deafening wind, "Mac that was dumb!"

As my mind started to fade into the darkness and with a half-hearted feeble reply, "No shit!"

I woke to the sing - song of several bellowing bullfrogs as they splashed from the bank into the water of the nearby watering hole. I blinked my eyes several times and rolled onto my back looking at the now empty blue sky overhead; by the position of the sun, it was mid-morning and it would seem I had slept through the storm.

I sat up slowly because I was still weak, but after feeling my forehead, it drove home the fact that I no longer had a fever. I was even dressed in dry clothes. My back and burns were no longer on fire, and the thought crossed my mind how it was almost a miracle that I had recovered in less than a day.

Horse and Sammy were unsaddled and grazing peacefully getting their fill on the long summer grass in the shadows of the trees next to the cattails.

As I looked about my surroundings, it would seem that Keegan had been more than busy during the night. From the tendrils of smoke still rising from the almost extinguished campfire, I saw behind me where the tree branches were propped up and woven into a makeshift blind between two elm trees for a windbreak from the storm. It was obvious the young Irish girl had survival skills.

Just when I was wondering where Keegan and Hugo were, the cattails in front of me started swaying back and forth as she and the man killing dog made their way back to camp carrying the canteens still glistening from water droplets from being refilled.

Behind Keegan, Hugo saw me sitting up and his tail started arcing back and forth in his happiness. He ran toward me and tried to hurdle into my lap with a mistimed jump, catching my knee which buckled him to the ground. Smiling and shaking my head, I reached down and scooped up the furry bundle and pressed him to my chest.

In between the numerous licks and barks, I pointed to the campfire and the shelter that had been built and looked at Keegan and said with pride, "My Lord Keegan, you were very busy last night."

Keegan stopped in front of me with a huge smile on her face. "You look better Mac - a lot better. You had me scared for the first couple of days."

Blinking my eyes and with some confusion, I replied, "Couple of days? How long have we been here?"

Handing me a fresh canteen of water, "This is the fourth day since the storm. I was so scared the first night with the lightning and thunder; the rain was so thick I could not find anything dry enough to start a fire. I tried to keep you warm by holding you and I was sure you were going to die. The morning after the storm, I was able to finally get a fire started; then I dragged you closer and built the wind blind. I then saw all the horrible burns on your back and after heating the blade of your Bowie knife, I first drained the pus from the burns and then scraped the infection out with a red hot tip of the blade. I hope you don't mind, but I went through your belongings and found an open tin of chokecherry poultice and have been applying that twice a day. Just this morning the burns now seem to be healing fine with no more sign of infection. When your fever was at the strongest, you kept shouting out names - Sandy - and that son of a bitch Captain Merna. You seemed sad when you would say Sandy and mad when you spoke of the Captain."

Wow, four days! How brave and strong this little girl was. Most grownups, be it a man or a woman, would have given up. Reaching out and grabbing Keegan's hand and looking her straight in the eye before speaking, "It would seem lass you have saved my bacon and I will always owe you a debt of honor in that regard. I am still very weak and tired and need some more rest. This evening or in the morning when I feel stouter, I will tell you the stories behind the names I raved about."

Keegan was all grins when she gently pulled Hugo from my arms. "I am just happy you are feeling much better Mac! I don't think I could handle losing you after losing my folks. You get some rest and I will try and keep Hugo from waking you up."

Lying back down and closing my eyes, I had two things cross my mind. First was Keegan was one hell of a good kid. The second thing was I still had a score to settle with Captain John Merna.

CHAPTER 14

My fever had left on the fourth day after the storm, but it was not until the fifth day that I could stand and walk without a drunken wobble to my step. The whole time during my recovery Keegan, the eleven year old Irish lass, took care of all the camp chores while she doctored me back to health.

About twice a day I would catch Keegan looking back to the east toward Dighton and what used to be her home in the faraway horizon, and she would wipe a tear that had formed. I didn't know how to comfort such a young girl - hell, I didn't know how to comfort anyone.

What I lacked in response to the young girl's emotions, Hugo made up for in just being Hugo. He was a joy to have around the camp and he loved the Irish girl like no other. Hugo tolerated me of course and had taken a liking to my boot and damn near had a hole chewed into it. If Hugo had his way, I would be walking and riding in just my socks.

Once I had awoken from the fever sleep, my first thought was of Keegan, and my second thought was that of Captain John Merna and his band of renegade Redlegs. Merna and his men would now have over a week's head start which meant they were maybe already in the Colorado Mountains. If the story was true about his having the map to the loot that the Reynolds gang had hidden, they might already have that in their possession as well.

Fate and destiny had slowed my vengeance trail against the Captain and those that had killed Sandy and the O'Rourke's with having the task of getting Keegan safely to her Aunt Risa in Blackhawk. Once Keegan was safe, I was going to track down and kill the son of a bitch Merna if that was the last thing I did in this life. It would not be an easy undertaking and would probably in the end get me a seat in hell right along with the murdering Captain and his Redlegs.

One thing I had learned in this life is that having money and land didn't make it a worthwhile life and that friendship and honor were the true measure of a man's success. In my eyes after killing the one and only true friend I had in Sandy, it was the only honorable thing to do to make sure justice was done. Captain Merna had his judgment day coming and I, Mac Patton was the judge, jury, and executioner.

The evening of the fifth day after the storm after a filling meal of bullfrog legs and fried wild onions, Keegan and I spoke of what lay ahead of us as we started back on the Keegan Trail in the morning. I also told her about the names I spoke of during the delirium of my fever pitch.

Keegan already knew some of the story about Captain Merna and Redlegs, but I gave her some of the back story as well. I tried to keep it simple thinking she was only eleven, but she kept asking questions that only a grown-up would ask and I felt at times that the young girl on the inside was older than her outside. She was what my Ma would have called an "old soul" - though she was only eleven; somehow, someway she had the wisdom of having already lived a full life. I also spoke of my lifelong friendship with Sandy and how it came to be that his death by being shot and burned to ashes was caused by Merna and his cutthroats. She didn't even bat an eye that I had a sugar sack of Sandy's ashes and bone fragments riding shotgun with Hugo in the saddle bag.

After seeing to Sammy and Horse and making sure they had been rubbed down and been given a small treat of sugar this evening, I threw a couple of more buffalo chips on the fire.

Keegan and Hugo were already fast asleep next to the fire. The night had cooled considerably as I arranged my saddle to be able to use it as a headrest. I pulled up my blanket to ward off the chilled night air as I watched the stars dancing their starlight dance in the heavens. The moon was just a sliver of a piece of pie this evening but still a wonderful sight nevertheless. As a child, I always thought the moon spoke to me and only me, and it was a comforting sight to see it every night when the clouds didn't cover the shine and the light. Listening to the night sounds I smiled, realizing the bullfrogs wouldn't keep us awake tonight since we had made them into a tasty supper. It wasn't long with a full belly before I drifted off to sleep.

Waking up in the morning, Horse, Sammy, and Keegan - the whole kit and caboodle - along with Hugo were in good spirits and after a quick breakfast of leftover wild onions and beans, Hugo's army was ready and anxious to get back on the Keegan Trail and headed west. I noticed Hugo had gained some length and weight when I secured him with Sandy in the saddlebag. Licking my hand and wagging his tail, he seemed willing and excited as he always was. Shaking my head and looking at the man killer, I wished my life was as happy and simple as Hugo's. I gave him a hug and a kiss on the top of his head when I saw Keegan watching us with a big smile. Raising my eyebrows and feeling a tad uncomfortable having anyone see a softer side of Mac Patton, I pointed at Hugo and said, "Just smelling him to see if he needs a bath. I don't want him stinking up my saddlebag."

Keegan's eyes got larger and her smile stretched from ear to ear and with a small laugh she said, "Sure Mac."

Stepping into the stirrup and planting myself into the saddle on Sammy, I pondered, "What the hell am I being punished for to get saddled with taking care of a kid and her mutt?"

Giving Sammy a slight jab of my spur, I took the lead as Hugo's army headed west toward Colorado.

By midday we came upon another almost town named Leoti with a train depot and a general store. We stopped and replenished our supplies and were able to buy another tin of chokecherry poultice from an old, skinny, and bald headed store owner named Samuel Reifschneider. Samuel seemed right proud that he was what he called a "pharmacist." I wondered what being a pharmacist was and what they did and was a little embarrassed that Keegan seemed to know what it meant. All I cared about was that he had some chokecherry poultice along with the rest of the items we were in short supply of.

We were able to get information from Samuel that it was roughly thirty-eight miles to the fairly new state of Colorado. He also warned us that he had received a telegram the day before about a band of Kiowa Indians that had left their reservation down in southwestern Oklahoma and had made their presence known on their old ancestral stomping grounds on the eastern plains of Colorado. He mentioned so far they had not been causing a ruckus and they just seemed to be homesick. He cautioned us to be more aware and keep my weapons loaded. I sort of shrugged my shoulders thinking my weapons were always loaded - didn't make much sense to keep them unloaded. Although he seemed nice enough and well-meaning, Samuel the pharmacist was a strange duck indeed.

The next two days were uneventful as we finally by my calculations were now in the state of Colorado. The weather had been decent and not too hot, and the nights had been pleasantly cooled for good sleeping weather. The high grass around Dighton had been replaced by sagebrush and rolling hills with little or no grass or trees here in eastern Colorado. And the Rocky Mountains had yet to make an appearance on the western horizon. Keegan and I were both looking forward to seeing them in all their grandeur.

We had not encountered anyone nor seen any homesteads on the Keegan Trail, and there were no recent tracks in the dirt. We knew the train tracks were in the north some distance because we could see the telegraph poles that followed alongside of them. In two days we had not seen a train which seemed odd to me. It always seemed back east in Missouri that the trains never quit and became part of the landscape. It would appear to me that the eastern side of Colorado was desolate and empty and not much to look at.

Even though Keegan, Hugo, Sammy, Horse, and I seemed to be all alone in this godforsaken country, I had this nagging feeling in my gut that we were not. I kept looking for any indication that we were being followed or tracked and saw none. I was not a greenhorn in this regard and from my experience in the war and since then, I learned to trust my gut instinct. I knew someone was out there watching us, and whomever they were - they had skills.

I did not mention any of this to Keegan of course about my gut feeling because right now that was all it was. My mind kept returning to what Samuel the pharmacist had said about the Kiowa Indians that had left the reservation to return home. Home? Looking about, I could not imagine how southwestern Oklahoma could look any bleaker than this country and why anyone would make tracks back here. The pharmacist had also mentioned the Kiowa had not been causing a ruckus as of yet, but if it was them that were indeed watching us, the horses, our supplies, and the young girl, it might be tempting enough for them to start a ruckus.

CHAPTER 15

B y my reckoning on the third day after leaving Leoti, Kansas we were thirty-eight or forty miles into the state of Colorado and still heading west with a northern tilt. Even though the Indian Wars had long been over and all the plains Indians such as the Cheyenne, Arapaho, and of course the Kiowa had been sent to reservations, I was still as nervous as a long tailed cat in a room full of rocking chairs. Although we had not seen hide nor hair of the Kiowa that had escaped their reservation in Oklahoma, I knew they were out there watching and trailing us. My gut told me so and it had never been wrong before.

Every time we would breach the top of a gully or small incline ahead of us, I expected to see the band of renegade Kiowa. We had been moving more slowly than I would have liked westward because I was being extra careful. My Winchester was not in the scabbard on the saddle but with a shell in the firing chamber and in front of me just in front of the saddle horn.

Thinking it was important for Keegan to know how to use the Colt and the Winchester in case we actually had a run in with the

Kiowa, I spent a half of an hour to a full hour each morning to let her practice shooting. She was getting proficient with the Winchester if she steadied it on a rock or the tree limb I had fashioned for her into a shooting bi-pod. The Colt was more difficult for her since it was heavy to hold and she struggled with that. Been my familiarity that women in general had a natural eye for when it came to shooting firearms. And Keegan was no exception in that regard.

About two hours before sunset, I could see in the distance the tops of some trees that followed in somewhat of a line going north to south, which told me that there was a river or creek ahead which would be welcome relief for all of us especially Sammy and Horse.

The wind had picked up some, and the sagebrush tumbleweeds were starting to dance and roll with each gust of wind. Some murky clouds were starting to move in from the north and had the look of possible rain in them. Pulling back on Sammy's reins, I brought her to a halt, and Keegan followed suit with Horse. Taking out my binoculars, I surveyed the trees in front of me looking for possible movement. I would not be the only one that thought the river or creek to the west would be a suitable spot to stop for the night. If the Kiowa were close, they may have already claimed it and I was not in the mood to tangle with them on this day. Looking far away and then nearer, I spotted some sun bleached white ribcages of what I thought to be a couple of horses just ahead. Curious on how the two met their death so close to the water, I gave Sammy a little spur and moved forward toward the bones that stuck up out of the Colorado prairie.

Bringing Sammy up alongside the horse bones, I dismounted and got Hugo out of his saddle bag so he could unload his bladder. After making sure he was not going to run off, I squatted to study the long dead bones to see if I could decipher how they had come to die in this place. Picking up a handful of dirt, I almost cut my hand on an old arrowhead. I kicked about in the dirt and uncovered a couple more. So it would seem these dead horses had been a couple of Indian war ponies. Keeping the arrowheads to give to Keegan, I remounted and we continued on toward the water ahead.

I was in the lead and we were close enough that Sammy and Horse could smell the water when I heard Keegan in an excited voice, "Mac, look!"

73

Looking back, she was pointing toward Sammy's rear hoof, and it would seem that she had kicked up half of a human skull. Raising my eyebrows when I looked and spoke to Keegan, I calmly said, "Must have been the fellow that owned those two dead horses back yonder. Any story that could have been told about why they had perished had long ago been lost in the dust."

Keegan spoke in a respectful tone, "How sad. His family probably never knew what happened to him."

Giving some spur to Sammy while moving west, "I reckon that would be just about the gist of what happened."

Several minutes later we discovered a creek instead of a river, but still it was plenty of water and the trees were plentiful enough to give us some protection against the weather that was building in the north.

Since there were trees, Keegan was able to start gathering enough downed limbs for firewood for our cook fire this evening while I took care of the horses. Stripping Sammy and Horse of their saddles, I brushed and combed them with my wooden curry comb. After grooming their manes and tails the best I could, I gave each of them a generous portion of sugar for a treat.

Deciding with the weather moving in and the possibility of the escaped Kiowa being close, I would hobble both horses near us tonight. It would make it more difficult for the Kiowa if they were so inclined to steal Sammy and Horse. Also, it would give me their eyes and ears to help alert me in case of any danger that may present itself. My gut instinct was working double time this evening.

As I was preparing the jackrabbits I had shot earlier, Keegan struggling with another armful of wood, handed me something that she had found that I was more than familiar with. Keegan spoke in a confused voice, "Look what I found down by the creek."

What she had was a beat up old wooden stock of a Springfield Model 1861 musket rifle that was widely used in the Civil War. Sandy and I both used to carry one each and Sandy was deadly accurate with his. If the barrel had been present, it would have been forty inches long. The Springfield fired .58 caliber minié ball, and the complete rifle was sort of heavy to tote around and weighed about nine pounds.

Setting the rabbits on a spit over the fire, I sat down on a log I had dragged up from near the creek to sit as I pondered the Springfield stock. Keegan was busy frying up some beans and some more wild onions we had located on the trail today.

Looking about our camp and then down toward the creek, I said to Keegan, "I will be damned. I think this is the Big Sandy Creek."

Keegan stopped what she was doing and replied, "Not sure I have ever heard that name. Should I know it?"

Thinking back on everything I knew and had read about this place, I finally remembered enough to tell Keegan. "Probably not Keegan. It happened before you were born, and this part of the country was called the Colorado Territory back then. After seeing the skull and the horses' rib cages and now the Springfield, I believe we have stumbled onto the location of the Battle of Sand Creek. Toward the end of the Civil War, the Indians had all been sent packing to reservations and some of the tribes refused to go since the US government had not lived up to the promises in the treaties they had negotiated with the various tribes. As I recall from the stories, I heard it was here on the banks of the Big Sandy Creek that some Cheyenne and Arapaho had made a village thinking they were safe from the US Calvary. How wrong they were, Keegan. The military saw it as a huge victory against the Indians, but it was really a massacre of mostly women and children."

"A volunteer force called the Colorado 3rd Calvary of about 650 men was formed under the leadership of a Colonel John Chivington, and they were dispatched down here to end the Indian problem. It was a surprise early morning attack that wiped out 150 or so of the Indians with only about ten casualties for the Calvary. After the slaughter was done, they burned the village to the ground. Some call Chivington a hero for what happened here; others call him a coward for what happened. The funny thing Keegan, the nickname of the Colorado 3rd was the Bloodless 3rd."

My retelling of the battle and the death of those on that morning had brought a few tears to Keegan's eyes and in a quiet voice, "How sad that they all died just trying to live their lives. Just like my folks did. There is so much sadness out here and bad people."

Feeling guilty that I had triggered a horrible memory for the young girl about her folks' deaths, I stood and walked over and gently wiped the tears from Keegan's face. She latched on to my hand and pressed the back of it to her face, holding it there for some time. At that moment I decided there was nothing I would not do for this young girl. She deserved a full and fruitful life, her heart was pure, and the goodness of her soul was more than evident to me. I am sure that her folks when alive were proud of her. I know I was.

The sun just before dark had hidden itself behind the menacing clouds that had moved in from the north. The dimness of the light told me that the sun was dropping beyond the western horizon, bringing an end to the day. The wind was slightly gusting and I could smell and savor the scent of the crisp, cool water from the Big Sandy Creek, and it was refreshing after eating and smelling dust all day.

Keegan and Hugo had fallen asleep about an hour before. Even though Sammy, Horse, and Hugo were calm and acting normally, my gut was telling me it was not going to be long before the Kiowa showed themselves to us. Sensing the danger of what was ahead, I checked my loads in the Colt and Winchester to make sure I had a 44 shell in the firing chambers as I lay down and closed my eyes.

CHAPTER 16

Waking suddenly, I was pissed because I had fallen into a hard sleep. The older I had gotten my alertness was starting to falter and a man with a gunfighter reputation - whether he deserved it or not - losing the edge would only get him killed. I looked quickly toward the horses for any sign of danger. Sammy and Horse both were grazing peacefully, and Sammy turned her head in my direction as if she was trying to figure out why I was so nervy. I turned toward Keegan and Hugo, and they were both still sound asleep with Hugo all cuddled up in Keegan's arms.

I sat up slowly realizing my innards were all knotted up with tension. I rolled it around some trying to ponder why this was so. It could be I was feeling the sadness of what happened here on the banks of the Big Sandy so many years ago or that the Kiowa Indians were close, or maybe it was my knowing that my kind of justice had yet to be served on Captain Merna and his Redlegs. The more the thoughts passed through my brain pan, I reckoned it had more to do with how now I was answerable for the well-being of

Keegan and Hugo. It had been a long time since my actions or mistakes would determine the outcome of someone I had grown to care about. Sandy didn't really count in that regard because we both were capable of taking care of ourselves; it wasn't the same as having someone whose life depended solely on me.

I probably should have just put the young girl on the train and been done with it. I still wondered why I did what I did until I just saw Keegan now in her sleep pull Hugo in tighter with a gentle loving embrace, which drove home the fact and told me that seeing her safe to her Aunt Risa in Blackhawk was the only choice I could have made. Speaking in a whisper to myself as I slapped Keegan's Pa's hat on my head and started to stand, "Shit! McCall Patton you have gone soft in the head!"

Sort of angry with myself for reasons that somehow escaped me, I quickly stirred the embers of last night's campfire to try and bring the hottest to the surface and give them some air so the flames could have a new life.

The dark clouds that had looked like rain last night had failed in their attempt and had moved on to parts unknown this morning. The sun was a deep orange this dawn as it broke the skyline in the east. The sound of water flowing in the Big Sandy Creek was loud and clear as the day began.

Keegan and Hugo were up and moving as well. Hugo, after relieving himself, decided he was going to eat my boot for breakfast which just happened to be on my foot. Bending down and picking up the man killer, I hugged the little shit just as Keegan had hugged him in her sleep. Grinning, I put him back down, and he immediately attacked my boot again and all of the feeling out of sorts with myself seemed to disappear. Scooting him gently to the side with the edge of my boot, "Out of the way buster, I need to start some breakfast."

Hugo moved a couple feet away and plopped his butt down into the dirt with his tail still wagging and his tongue hanging out of his mouth because he was smart enough to know "breakfast" meant he was going to get some bacon. Once a flicker of flame started to dance, I added enough medium sized kindling to get a decent fire working to be able to fry up some fatback bacon for breakfast.

78

After breakfast Keegan started her daily chore of cleaning the campsite and extinguishing the fire as I saddled and packed the horses and made them ready for travel.

Horse and Sammy after being saddled started to snort and toss their heads looking toward the east. Stepping away from them both, I looked in the same direction toward the rising sun and after blinking my eyes several times to help them adjust since I was looking directly into the sun, I could then see what they saw. About sixty yards out, there were five horses and riding on three of them were three Kiowa Indians. The Kiowa were facing us and not advancing for the moment and seemed content to just observe us for now.

I slowly pulled the Winchester from the saddle scabbard and Keegan's bi-pod shooting stick and without any fanfare used the lever action of the rifle and placed a shell in the firing chamber. The sound of my loading the rifle caused Keegan to look at me, and I nodded and indicated by my head for her to look east. Keegan, once she saw the Indians in the distance, calmly walked over and after I handed her the Winchester and her shooting stick, she asked, "Where do you want me?"

I could not have been more proud of her than I was just at that moment. Though she was only eleven, she was calmer than any girl her age should have been in the face of uncertainty of what was going to happen. Bending down to get eye level with her, I could see her eyes dancing with a tad bit of fear of the unknown. Speaking in a calm and reassuring voice, "Not sure what they want Keegan, and you just follow my lead. Understand if this all goes south, do not hesitate to shoot them. The one that will be doing the speaking for them will be their ramrod, so keep a bead on him. This is about us living another day and if they intend us harm, then they have given up any right to live beyond this day. Do you understand?"

With her eyes locked on me, she slowly nodded her head "yes" and her voice cracked some as she answered, "I understand Mac."

Pointing north and indicating a rock about thirty feet away, "Set up over there Keegan and don't do anything until I tell you."

As Keegan moved into position, Hugo followed her and all his playfulness had vanished as he seemed to sense the now mounting tension. Standing and facing the Kiowa, we watched as they spurred their horse into our direction at a slow trot bringing the two extra horses.

When they got within forty feet of us, I said in a loud and clear voice, "That's far enough."

Once they had brought their horses to a halt, I was able to size them up. All three had two long black braids with eagle feathers woven into the end of each braid. They wore leather breeches and leather shirts with rawhide fringe for decoration. All were heavily muscled and seemed to be in the late twenties or early thirties. The two hanging in the back were a lot smaller and looked to be kin such as brothers with hard, lean faces. The one in front holding on to the two spare horses was clearly the leader by his demeanor. The leader's face looked as if it had been chiseled out of marble and if I had been a woman, I probably would have called him handsome. All three seemed to be capable men, and they were armed with a Winchester just like mine, which they held in front of them crossways across the manes as they were seated on their ponies.

As I was sizing them up, they were sizing me up as well plus the lay of the land so to speak. Keegan was off to the side far enough that they had to turn their heads to look at her, and there was no mistake that she had the Winchester pointed at the one out front, and it made me smile that she had already thought it through who the leader was.

Still in a clear and confident voice I said, "You rode here, so what can I do for you gents?"

The leader of the Kiowa in perfect English said, "We want to trade."

So that explained the two spare horses. All five horses were branded and each had a different brand which indicated to me that they all were probably stolen. Shaking my head "no" and still with a calm voice, "Looks like a wasted trip for you fellows because we have nothing to trade."

The Kiowa leader lifted his hand with the two ponies' reins and then pointed to Keegan and said, "We trade for her!"

What these renegades did not know was that they were bunched tight enough that I could kill them all if it came to a shooting match. My fear was that they could get a shot or two off and Keegan might catch one, so I was going to try and avoid one if possible, but my mind had already moved in that direction that gave me a total awareness of my surroundings. I could see every wrinkle and crease in their sun burnt faces. I could even smell the dirt and the griminess of the trail on their bodies. In my mind I saw myself drawing my pistol and what the outcome would be. I was ready for whatever fate had to throw in my direction when I spoke again, "She is not for trade so you assholes just turn around and head back to where you came from."

The leader looked me in the eye and saw no fear whatsoever and he wasn't used to that. He probably has been scaring white folk since he was old enough to ride. After a full minute of eye-to-eye contact with neither of us flinching or blinking, he spoke again, "Maybe we take her."

CHAPTER 17

Enough is enough flashed through my mind when I palmed my Colt with lightning speed and pointed the killing end at the leader's chest. My reaction was so quick it took the Indians by surprise. Even Keegan said out loud, "Whoa!"

The Kiowa had no chance to raise their rifles, and I think it was starting to dawn on them that they were tightly bunched and in trouble. Speaking in a loud and clear voice, "How about I ventilate all of you and leave you for buzzard bait? Make no mistake, I have had a rough couple of weeks, and I am just itching to shoot somebody, so I would suggest to you to take your stolen ponies and get your ass out of here before I get mad."

The two Kiowa in the back darted their eyes back and forth in between Keegan and myself now that we had two weapons pointed in their direction. The leader's eyes locked on me - and only me. His eyes showed anger and if he didn't have a Winchester and a Colt pointed at him, I had no doubt he would have pushed the issue. He was smart enough to realize he would not survive the encounter, which made him a heck of a lot keener than the one in the back on the right who started to raise his Winchester.

Maybe he thought I would shoot the leader first, maybe he was just stupid, and maybe it was both. Without hesitation, I shifted my sight slightly to my right and shot him off of his horse. Even before he hit the ground, I spoke loud and clear again, "Keegan! Anyone else twitches a muscle you shoot the bastard in front!"

Keegan in a loud and clear voice replied, "Yes Sir!"

The downed Kiowa had not moved and was dead to this world. He had taken my slug center mass in his chest as the bullet pierced his heart. His soul would have already been departed before he hit the dirt.

The leader didn't even flinch when I shot his compadre and had yet to look at him. All the remaining Indian in the back could do was keep looking at the one that had lost his life. The silent standoff between the head honcho and myself lasted another full minute…and I was starting to get annoyed. Pulling back the hammer on my Colt, I still pointed it at the leader and in a calm but loud voice, "You still here, Chief? Either jump and let's finish it here or take your man and leave. There is not another option. Daylight is burning and I got things to do. Your choice and you now have ten seconds to make up your mind."

With the silent count in my head to eight, the head renegade slowly turned his horse and started to move out in the same direction from where they had come and when he passed the dead man, he said to the other living Kiowa, "Leave him!"

The second Kiowa grabbed the dead man's horse's reins and now with all five horses in tow, they started into a trot.

Watching the two Indians, I replaced the spent cartridge in my Colt with a live round and turned to Keegan, who was still following the retreating Kiowa with the tip of the Winchester when I spoke to her, "Miss Keegan Doreen O'Rourke, you did well, and I will never worry again knowing that I have you now to back my play. I am proud of you, very proud of you."

Keegan stood and stumbled and I could she was struggling trying not to cry; with her voice breaking with emotion, "I was so scared Mac!"

Walking over and taking the Winchester from her, I hugged her and she then started to cry. Bending down, I held her at arm's length and in a soothing voice, "I was scared also Keegan. It took courage to do what you did and you should be proud of that. The fear and being scared is normal; it is what makes you and me better people than the bad guys."

Hugo had leaned into Keegan trying to comfort her in the only way he could. The young Irish lass wiped the tears away from her face when she asked in an almost whisper, "You were really scared, Mac?"

Looking at this brave girl who had been through so much in the last couple of weeks, I brought her in tight and hugged her again. "Of course I was, Keegan. I have just had more experience than you at this. Now we got to get moving and keep alert because I am afraid we have not seen the last of those two."

Releasing me, Keegan stepped back and said, "You think they will come back?"

Standing and looking down at her, "I have no doubt. I could read it in the one Indian's eyes. He will feel insulted from what happened here today and will not forget it. Yes, I think they will be back. We just need to be alert and ready and have no hesitation in finishing what was started. Do you understand?"

Keegan now was starting to calm down and shook her head slowly "yes." She then pointed at the dead Indian and asked, "What do we do with him?"

Thinking before I spoke because I knew my answer was not what Keegan thought it should be, "We leave him lay. His own people didn't respect him enough to give him a proper send off, so we will not either. Not that I am against burying him, it is just leaving his body is a message for that leader that we are just as harsh and brutal as he is. That we don't cotton to what they tried to do with kidnapping you and killing me. Life is tough and only the tough survive. Does that make any sense to you?"

Keegan looked as if she was about ready to cry again. "No, I really don't understand, Mac."

Reaching out and softly wiping a tear from her face, "Let's hope you never do Keegan. Now we wasted enough time here and I think the Keegan Trail is calling our name."

After making sure the canteens were topped off with fresh creek water, I then secured Hugo with Sandy in the saddlebag, and it was evident once again he was gaining some weight. It would not be long when he would no longer be a puppy. Since Horse and Sammy were already packed and saddled when the Kiowa made their visit, it was only a matter of minutes and we were back on the trail. We started in a more northern than a westerly direction.

Looking back only once, I could still see the dead Kiowa in the same spot he had landed once I shot him. If the others never returned to bury his body, he would join those many other ghosts that roamed the banks of the Big Sandy. I felt a little guilty about leaving his body, but I still felt it was the right thing to do, and that was to leave a reminder to the others that we were not to be trifled with.

As I looked northwest, the sun was already at its mid-morning point as I thought about our next destination which would be Wild Horse, Colorado.

What I had learned about Wild Horse from the pharmacist in Leoti, Kansas was that it used to be an army Calvary outpost established after the Battle of Sand Creek and was located in this remote and lonely part of Colorado. He also mentioned it had a railroad station and a town had sprung up around it.

It was evident that Keegan was very alert, and she kept scanning the east and west horizons and each one of the gullies as we came up on them. It was good to have another set of eyes searching for any sign of the Kiowa. My gut, just as I had told Keegan, was that we were not free of them. It would be just a matter of time before they tried to take her. Women and young girls were prized possessions in their culture and if the women or young girls became too bothersome, they would travel south and trade them to the Comancheros. It would be a life that would not be pleasant or desirable for her or any other woman or girl. It was not even a question that I would take a bullet to keep Keegan Doreen O'Rourke safe from those that would take her freedom away.

Staying always alert to my surroundings, I quickly went through what had happened in the last several weeks. Sandy and my big adventure seeking fortune in the Colorado gold camps had quickly turned into a revenge trail against Captain Merna and the other Redlegs. The misery of losing my best friend had also turned into a tale of survival for not only me, but also for Keegan since Merna and the others had butchered her folks. Looking at the young girl riding by my side got me thinking how she at the age of eleven had stepped up and saved my life when the fever sickness got ahold of me. I realized my life was hers until I got her safe to Blackhawk and her Aunt Risa. Getting her there safely was my sole mission at this time. Then I would concentrate on Captain John Merna.

CHAPTER 18

After the encounter and the shooting of the one Kiowa Indian, Sammy, Horse, Keegan, Hugo and I seemed more attentive of all that surrounded us. I had no doubt we had not seen the last of the other two reservation runners. The leader's eyes told his story and in just those few moments of time when I looked at them, I read his hatred for all those that had white skin. His animosity may in a fact be justified, but Keegan and I had done nothing to be the center of his loathing for all that were white. I for one had sympathy for the plains Indians and the broken treaties that had befallen them, but in the same token, I was not a man to stand by and let others take what is mine without a fight. My gut told me that I was going to have to kill those two that had escaped the reservation. If they pushed the issue, I would not hesitate to defend what is mine and Keegan and myself.

Toward mid-afternoon the trail toward Wild Horse was vacant except for a few tumbleweeds as the wind in the north started to build. The clouds once again had the nasty, dark look of rain and even from this distance I could see the flashes of lightning as it danced in the heavens. Turning back and looking northwest forward on the Keegan Trail, I saw no trees nor any type of shelter that would keep us safe from the approaching storm. Matter of fact, I had not seen one tree since leaving the banks of Big Sandy Creek. It would not be a pleasant night if we had to hunker down and ride out the storm in the open prairie.

A spattering of raindrops started to fall just as we crested a small rise of an arroyo and after giving up any hope of finding shelter, I spied not a hundred yards away an old abandoned homestead.

Stopping Sammy, I reached in my saddlebag and produced my binoculars and studied the old depleted wooden house for a few minutes. Now the last time I took shelter in such a place, Sandy had met his untimely death. If it had only been me, I might have chanced to ride out the storm on the prairie, but I had Keegan and the man killer mutt Hugo to ruminate about. Without speaking, I pointed toward the old house so Keegan would know that was to be our destination for camp tonight.

As we reached the old ranch house, it seemed the roof and the walls were still stable except where the front door on the west side used to be where part of the framing and wall had collapsed. Thinking that this actually might be to our advantage, Keegan and I took about a half of an hour and moved a few logs out of the way so Sammy and Horse could spend the night sheltered from the storm in the house with us.

Once we had enough room, I walked Sammy and Horse into the house and when I had them settled down some, Keegan gathered enough of the wood lying about to start us up a cook fire. It looked as if it was going to be fried beans and a fatback bacon type of evening.

After unsaddling Sammy and Horse, I took the binoculars and went to the buckled wall and looked north toward the storm that was almost upon us in earnest. Just as the rain started to mist the sky, I looked at our back trail down the Keegan Trail, and I caught a glimpse of the two Kiowa reservation runners as they crested the same small rise in the gully where I first saw this old house. Sure enough, they had been trailing us as I knew they would. As quickly as they crested the rise, they retreated, not knowing that I had seen them for that split second. It would seem chance had put this old house here for the showdown with the Kiowa. As I was pondering if fate was mocking me or not, I began looking about the inside of this house to see how easy it would be to defend it. The opening in the wall where the door used to be and the only window facing south gave me the conclusion that even in daylight this old house had limited sight of the surrounding countryside, but it seemed that since I knew the Kiowa were close, it now seemed that fate had dealt us a royal flush. This old homestead provided us shelter from the storm that now was cranking up the old windmill as the rain started to come down in sheets. The flashes of lightning and the drum roll of thunder were not far behind and then came the hail.

The darkness of the night had already started in the east and was making fast tracks our way as the sun dropped behind the clouds in the western horizon giving us the start of the night.

The hail at first started off as pea size, but quickly the hardened ice grew to that of small chicken eggs. The ferocity and abundance of the hail were damn sure going to beat those Kiowa to a frazzle since there was no shelter to be had except what this old house could provide, which told me that when the storm had a lull, those that wanted Keegan and the horses would not be far behind thinking they could take us by surprise.

Keegan had already gotten a fire going in the fireplace; the stones and hearth seemed solid and were still intact. As soon as she was finished with that chore, I told her of the Kiowa and what I believed they would do when the storm calmed down some. Taking my extra Colt from the saddlebag, I loaded it and gave it to Keegan, who was hesitant in taking it since she had not fared as well in her shooting practice as she had done with the rifle. Gently I took her hand and handed it to her as I spoke, "This is to be used only if I fail in stopping the Kiowa. Make no mistake Keegan, if I fail in doing so, your best interest is not what they have in mind. You stand your ground and you have to be as ruthless as they can be. It is the only way out here where there is no law. The law rides with what we carry in the cartridges of our pistols and rifles. That Colt in your hand makes you equal to your enemy no matter how big or strong they are. Now go about your supper fixing while I make ready for our uninvited guests."

The rain and hail had been beating relentlessly on the rooftop for an hour now and was causing even more damage to the old wood shingles, and the old house had sprung more than a few leaks. My thought was the Kiowa were hunkered down for now trying to stay safe from the storm. Keegan and I were able to eat our supper in peace even though eating without speaking, we both kept alert and our eyes on Sammy and Horse to give us an advance warning.

Knowing it would be a close quarters' battle, I kept my Winchester loaded but off to the side since this would be a battle with the Colt and my Bowie knife if needed. It really did not matter which, for I had skill in both. Sandy used to say I was a warrior many times in my past lives and that it was not until this life that all that fine tuning came together in one total warrior package. My only fear tonight was of failure and what would then happen to Keegan. Hugo was eating bacon and wagging his tail, seeming oblivious to the storm and the tension of the room.

It was not until shortly after finishing my supper that the hail stopped and the rain lessened to a sprinkle as the storm and its center moved further south. Looking at Keegan, I spoke in a whisper, "It will not be long now. Let me handle this attack myself unless I go down."

Keegan was scared even though she was trying her hardest to hide it, and she had every right to be scared. Her life and that of her dog depended on me. Life in this country could be harsh as she had already found out. I was going to do everything in my power to get her and the dog through the evening.

Just like every time before an encounter that could bring about my death, my mind and body fine-tuned itself to all of my surroundings. I could hear the thunder now in the far distance south of me and the last of the raindrops as they fell to their demise on the roof above this abandoned house. I could also hear all of us, including myself, take in the air and exhale as we breathed. Even heard the sound as Hugo shuffled across the ground trying to get Keegan to pay attention to him. My eyes had adjusted to the half-light of the flickering fire as the shadows danced around the room. The tension was in the air and was supplied by both Sammy and Horse as well as Keegan and myself. I was ready for what would come out of the wet and darkness of the night.

Sammy gave the first indication that something was amiss as her ears stood straight up, and she looked toward the opening in the wall.

A few seconds later with a war cry to paralyze the enemy, the one Kiowa which was not the leader rushed in and tripped over the log I had placed in the shadows to slow their advance. He face planted hard on the ground and knowing he was out of the fight momentarily, I turned my full attention to the window as the leader made his attack which was cut short as I placed two 44 shells in his chest just as his feet hit the ground. The now dying leader dropped his knife and fell to his knees and looked at me in confusion as his life blood seeped from the wounds in his chest. I could hear the sound of his wounds sucking air as I aimed my Colt once again and before shooting him in the forehead, I said in a calm voice, "You should have stayed on the reservation, son."

CHAPTER 19

N ow that the leader of the reservation jumpers was down and dead, I now turned my attention back to the other one that the leader had used as bait and for a distraction so the now dead Indian could make his attack through the window. The second Indian was still stunned from his face plant after tripping over the log when he sprinted through the collapsed wall and doorway. The last remaining Kiowa was slowly doing a pushup to at least gain his knees as he shook his head trying to shake the cobwebs loose from his thinker.

The smell of my three spent shells was heavy in the air as I pointed the deadly end of my Colt toward the dazed Indian. Speaking calmly and slowly, "Now if you can speak English, I would suggest to you that you move slowly and cautiously so that I don't do the same to you as I did the last two fellers you jumped the reservation with. It would seem that your friends had a bad day today."

The Kiowa had gained his knees and his first glance told him everything he needed to know as I had my Colt pointed at him, and it was obvious I knew how to use it. His eyes lingered for a short spell on the one lying dead at the foot of the window, and I could read it in his face that he was not angry and he looked sort of relieved. After taking in the situation, he looked me in the eye awaiting his death if that was what I had intended to do. In that moment I saw that he was a proud man and he did not fear death. Thinking before I spoke again, I asked, "What is your name?"

He hesitated because that question is not what he was expecting at all. In a clear and strong voice he answered, "My name is Lucius Aitsan."

Raising my eyebrows after hearing his name, "Lucius Aitsan? Aitsan must be a Kiowa name. Lucius I am sure you know is a Christian name and it means light in Latin. Interesting. How did it come to be that you have a Latin name?"

Still with no fear he once again answered, "I was sent to a Christian school when I was eight and given a white man name. I like the sound of it, so I kept it."

Looking quickly at Keegan and then back at Lucius Aitsan, I rolled it around some of what to do now with this Christian Indian. He, along with the other two, had tried to kidnap Keegan and steal the horses and kill me in the process. He might have spent some time in a Christian upbringing, but he was still a savage in his soul. My gut instinct was telling me, although he was a savage, that he was different from the other one that I had just shot. It was possible that he had fallen in with the wrong fellows when he left the reservation and had no choice in the matter.

After a full minute of pondering, I looked the man in the eye and asked a couple of questions. If I believed his answers to these questions, his life may be spared. Clearing my voice to make myself understood, "Lucius are you an honorable man? If I let you live, will you take your friend here and leave with the promise that I will never see you again on my back trail?"

Lucius stared at me without speaking for a spell and then he asked, "What is your name?"

I respected that he was not pleading for his life and he wanted to know the name of the man who now held his life in his hands. "My name is McCall Patton. Most folks just call me Mac."

Lucius' eyes widened some when he heard my name. "The gray rider? The one who fought the blue riders? I heard it before today, but I now know it to be true that you have the heart of a warrior and fast with your pistol."

Shaking my head "yes" I answered, "I rode for the gray soldiers and it is true that I fought the blue soldiers, but that was a long time ago. As for being fast with my pistol, I have been given the talent and it has kept me alive so far. You didn't answer my questions, Lucius. If I let you live and I see one hair on your head or even if I have a second thought that you might return and try to harm this little girl, I will track you down and send you to your grave. So Lucius, you need to answer my question. Will you take your dead friend and leave and never follow us again?"

Lucius shook his head 'yes" and then said, "I will need two horses to do what you ask."

With a small laugh, "Hell son - take all five. The last thing I want is to get hung for a horse that you and your compadres stole."

Indicating with the tip of my pistol for him to stand, "Now drag your friend on out of here and go fetch your horses. After loading him on one, I want to see your backside heading in any direction but northwest. Is that clear?"

Slowly standing to get the kinks out of his knees from having been on them for a spell, he nodded his head "yes," seeming to understand the agreement between himself and me. He then dragged the dead Kiowa out of the old house, and I followed him still keeping my pistol ready. Standing at the collapsed wall, I watched as Lucius walked eastward and within a few minutes I could hear him returning with all five horses.

Lucius Aitsan was good to his word after returning with the stolen ponies, and he loaded the dead Kiowa on horseback and with one last look at me and a nod with his head and without any further fanfare or even a "kiss my ass," he headed back east into the darkness.

Keegan stood next to me and held my hand as we watched the Kiowa ride away as she asked, "Do you think he will be back Mac?"

Realizing just now that Keegan had grabbed my hand out of instinct and I let her, I held it until she let go. Thinking about her question before I replied, "My gut tells me we have seen the last of Lucius Aitsan. He is still a savage, but he also has honor. He will not trail us again."

Still staring into the hole in the darkness that Lucius had ridden into, Keegan asked one more question, "Mac, what do you think will happen to him?"

Bending down to get eye level with Keegan and still holding her hand, "I reckon whatever happens to Lucius Aitsan will not be a good thing. He is off the reservation with five stolen ponies and all alone. He, like the other Kiowa and the other tribes of the plains Indians' way of life, has vanished into the prairie dust and wind. Fate has dealt Lucius a tough hand, and I recollect it will end badly for him."

Keegan's eyes clouded over with a few tears, and she pulled me tight to give me a hug. It was the second hug we had shared in less than two days. The emotion that I felt for this child confused me, but it seemed now to be the most natural thing in the world. Holding her tight, I felt that Keegan Doreen O'Rourke had given me a gift - the gift of caring. It had been so long I could not even remember the last time when I was able to give someone comfort in just having me hold them.

Hugo was jealous that he was not getting any loving, and he jumped up on Keegan's leg several times until she let go of me and picked him up with a smile and crushed him into her face. Hugo, just like Keegan, I had grown to care for. Even if the little shit was a tad irritating.

As Keegan cuddled with her man killing mutt, I looked toward the sky and there were not any clouds left to hide the stars as they twinkled and showed me their starlight. The storm had long since passed and the air smelled fresh and clean. There was nothing like the musky smell of the earth after a good hard rain. The moon had risen and had given enough light to bring forth the shadows of the night. After the tension and death from the encounter with the Kiowa, it was a pleasant impression.

After rubbing down Sammy and Horse for the night, Keegan, Hugo and I settled in for some much needed sleep. The air had chilled some, and I kept a small fire burning in the old house fireplace for some extra warmth.

After watching Keegan and Hugo fall into a deep sleep, I found it difficult for me to do likewise. The faces of the two Kiowa that I had killed kept invading my sleep and just like the others that had died in the past by my hand, I knew that they would forever haunt me. I tried to think of Sandy and the good times of our friendship to ward off the new death faces, but it was to no avail. It was going to be a long night.

CHAPTER 20

After tossing and turning most of the night, it was just before dawn that I came to a full awakening still feeling the effects that the haunts of the two dead Indians had on my sleep.

Sitting up I watched Keegan sleep as Hugo wagged his tail and then sauntered over to my feet and started in again gnawing at my boot. It would seem that he never tired of trying to eat a hole in my boot. Hugo made me feel somewhat better just by looking at him, so I picked him up and brought him close to my face, and he promptly tried to lick my nose off. Of course the little shit made me smile and helped in easing the memories of the death faces. Holding him out further to get a better look at him, I realized he was getting even heavier, and it would not be long that he would no longer be a pup.

Seeing movement beyond Hugo, I watched Keegan sit up smiling and staring at me holding her dog. Keegan watched for a second or two before she spoke, "You know you like Hugo; you just can't admit it Mac!"

I put the dog down and ruffled the top of his head before he bolted and jumped into Keegan's lap and I thought a moment before I replied, "I was just checking his weight is all. Won't be long and he will not fit in the saddlebag anymore. Might have to leave him behind if that happens."

Keegan burst out loud with a full belly laugh as she began to speak, "Yea, right Mac! Hugo is just as much a part of you now as he is part of me."

I stood and slapped Keegan's Pa's hat on my head when the thought crossed my mind that she was right. I tried for a real serious look and failed in doing so before replying, "Are you sure you are only eleven years old? You act like my Ma sometimes."

Still laughing and smiling, Keegan stifled another laugh before speaking again, "You just got a soft spot in your heart for Hugo is all, and you are afraid to say it is true."

Looking straight at her, "And to think I turned down two horses to keep you around!"

Keegan's smile on her face evaporated as she thought about what I just said before she replied, "They were beautiful horses."

Now that statement made me laugh and laugh hard - the first time I had such a laugh since before Sandy had been killed. Still laughing and shaking my head, I pointed to Keegan, "Beautiful horses? Beautiful horses indeed. Too late for the trade now; that Indian is probably half way back to Oklahoma with my herd. You need to shut your pie hole and stir them embers to awaken us a cook fire as I get Sammy and Horse ready for the trail."

Setting Hugo down, Keegan stood up with a gleam in her eye and a shit eating grin from ear to ear as she headed to the fireplace. "Yes sir!"

After saddling the horses and getting mostly packed, I helped Keegan cook a fine breakfast of more bacon and beans, but since we had a nice fireplace working with us this morning, I took the time to make a batch of Dutch oven biscuits to mop up after the bacon and beans. Keegan and I both agreed the biscuits were a perfect addition to our breakfast this morning. We had several extra biscuits left over which we packed away for later.

After topping off our canteens from a small brook that was running full with rainwater behind the old house, we settled into our saddles, and then I pointed Sammy northwest and gave the reins and her head, and with a slight jab with my right spur we headed back onto the Keegan Trail with Keegan, Hugo, and Horse trailing behind toward Wild Horse, Colorado.

The wetness from the hail and rainstorm last night left a lingering mist and fog this morning, and visibility was down to less than a quarter of a mile. Back during the war a morning like this was a disadvantage for you, but also a disadvantage for your enemy since they also had limited visibility as well. It would even the battlefield, giving no one the advantage. It seemed to me that no one ever attacked during a foggy morning.

By noon the fog had long been gone from the eastern prairie southeast of Wild Horse, and I was able to spot the town in the distance of about one mile. As I got closer, I looked through my binoculars and the town was bustling with the normal activity of the day. Studying the town for several minutes, I was able to observe along with the normal doings of the local folk that the town had a Calvary presence along with what looked like a brand new railroad depot. After I saw the soldiers, it was my assumption that Wild Horse had started out as a remote Calvary outpost here on the eastern plains of Colorado. Now concentrating on the new wood building that served as the railroad depot, I could see the telegraph wires stretching down to the roof of the building which gave me the idea that I should send another telegram to Keegan's Aunt Risa in Blackhawk giving her an update on the arrival of her niece. My hope was there was a message waiting for me from her stating she had received my first telegram and was expecting Keegan's arrival. It would seem nothing was off kilter, so we ventured forth until we made the main street of Wild Horse.

After replacing some supplies that had been used on the trail, I also bought four cans of peaches and some hard candy for Keegan as a surprise once we got back on the Keegan Trail.

While talking to Jason and Robin Ridenour, who were the friendliest couple I had ever met who owned and operated the supply depot in Wild Horse named Ridenour Supply, I was able to gather much needed information on the trail to the northwest. It would seem that thirty-three miles ahead would be the town of Hugo, Colorado. They warned me that Hugo and the surrounding area for many miles was owned by three very large cattle operations that were run by men that called themselves Barons, and they did not take kindly to strangers that wandered through their area of operations. They also warned me that the cowboys that worked for these brands and the cattle barons were a hard lot and sometimes took a hankering to hang someone. They would call them cattle thieves, which gave them a right to string them up. They recommended that we should not linger long in the town of Hugo. It sounded like advice that I would follow.

Jason was roughly forty or so with a shaved bald head and a dark, small well-trimmed beard. He was about 5'8" and more muscled than most shopkeepers I had seen, and it was my guess he had led a wild side of life before meeting his wife. It was my guess that Robin was slightly older than her husband. She was of medium build and very attractive with brown hair with a beautiful streak of gray hair that offset the soft line of her beautiful face. It would seem that Robin's personality matched her looks and she had taken a shine to Keegan.

Jason and Robin had given Hugo the run of the store, and his tail never stopped wagging as he went from gunny sack to gunny sack sniffing and exploring all the new scents that were down on the floor. Jason even fed him a generous portion of beef jerky which made him a friend for life with Hugo.

Robin and Keegan seemed like two peas in a pod and so in tune with each other that they did not notice that after a small nod with my head to Jason that I would be back shortly. After Jason acknowledged me, I slipped out the door to go to the railroad depot to send the telegram to Keegan's Aunt.

There were no telegrams waiting for Keegan or myself and it was worrisome that Keegan's Aunt Risa had not replied to the first message. It was still a mystery if the elusive aunt was still living in Blackhawk or for that matter still alive. Not knowing if my message would ever be read, I sent another updating our whereabouts and that Keegan and I were still heading toward the Rocky Mountains and the town of Blackhawk in the west.

Before leaving Wild Horse, Keegan and I had a very good and tasty meal of beef steak and fried taters and a slice of apple pie at a tent that served as an eatery next to Ridenour Supply.

If the town had a hotel, we would have stayed the night, but since the hotel was just in the beginning stages of being built, we saddled Sammy and Horse and packed Hugo away in his saddlebag with the ashes of Sandy, and we headed northwest toward the town that had the same name as Keegan's killer mutt.

Once back on the Keegan Trail, I thought about the warning from the Ridenours about the cattle baron's land to the northwest we were about to cross. It had been my experience that men that controlled large cattle herds and vast amounts of land were full of themselves and looked down on those that they did not deem worthy. They usually employed cowboys who were loyal to the brand and never questioned the boss's orders. These men - these cattle barons and cowboys that rode for them - were always hard and dangerous men. It would be wise, just as the Ridenours suggested, not to linger in their country for long. I was not a man that would seek out trouble, but I was the type that would not run from it either.

Pondering the trail ahead and the possible trouble we might encounter put me in a foul mood and got my thinker started on those that would be getting my full attention once I delivered Keegan and Hugo safe and sound to Blackhawk, Colorado. As the sun started to settle below the western horizon, John Merna and his remaining Redlegs occupied my mind.

Captain John Merna, John Loveless, Allen Wells, and Larry Brown the gunfighter known as LB didn't know it yet, but McCall Patton was going to send them to hell for what they tried to do to me and for killing the only true friend I ever had. After Keegan and her dog were safe, they would become my mission in life. And I never shirked from accomplishing a mission.

CHAPTER 21

The night and the following day and then another night as we ventured northwest toward the town of Hugo were uneventful. The weather had been pleasant during the day, and the nights had been cool and perfect for sleeping.

Hugo was getting so big now that I was afraid he would tip out of the saddlebag on the trail so I had to take the sugar sack containing Sandy's ashes and bone fragments out of the saddlebag to give the man killer more room.

Holding Sandy's sack with his ashes to my nose, I sniffed it and all I could smell was the dirt and grit of the ashes and the lingering smell of dirty dog. Not sure what I was expecting to smell, but suddenly I was overcome with grief once again as I held the sugar sack tight to my face as a lone tear stained the letter "S" of the word sugar which had been penned on the exterior of the sugar sack.

I didn't want Keegan to see my sorrow, but she did and she came to me and hugged my side before stepping away. She then looked up with a few tears in her eyes as well, for my actions had probably reminded her of the death of her folks and then she spoke in the most angel like voice, "Sandy was more than your best friend, Mac. He was your brother in heart and soul; my Pa used to tell me it was okay to mourn those that you loved, for they would have mourned you. So that's what I do when I think of my folks. You should not hide your grief Mac or at least not from me. I understand."

I stuffed Sandy and his ashes into the saddlebag on the opposite side of Keegan's horse - Horse - away from Hugo's saddlebag and once my friend was safely secured, I turned to the young Irish girl and wondered how I had been blessed after losing Sandy to have Keegan Doreen O'Rourke cross my trail. I realized at that moment how much she needed me that I needed her as well. Fate had put us together on this trail because without each other we would have been lost, but together we were strong and capable of dealing with the death of our loved ones that had befallen us. Reaching out, I carefully touched her shoulder and then lowered myself to look into her eyes before I spoke, 'You truly are a gift Keegan and an old soul for someone that is only eleven years old. Thank you…for being you!"

Even though after hearing from the Ridenours about the cattle herds in the countryside around the town of Hugo, I was amazed at the herd we saw before us. The vast herd was so much that there could be no way anyone could have ever counted them. I now understood why the cattle barons seemed like such a ruthless lot, because they had to be. I could only imagine that every rustler that had a horse had tried to steal from these men. They could only protect their cattle and their investments from those that would pinch their cows from them with the barrel of a Winchester rifle or a Colt pistol. I am sure if they even thought you were rustling, they would be the law, jury, and judge and hang you from the nearest tree or windmill. After using my binoculars for a full fifteen minutes to find the easiest route through the ocean of cowhide, I decided there was none that would be safe from spooking the herd. Since the herd was drifting south, we drifted north to find the edge of the moving wave of endless cows.

It was midday when we found a suitable route around the herd and finally pushed on into the town of Hugo, Colorado. We had not seen one traveler or cowboy on the Keegan Trail since leaving Wild Horse, and that suited me just fine.

Keegan and I were both hungry, so we stopped at the hotel that served as a saloon and eatery for a bite to eat before continuing on to the next stop in Limon, Colorado. It was my hope that as soon as we filled our bellies that we could resume the trail and put the cattle barons and the men who rode for them behind us.

After hitching Sammy and Horse to the hitching post outside, Keegan, Hugo, and I found a seat in the rear of the dining room. Since it was midday, it was fairly busy with numerous cowhands who must have ridden for the same brand since they seemed to be friendly with each other. I could make out everyone's faces except two that were facing away from me that were focused on eating the carved turkey and taters in front of them. My gut instinct was on alert, but nobody was really paying any attention to us. Sitting with my back against the wall so no one could approach me from behind, I felt somewhat at ease.

Since the only thing on the menu was turkey and taters, that is what we ordered. As we waited, I drank a warm beer and Keegan drank a sarsaparilla along with a glass of water for the each of us, which seemed to quench our thirsts for the time being. Keegan was talking about the cows and how she never thought there could be so many in the whole world. She started talking almost nonstop about Mrs. Ridenour in Wild Horse and what a sweet woman she was. As Keegan went on and on about Robin, Hugo went back and forth from gnawing at my boot to standing on his hind legs pressed against Keegan's leg so she could reach down and pet him.

Hugo was bothering no one except Keegan and myself until he saw or scented something across the room and bolted for the far side. In doing so, he ran in between one cowboy's legs that had just walked into the dining room and made him stumble slightly before he caught his balance. Hugo stopped to make sure the man was okay as he wagged his tail in friendship. The cowboy was a big man and stood 6'4" or better with short blonde hair under a cattleman creased Stetson hat that was sweat stained with trail dust. He had to weigh in the neighborhood of 250 pounds and looked strong and heavily muscled. This cowhand was a man that was used to bullying his way through life. It would seem I had a knack for running into these types of hard cases. The cowhand also wore a two gun rig which told me all I wanted to know about the man. He fancied himself a gunfighter, which was not a good sign at all.

The cowboy that Hugo had tripped looked down with a frown because that was all he had. He seemed the type that if he ever smiled it would crack his face in two. With an unpleasant voice he said, "Damn dog!" He then promptly kicked Hugo ten feet across the room into a dining table leg. Hugo landed with a solid thud when his body hit an oaken table leg, and he started to whimper.

Keegan looked at me with astonishment and with a nod of my head toward Hugo, I said in a calm voice, "Go get Hugo and see how bad he is hurt, Keegan."

Keegan shot from her chair and gathered up her dog in her arms with a tear or two in her eyes as she looked at the cowboy and said loudly, "He didn't hurt you none mister, and there was no need to kick him like that!"

The cowboy being the unpleasant fellow that he was said in a loud and boisterous voice, "Drop the dog girly - I am going to teach that mutt a lesson!"

I stood slowly as I took in all the sights and sounds of the room as my focus became intense. I could smell the sweat, stale tobacco, and even an outhouse that was near. Behind the bar, the clock's ticks of the second hand seemed to echo in the room as time in my mind slowed down. Speaking loudly and with a clear voice so there would be no misunderstanding, I said, "Mister you try to kick that dog again, then you will have to deal with me. He is not bothering you anymore, so let it go!"

Now you would have thought I had yelled fire as the rest of the men in the room backed away from us both as they tried to find a place that would be safe from catching a stray bullet. As his friends made for the outer walls and made the center of the room larger, the gunfighter cowboy turned to face me as he squared his shoulders over his feet in the typical gunfighter stance. Still with a frown on his face, he spoke, "If that is your dog, then I don't care much for you either, mister."

As I watched the cowboy's eyes that I was getting ready to kill for any sign that he was going to go for his pistols, another loud voice joined into the tension that was a mounting crescendo in the room from one of the men that had been seated eating his turkey and taters that I couldn't see his face earlier. He now stood standing watching the events in front of him and spoke loudly enough for all to hear, "Well, I will be damned if it isn't McCall Patton from down "Little Dixie" Missouri. For those in this room that do not know who McCall Patton might be, he is better known as Rebel Mac. Chris Grable, this is not a man to get shot down by over a dog tripping you. Make no mistake he will kill you."

After hearing my name, Chris Grable the wannabe gunfighter that had kicked Hugo, turned pale as the blood ran out of it. It would seem my reputation as a man not to be trifled with had reached as far west as Hugo, Colorado. Looking at Grable, I knew the fight in the man had been replaced with the fear of a sudden death. From the look on Grable's face, this was the first time he had tried to bully a man that would not be bullied. I could see his demeanor went from amusement to outright distress. He would no longer be a threat to Keegan, Hugo, or myself.

Dismissing Grable in my thoughts, now I focused on the man who had told everyone in the room who I was. He looked older of course with now long gray hair, but he still had the swagger of his youth and looked like he weighed about the same as I remembered him at about 180 pounds on a 6' 3" lanky frame. Speaking without smiling, I said, "It would seem Bogart that you are far from home yourself. What is your story here in Hugo of all places?"

Deforest Bogart was from "Little Dixie" as well and he rode with Sandy and me in the war up until Quantrill's Raiders' massacre at Lawrence, Kansas. Bogart was one of Quantrill's loyal followers and relished in the death and rape of those poor folks that had been slaughtered in Lawrence.

Bogart with a smile and with self-importance said, "I am the foreman and ramrod of these yahoos. We ride for Mr. Deter of the Double D."

Still in a foul mood and not over the fact that one of Bogart's men had taken his boot to Keegan's dog Hugo, I looked Bogart in the eye and said matter of fact, "I reckon Bogart I don't cotton to you much either!"

CHAPTER 22

Keegan had gathered up Hugo and had retaken her seat as she comforted her dog while I was still standing and facing Bogart. Hugo seemed unhurt from Chris Grable's boot kick and was happily eating up all the love that Keegan was giving him.

Bogart was not sure how to handle my remark, and it took several seconds as he pushed it around in his thinker before he responded. A smile slowly crossed his face before he spoke, "Slow down Mac, what happened was a long time ago and I was just following Quantrill's orders. Nowadays I wished I had taken the high road with you and Sands. Where is ole' Sandy?"

I thought it was best not to push the matter anymore over something that was done and could not be undone from so many years ago. Looking Bogart in the eye with a slight nod of my head that indicated the past was the past before speaking, "Sandy was killed by Captain John Merna and some renegade Redlegs several weeks ago as they pushed their way to the gold fields in the Rocky Mountains. As they move west, they are killing any former confederates they cross trails with. They also killed this Irish girl's folks because her Pa had fought for the gray as well. Once I see her safely to her aunt in Blackhawk, Colorado, I will then finish the task of hunting down Merna and the remaining Redlegs and bring them the justice they deserve."

Bogart nodded his head and in a voice that spoke of understanding, "You always were the avenging angel, Mac. If Merna passed this way, it might explain how two former confederates might have met an untimely death northwest of here forty miles in Agate, Colorado a couple of weeks ago. The two ex-confederates' deaths were unusual in that they were shot and stabbed. Now it makes sense because the Captain always carried that damn saber into battle and had no qualms about using it to finish off the dying. I wonder what prompted Captain Merna to head to the gold fields in the first place."

Hearing of the death of the two former gray soldiers sounded like Captain Merna, and my gut told me that it was Merna and his men that had done the killing. That bit of news just rammed home the fact that Merna was not playing with a full deck. The man's mind I was convinced was coming undone just as Randy Vaughn had said. Before regaining my seat I said, "I spoke with one of Captain Merna's men in Dighton, Kansas named Randy Vaughn, and he told me Merna had in his possession the map that told where the Reynolds gang had hidden their loot before they were captured. It sounded as if he and his Redlegs were going to try and recover it."

Bogart's eyes got slightly larger when he asked, "Is Randy Vaughn dead?"

Without speaking, I just nodded my head "yes" like of course he was dead. I sat down to finish my meal as Bogart still stood smiling and spoke, "That is one hell of a story, Mac. I have heard of the Reynolds gang's loot and that really would be something if Captain Merna had the map. I would give my right arm to have that map. Yes sir Mac that is one of a kind of story. Are you going for the map and the gold?"

I could see the desire for the gold and loot in Bogart's eyes as he pulled out a chair to sit at the same table with Keegan and myself. Looking into the man's eyes that killed and raped so many in Lawrence, Kansas so many years ago, I said in a voice that was calm and just loud enough so not to be misunderstood, "It is not the map I am after you asshole, and I could care less for the loot. It is the vengeance and justice I seek against those that killed my best friend and Keegan's parents. And just because we are having this chat does not make us pals or compadres. What you did in Lawrence, Kansas while under orders or not does not sit well in my craw. So I suggest you remove yourself from the seat at this table and lose yourself in the crowd!"

Bogart's anger was evident as he so quickly and violently stood that the chair he was sitting in shot backwards and toppled over into the middle of the room with a loud clunk that made the cowpunchers present go silent once again as all their eyes now locked back on Bogart and myself.

The anger of Deforest Bogart from "Little Dixie" was getting the best of him as he stood before me. I could now see it in his eyes that the thought crossed his mind that he might now have the advantage against me since I was sitting down at the table. That all changed as the sound of the hammer of my Colt overcame the silence of the room when it was cocked back as I pointed the killing end of my pistol at him from under the table. I had drawn it as soon as I had sat down. The anger in Bogart's eyes was replaced with the knowledge that if he flinched a muscle, I would kill him where he stood without batting an eyelash. Still looking into the ramrod of the Double D rancher's eyes as I calmly spoke, "You can leave now Bogart, but slowly remove your Colt from your holster and place it on the table. You can retrieve it after we have left. The key for you to walk out of here alive is that you do it slowly!"

Bogart did not move for a full fifteen seconds, and it looked as if he was going to make a very bad life and death decision until the man who had been sitting next to Bogart while he was eating when I entered the room finally stood and said with a voice of a man who was used to being heard, "Hold on now Bogart, don't do anything stupid! Place the gun on the table in front of the man slow and easy like."

Bogart turned his head and looked at the older man with white hair, and then he looked back at me with what I saw was relief in his eyes and said, "Yes sir, Mr. Deter."

Bogart then slowly placed his gun on the table in front of me and turned and spun around and started out the door as he shouted, "Enough of this shit, everyone back to work and I mean - NOW!"

It took several minutes for all the men to file out of the room, which left the room empty except for Mr. Deter, Keegan, Hugo, and myself.

Mr. Deter was an older man with pure white hair and a goatee to match. He stood I would guess at least 6' and weighed about 175. His nose was big and had what looked like a knuckle in the bridge, probably from being broken a time or two. He was wearing dark wool pants with a single holstered Colt pistol. He also had on a dark wool shirt with a dark leather vest with a black cattleman creased Stetson on his head. He was dressed expensively but not showy. He had the presence of a man who knew how to command men and that was quickly evident as he took control of the situation today. The cattle baron of the Double D walked over with a huge smile on his face and said, "Mr. Patton, do you mind if I take a seat?"

Taking my pistol out from under the table, I released the hammer almost silently and placed it on the table in front of me and grabbed my fork before I said, "I have no quarrel with you, Mr. Deter."

Once all the cowpunchers had left the room, Keegan placed Hugo back on the floor, and he promptly wagged his tail and then jumped up on Mr. Deter's leg wanting to be picked up. Deter still with a smile picked up Hugo and started to pet the man killing pup, which told me that this man that ran a cattle empire may be ruthless in his business dealings, but he had a good heart.

Still petting Hugo, Deter spoke in a calm voice, "My name is Bob Deter and as you may have gathered, I am the owner of the Double D ranch. You sir, have backed down two of my toughest men today, which I assure you is nothing short of a miracle. You also may have surmised that I have the need for tough men such as yourself, and I would like to offer you a job as a foreman here at the Double D. Would you be interested in the job?"

I smiled at Mr. Bob Deter because my gut instinct was telling me he was true to his word and had morals and probably did not know the background of the foreman he had in Bogart until this day. I had the feeling that Deforest Bogart's days as ramrod at the

Double D will be at an end as soon as Deter could find a suitable replacement. Taking a pause from eating what was now cold turkey I replied, "I respect you Mr. Deter for what you have accomplished here. And thank you for the job offer, but I have a few things I need to settle first before thinking about taking on a full time job. So, I respectfully decline your offer."

Sitting Hugo back on the floor, Bob Deter stood. "Thought it was a lost cause, but thought I'd give it a shot since it seems I will be needing a new ramrod soon. Until this day I had not known the full extent of Bogart's background, and I thank you for bringing that to light for me."

Placing a five dollar gold piece on the table, he said, "I would like to buy you and the young Miss your meal. And I will send riders ahead to the other ranches giving you safe passage as far as Limon. If you ever finish your business and rethink the job offer, it will always be open, Mr. Patton."

As Bob Deter turned to head out the door, I said, "Much appreciated, Mr. Deter."

CHAPTER 23

A fter paying for our meal with Deter's five dollar gold
piece, I left the change for a tip for the bartender, and
then we walked out into an empty street in the town of
Hugo. Every cowpuncher including the owner of the Double D,
Bob Deter and ramrod Deforest Bogart had left. Keegan, while
holding Hugo, looked both ways and with a half laugh said, "You
sure know how to clear out a town, Mac."

Looking at her smiling eyes and with a small chuckle myself, "I
assure you Keegan, it is a skill not for the faint hearted."

The next several days on the Keegan Trail were unexciting, and
it would seem that the Cattle Baron Deter was true to his word as
we passed by numerous cowhands on the open prairie between
Hugo and Limon, and no one paid any attention to the strangers in
their lands and gave us a wide berth. We never even stopped in the
tiny outlying stations of Limon and Agate as we made our way
more north than west until we came across the railway station in
Deer Trail.

After studying Deer Trail from the distance for a spell and
seeing nothing out of kilter, I decided it was time again to send

another message to Aunt Risa in Blackhawk and hopefully pick up one from her saying she had received the previous messages and was waiting for Keegan's arrival.

I was a little dismayed after reaching the Deer Trail telegraph office in the railroad station depot that there was no message from Keegan's aunt. That of course did not stop me from sending another message that updated our travels and that we were still heading to Blackhawk. After paying for the message, I stood on the boardwalk and ran it through my mind the very real possibility that Larisa Devin O'Rourke was no longer in Blackhawk. It was also a good possibility that the elusive Aunt Risa was not even among the living. As I bounced that thought around in my brain pan, Keegan ran down the boardwalk with Hugo keeping stride for stride with her. The little Irish girl was all smiles and excited as she pointed due west and with an almost shrill in her voice, "Mac, can you see them? Can you see the mountains?"

Following her finger pointing, I was now looking due west and with a little concentration and focus I saw what had excited her. As the very faint blue outline against the far western horizon came more into focus, I felt the same buzz and childlike wonder that Keegan was experiencing. Just like her, it was the very first time that I had ever seen the mighty Rocky Mountains. Stepping back into the Telegraph office, I asked the man that had just sent my message, "How far away are the Rocky Mountains?"

With a slight smile as if he had been asked this very same question numerous times, "Roughly ninety miles to the foothills of the Rockies."

Stepping back outside, I found Keegan and Hugo with his tail wagging nonstop sitting on the edge of the boardwalk looking at the western horizon as if it was a parade going through the town of Deer Trail. As I sat down next to Keegan, she instinctively leaned into me and without thinking, I put my arm around her and held her close. I turned and looked at the young girl as her eyes were wide and bright as she looked at the faraway blue mountains. Once again I was hit hard with how much we had grown to care about each other in such a short period of time. It was almost as if we were meant to be blood and kin. Our relationship that was born out of tragedy had become almost like a grandfather and granddaughter. I was no longer going to question it; from this moment on I was just going to accept it as fact. Sandy my poor departed best friend, of course, would have said, "You have gotten soft in the head old man!"

Sitting here on this boardwalk with Keegan and Hugo was probably the most peaceful moment that I have ever had in my life or at least since I could remember. As we looked in awe and felt the mystery of the mountains of old that reached out to us from the west, I spoke in an almost whisper, not wanting to disturb our slice of heaven, "The man inside said the mountains are ninety miles away. Think about that for a moment - ninety miles - how majestic to think we can actually see the Rocky Mountains from that great distance. It just baffles my mind, Keegan."

Keegan turned slowly to look at me and after a second of studying my face, she buried herself into my arm even more and she spoke with the tenderness that can only come from one that is so young. "They are wonderful, Mac. Just wonderful and thank you for taking care of me and Hugo."

Looking at Keegan with a half-smile, "Hugo has been a pain in the butt since the first day and to think I could have had a couple of fine looking horses for you. Right or wrong a man has to make decisions."

Keegan backed away slowly and after some thought she said, "They were beautiful horses!"

Of course that made us both laugh so hard that it brought tears. I stood up quickly, and Hugo immediately attacked the toe of my boot trying to gnaw a hole through it once again. Grabbing Keegan's hand, I helped her stand as I spoke, "We are burning daylight kiddo; we got to keep moving west."

As I readied Sammy and Horse to move out and was rearranging the saddlebags, I pulled out the sugar sack containing Sandy's ashes and bone and I stared at it a full minute, and the pleasure I had just experienced with Keegan on the boardwalk was suddenly replaced with the sadness and anger I felt losing Sandy to Captain John Merna and his men. I could not let the happiness I felt with Keegan replace what I saw as my duty to avenge my best friend's murder. Keegan was my duty for now; then Captain John Merna would get my full attention after that. It was the way it was supposed to be. As we left Deer Trail pushing Sammy and Horse due west now towards Denver, I was overcome with a sense of dread.

The rest of the late summer day was pleasant enough and not too hot, but black and menacing clouds started to form in the north and were moving south in our direction. Remembering the hail storm that we experienced not long ago, I did not want to relive that again anytime soon. I kept my eye looking north to keep alert if the weather took a turn for the worse.

The wind came first and it felt good and gentle, and then it turned into an outright roar that was nasty and brutal. After chasing down my hat once for over a quarter of a mile after it was blown from my head, I stuffed it in my saddlebag on top of Sandy's ashes. Once back in the saddle on Sammy, I looked north and in just under a minute, the sky turned from light gray color to black. This storm was moving faster toward us than I could ever imagine. Hugo was trying to bury himself deeper into the saddlebag to hunker down out of the wind and the storm. He was getting so big now it was not possible for him to do so. With my eye to the north and the storm, I knew Hugo was the least of my worries at this moment.

Realizing that we might be in trouble, I yelled to Keegan over the sound of the wind that we needed to find some sort of shelter to outlast the storm. She shook her head in understanding, and I could see a tad smidgen of fear building in her face. It was starting to dawn on her that this was a very dangerous storm that was almost on top of us.

We rode another 100 yards or so when I spotted a gully to the south of us and looking west and east, I saw nothing else that would provide any type of shelter, so it would seem the gully was our best bet. Waving my left arm to get Keegan's attention, I pointed toward the south and the gully and she shook her head "yes" and reined Horse in that direction. Before reining Sammy, I looked again toward the north and saw a wall of white that stretched from the prairie to the black sky not more than a mile north of us. Took me a second to realize what I first mistook as a wall of rain was in fact a wall of hail. Giving Sammy some spurs, I raced after Keegan, Hugo, and Horse.

Keegan and Horse reached the gully first, and she dismounted like a fully mature horsewoman that she had become and was grabbing Hugo from the saddlebag as I brought Sammy to a sudden halt beside her. Grabbing both reins of Horse and Sammy, I pulled them down into the gully. Once we were all down and out of the wind somewhat, I told Keegan about the approaching wall of hail. I also warned her that we also had to be aware in this dry gully of a flash flood that could be caused by this storm, but for now we had to ride out the hail first and play it by ear and gut instinct on the other.

I pulled both Horse and Sammy to the ground to get them both as low as possible so that Keegan, Hugo and I could cuddle up next to them. The air just before the hail hit turned cold enough that we could see our breaths, and Keegan and I shivered in the sudden cold wave.

The sky now was midnight black above our heads and seemed almost so close that I could just reach up and touch the dark clouds. The hail first started as hard sleet and reminded me of the ice storms we used to experience in "Little Dixie." Then the sleet turned to hail and peppered us with hail the size of corn kernels which lasted a full ten minutes. Once the corn kernel hail stopped, so did the wind, and the Colorado eastern prairie around us turned into complete silence.

Keegan and I looked at each other in the surrounding stillness - waiting. We waited and waited some more. Keegan started to laugh and said, "That was nothing, Mac."

We looked straight above us in the sky and it turned from black to dark grey right before my eyes and it made me smile when I returned to gaze at Keegan. "It would seem Keegan that might have been the worst of it. I truly believed we were in for a hell of a lot more."

Slapping my hands on my damp pants, I stood up and stretched to get the kinks out of being tightly cramped up. Smiling, I took three strides to get back to the top of the gully, and I looked toward the north.

The smile and good feeling of getting out of this scrape with the Colorado plains weather without hardly getting wet turned into a sour mood as a mile to the north, I saw a two-headed tornado barreling straight for us.

CHAPTER 24

I t was obvious now that the calm and serenity that we were experiencing right after the hail had stopped was just the calm before this maddening storm now approaching. Looking back towards Keegan and with urgency in my voice, I told her, "Grab hold of Hugo and lay down in between the horses and north bank of the gully; we have one hell of a tornado heading our way!"

Keegan looked at me with confusion and uncertainty as she tried to decipher my words. Not wanting to overly alarm her, I once again spoke, but in a calm manner, "Do it now Keegan, the tornado will be here in just a few minutes. I will join you before it goes over the top of us."

After what I said had finally sunk into the young Irish girl, she gathered up Hugo and crouched down into a ball between the north side of the gully and Horse and Sammy holding the dog as if her life depended on it, which by the looks of things - it did.

Turning back toward the north, I watched this tornado and it almost seemed alive and very angry with lightning bolts lighting up the exterior of the dark mass of wind and dust. It was a fascinating turn of events because I had seen a few tornadoes in my life but never one that had two heads as this one making a beeline toward the gully and us. There were no trees in its path to gauge its destructiveness, but it seemed that every tumbleweed in eastern Colorado had been sucked up and was being shredded inside the belly of the beast that now was about a half mile away.

When the tornado was a third of a mile away, I could feel the air surrounding me start to change and the hair on my hatless head began to dance and sway toward the north and the storm.

Taking one last look at the storm, I swore I saw a cow being swirled about inside of it. Sandy of course would have had some smart ass comment to make about that if he had still been alive. Not wanting to join Sandy in the hereafter, I joined Keegan and Hugo and I lay down holding her tight to my chest. Keegan was being strong and trying to stay silent, but I could feel her crying softly before she mumbled, "I am so scared Mac!"

Holding her and Hugo tighter to my chest, I said softly in her ear, "It is all right to be scared Keegan, because I am too. No matter what happens in the next few minutes, I will never let go of you or Hugo. You got to believe that."

Looking over my shoulder at Sammy and Horse, I could see the fear of the unknown in their eyes as the storm got closer. I had to give them both credit though because they did not try to stand and bolt. They looked at me for reassurance, and they actually tried to scoot closer to make a tighter circle. It was an all or nothing circle of life, and they seemed to sense it as well.

Holding tight and closing my eyes, I said a silent prayer more for Keegan's survival than my own. She had been dealt a raw deal of late and she deserved a full life. I have had mine and had seen both the beauty and the evil of life in my time, but this little girl merited more. She was just about the closest thing to a true angel I had ever known.

As the storm and the two headed tornado grew even closer, Horse and Sammy started to snort and blow air out of their noses in a frantic manner. Without even looking, I knew their eyes would be wide-eyed and full of distress. I kept my eyes closed which helped to keep the dirt and grit out because now the smallest piece of dirt, sand, and grit had started to dance and swirl as the storm grew close

Once the tornado reached the top of the gully protecting us, the unnerving and enraging sound of the twirling wind replaced the quiet of the Colorado prairie and became all encompassing. The two headed beast now upon us sounded as if a freight train was running over the gully time and time again. In my mind, I knew what was now just above us was deviously deadly, but in some ways it was also eerily beautiful. Why is it in all things of nature that have so much magnificence and splendor can also bring so much death and devastation?

The sand, grit, dirt, tumbleweeds and anything pulled up from the eastern Colorado prairie was peppering like small shotgun pellets along my back, arms and face as I huddled over to protect Keegan and Hugo from the worst of it. Twice when the storm was on top of us, I felt our bodies start to lift and the weightlessness scared the hell out of me, but both times it only lasted for a second or two before I could feel the weight of our bodies being pulled back to the earth.

After what seemed like an eternity, but in real time was probably less than a minute, the tornado moved on to the south of us, and the roar of the freight train moved south as well caught up in the twisting whirlwind. My arms, back, and face stung from the shotgun blast of dirt and sand. When I opened my eyes, I could see tiny droplets of blood that now were centered on each and every sting. I could only see the back of Keegan's head and the top ears of Hugo, and they were matted with dirt and sand. Even though my ears had still not recovered from the echo of the storm that was still ringing in them, I could hear Keegan's muffled voice, "Is it over Mac? I am too scared to open my eyes!"

When I replied I could taste the dirt and the sand pebbles crunching in my teeth as I spoke, "Yes Keegan it is over. Open your eyes slowly, for they will be full of grit and dirt."

As I released Keegan and the man killing dog, we shook off the kinks and then stood up. As soon as Keegan saw my face, she started to cry - the type of cry that when you have faced the specter of death and he decided it was not your time to die type of cry. I crouched down to the level of Keegan and held out my arms as she fell into them. Her spasms of tears of relief made my arms shake as she let it all out. Her tears and knowing that we all were going to live to finish the day brought a few tears to my eyes as well.

The sound of Sammy and Horse struggling to stand after they were also sand blasted from the tornado brought me out of my brief daze, and I released Keegan so she could tend to her pup and I could tend to the horses.

Both horses were peppered as I was with very tiny wounds that should heal without much difficulty. Both Sammy and Horse were having trouble breathing, and I spent considerable time clearing the nostrils of both horses since they were packed with dirt. Since I had not had the time to unsaddle Sammy or Horse, the areas on their backs and sides showed no wounds as the leather of the saddles had protected them from the onslaught of the wind and the sand.

With a nod of my head, I indicated to Keegan that we needed to get out of the gully that had saved us from what I felt was certain death. Grabbing both of the horses' reins, we slowly climbed out and were met by the most serene Colorado prairie. The tornado had long disappeared from where it had come as it returned to the sky. The sky above our heads was a magnificent blue that stretched as far as our eyes could see. The air seemed cleaner, for as I looked west, the outline of the Rocky Mountains seemed more defined, and I could see the white shrouds of snow that covered even the highest peaks even at this time of year.

Since it was late in the day, I decided we had enough excitement and that we would make camp here and clean and tend to the minor wounds that the horses, Keegan, and I all suffered. Hugo escaped the storm with no worse for wear.

The little shit had been the best protected and seemed as if he had even forgotten the tornado already. As I gathered the canteens for water to wash with, I tripped over the man killing dog as he once again attacked the toe of my boot. Looking down at Hugo, I realized he was no longer a pup and now was almost full grown. Gauging his size, I realized he had to be uncomfortable riding in the saddlebag. The problem was his legs were still way too short, and he would never be able to keep up with Sammy and Horse.

I looked at Keegan as she was giving me the ole' stink eye as she was wondering what I was brooding about, and then my eyes drifted back to Hugo. I finally made a decision that I knew I was going to regret sooner than later. Bending down, I picked up Hugo and brought him close enough to my face that he tried to lick my nose off once again. With a sigh, "Look here buster you are getting too big to ride in the saddlebag any longer, and you will now have to learn to share a saddle with me."

Keegan, once she had heard what I just said and with a smile from ear to ear, ran fast and hard and grabbed my side and gave me a huge hug.

CHAPTER 25

The first day of traveling with Hugo riding on the saddle with me made both of us irritable and cranky. Hugo fell six times and each time he landed on his feet and was uninjured, but it slowed us down a mite since each time I would have to ride back, dismount and then once again regain my saddle without dropping him. Every time I looked as if I was just about ready to pull my Colt and shoot the damn dog, Keegan would give me the eye like my mama used to do and put me in my place. At my age, it was not pleasant to ride with someone that acted like my mother. I even told Keegan this a few times, and each time she would just put her finger to her lip and shush me. Hard to believe a man my age getting shushed! It made me laugh.

The second day Hugo finally found his balance and was able to ride and share the back of Sammy without too much trouble and never once from sunup to sunset fell from the top of Horse.

On the third day after the tornado is when Hugo and I both felt comfortable enough with each other that it seemed we had been riding double all of our lives. Hugo seemed to enjoy it much more than being stuffed in that ole' saddlebag. After I roughed up his hair a mite on the top of his head, Hugo turned to me with his tongue hanging out and that doggie grin of his, and he seemed right proud of himself. I know I was proud of the little shit.

Took us a full three days after the tornado to reach the banks of Cherry Creek just southeast of Denver with the countless delays with Hugo and my learning how to share the saddle and the back of Sammy. Once at Cherry Creek we found a suitable place with fresh water to make camp and after doing so, Keegan made a friend of an old man named Marty Blake who was gold panning the creek.

Marty was bald headed, wrinkled, with barely any teeth left in his noggin, and it would seem his best years were far behind him. As we soon found out, Marty was a jovial timeworn man, and Keegan had taken a particular shine to the old man so we decided to feed him a supper of jack rabbits, taters, and a can of peaches for dessert.

Marty was surprised by the offer of a meal and readily accepted; it would seem he had taken a shine to Keegan as well. Hugo put his stamp of approval of Marty by jumping into his lap and promptly falling to sleep.

There was not much needed to carry on a conversation with Marty because he did all the talking and began to tell us some of his history. Marty told us he had been at the Cherry Creek diggings numerous times since the beginning of the Pikes Peak gold rush before Colorado became a state and it was still called the Kansas Territory. He went on to say he made two different fortunes from the yellow dust and lost them both because of his desires for gambling, drinking whiskey, and soiled doves. He had covered Keegan's ears with his hands and whispered "soiled doves" to me. Of course Keegan got a big laugh out of that because she could read his lips.

Marty was knowledgeable of the history of the area, and he gave us a quick lesson since this was as far west as either Keegan or I had ever been. He went on to say Denver was founded about twenty or so years prior on the banks of the South Platte River of which Cherry Creek was a tributary. Denver at first began as a gold camp, but the gold quickly dried up and the town became the main shipping point to the gold and silver camps that had sprung up in the mountains to the west. He also said Denver the town was not really very much to talk about until the railroads started using it as their main shipping point east of the great divide.

Keegan stopped Marty at that point and asked him what he meant by the "Great Divide," and I turned an ear to listen as well because I did not want to admit that I did not have a clue what the Great Divide was as well.

Marty went on to explain that the Great Divide was the spine of this great nation and that all rivers flowed downward from this point. It was the highest point in the mountains that ran from the farthest regions of the far north down into Mexico. Once Marty explained how the rivers got started, it all seemed rather simple of course. He said when it snowed in the high country and when it melted, all that water flowed downhill, where it gathered with more water at lower elevations, increasing in size until the now flowing water became brooks, then creeks, and then the mighty rivers. He went on to explain that is why on the west side of the Great Divide the rivers flowed from the east to the west and that on the east side the rivers flowed west to east.

After giving Keegan and myself the brief history of Denver and of the Great Divide, I asked Marty if he had ever heard of the Reynolds gang here in Colorado. Marty started to laugh and said not only had he heard of them, but actually he had been robbed of $300 of gold dust by them when he was working the north fork of the South Platte River just at the bottom of Kenosha Pass. He said other than robbing him of three months' worth of work, the two Confederate brothers and leaders of the gang, Jim and John Reynolds didn't seem to be as bad of fellows as the papers made them out to be. Marty went on to explain they had left him with twenty dollars and his mule and supplies to keep on gold panning. He said the rumor was that just east of Kenosha Pass was where the Reynolds gang had buried their stolen loot when they were tracked down by a posse out of Fairplay, Colorado.

Marty's tale was interesting about the Reynolds gang and it only confirmed to me that they were in fact a real gang robbing the gold miners in that part of the mountains of Colorado. I started to think it wasn't really a stretch of the imagination that Captain Merna had stumbled onto the supposed treasure map of the loot. As crazy as I thought the Captain was in regard to his ancient enemies that rode for the gray, he still had enough in his brain pan to understand the value of such loot if there was in fact any at all.

Since I was thinking of Merna, I decided to ask Marty if he had ever heard of Captain John Merna and the Kansas Redlegs from the Civil War. He said he didn't recollect ever hearing of Captain Merna, but he sure as hell had heard of those butchering Redlegs. Matter of fact old man Marty got so upset when I mentioned them that he stood up and started raising his voice and pointing his finger at me and then to the mountains in the west. It would seem he had gotten a telegraph message informing him of an old friend and former partner of his who had fought for the Confederacy and had been gunned down several weeks ago on the main street of Fairplay, Colorado, a gold mining camp west of Denver in the South Park region by one of those damn Redlegs named LB or something along those lines.

After the old gold miner got his anger out and in the open about the death of his friend, he calmed right back down and made his apologies to Keegan and myself for raving like a madman. As soon as Hugo jumped back in his lap, which told Keegan and myself all we needed to know about Marty Blake, we both at the same time told him that no apologies were needed.

After supper we invited Marty to roll out his bed roll here by our fire for the evening which once again he readily accepted. Once he got settled in, he started to tell Keegan and Hugo about the legend of a dance hall girl nicknamed Silver Heels and the town of Buckskin Joe in the South Park Region just west of Kenosha Pass. He even recited a poem that told of the legend he had memorized named - Silver Heels. Marty started his rendition obviously enjoying that he had a captivated crowd of Keegan and myself.

"In the Buckskin Joe gold camp, she arrived by way of the
Denver to Fairplay stage,
Exquisitely dressed in a long black dress no one could guess
her age.
She was inescapably beautiful, petite, quint, with raven colored
hair,
Lifting her dress above the snow and mud, she seemed to dance
in the air.

Gold miners, freighters, and men of the mountain were taken in
by the girl,
As she stepped up to the boardwalk and gave her parasol a
suggestive twirl.
Among the soiled doves she became the "Fancy Lady" in Bill
Buck's dance hall,
In the loneliness of the mountain winter snow - she won the
hearts of them all.
In this gold camp of Buckskin Joe in the Colorado high
mountains so remote,
The local newspaper it appeared of "The coming of an Angel" -
someone wrote.
Her real name remained a mystery - there were rumors, but no
one ever knew,
Adorned in tight-fitting satin gowns and silver heels - the
miners love for her only grew.
It was the girl's shiny silver heels that would give her the
immortal nickname,
Back then and forever in those isolated mountains "Silver
Heels" - she became.
With a vengeance in the fall of 1861 another visitor came to
Buckskin Joe,
Extremely painful, debilitating, and disfiguring - "Smallpox"
put on a show.
Death and disease was about to devastate the mining town of
Buckskin Joe,
During those cold and desolate days and months of the autumn
and winter snow.
Amid the heartbreak, disease, and death, that the Silver Heels'
legend would be made.
She cared for the sick and dying from cabin to cabin - heaven
sent and never afraid.
She held the sick miners and comforted them risking her only
asset - her beauty,
Songs and dance were lost in the panic - caring for those in
need became her duty.
In the final hours of the epidemic - tragically - Silver Heels
would catch the disease,

As the last of the sick - she was carried to her cabin down by the river and the trees.
In her isolated cabin Silver Heels declined deep into delirium and the darkness,
Smallpox had all but vanished from Buckskin Joe, but still proved forever heartless.
As the gold miners, children, women, and the town, healed and returned to what was,
Silver Heels, pockmarked, her beauty gone and would nevermore hear the applause.
Grateful miners gathered a purse of five thousand dollars for Silver Heels all in gold,
When they went to her cabin - she was gone - vanished - or so the legend is told.
Some say for numerous years following the smallpox epidemic of Buckskin Joe,
In the cemetery a mysterious veiled woman wearing a satin gown, silver heels - forever strolls."

I was watching Keegan's eyes as they widened from time to time as the old prospector told his tales and poems, and it reminded me of when I was a youngster and I would listen to my grand pappy tell of the days gone by and how much I enjoyed them. This would be a night around the campfire she would never forget, nor would I for that matter.

With Marty Blake still entertaining Keegan and her man killing mutt Hugo with strange tales of the mountains, I saw to Sammy and Horse and brushed them down with my wood curry comb. As I worked and gave some loving to the horses and after giving them some much needed grain, of course I gave them both a generous treat of sugar as I did every evening.

Once the horses were well taken care of, I looked toward the towering Rockies now not far in the western distance and once again marveled at a good ole' Rocky Mountain sunset. The late summer air had chilled some and it felt as if autumn seemed to be just around the bend. Looking at the white covered mountains, I could only think of how cold it got up above where the trees never grow.

Holding Sammy's neck and still looking west, I started to ponder about everything that Marty had spoken of this evening. It was of course interesting to hear his tales and poems of the mountains and also to learn some of the history of Cherry Creek and Colorado, but what weighed heavily on my mind was what the old man had said about the Reynolds gang's loot and of course the killing of his friend in Fairplay.

The man named LB that Marty had mentioned as the killer of his friend was of course Larry Brown the gunfighter and former Redleg that rode with none other than Captain John Merna.

As fate and destiny would have it, I had gotten a good clue and starting point in looking for those that rode with Merna that needed my full attention after I got Keegan safely where she needed to go. It would seem once Keegan was safe in Blackhawk that Fairplay, Colorado was where I would be heading.

CHAPTER 26

Gunshots in the distance woke me twice during the night. They came from the northwest and probably carried on the wind from the town of Denver. Stray gunshots at night could mean just about anything from an upstart town that was coming into its own. It was more than likely just a few cowhands letting off some steam from a long cattle drive. Such things normally would have been like flies on a fresh cow pie to Sandy and me, and we would have saddled up and headed in that direction to see what type of shenanigans were to be had.

Looking back at the still sleeping Keegan and Hugo, I knew that my precedence was with that little girl for now. Looking at the saddlebag lying on the ground beside me that had Sandy's ashes in it brought home once again that in regard of my best friend my priorities had also changed. Until I had brought justice to those that had killed my friend, any and all shenanigans would have to be set aside for now. Laying my head back down, I watched the stars as they twinkled on this cloudless night and after a few minutes, my head cleared enough for me to fall back to sleep.

Waking before dawn, I looked at the horses as was my habit to see if they were on edge and sensing only the peaceful morning, both Sammy and Horse were gracefully grazing on the tall grass on the bank of Cherry Creek.

Marty was already awake and he was already stirring last night's embers from our evening fire and after adding a few small logs had a breakfast fire going strong. He then produced some chicken eggs and was frying up some fatback bacon for what hopefully would be my breakfast this morning.

Marty saw me looking in his direction and held up an egg and said, "After last night's wonderful supper I thought it only right for me to get the fixings for our breakfast this morning. Do you and the young Miss like chicken eggs?"

Standing slowly to get the kinks of sleep out of my bones I said, "Who doesn't like chicken eggs, Marty? If you know of such a rascal, then they cannot be a friend of mine."

Marty showed his almost toothless grin and set aside the bacon as he cracked almost a dozen eggs into the skillet on the campfire. Then he began to scramble them. As the fire worked its magic on the eggs, Marty pointed to Keegan still sound asleep. "I take it you are not Keegan's Pa or Grandpa."

After slapping Keegan's Pa's hat on my head, I adjusted my holster and looked at Marty and in a thoughtful voice, "Not even any kin to her. I found her just outside Dighton, Kansas after her folks had been butchered by those same Redlegs that killed your friend in Fairplay and my good friend Sandy. Those men are led by Captain John Merna and he is an old enemy of mine and as soon as I get Keegan safely to her aunt in Blackhawk, then I will be hunting down Merna and his cutthroats and applying the justice that they have coming."

Marty set the frying pan aside and looked at me with the knowing eyes of someone only as old as him from living a rugged life in the west. Squinting his eyes, he asked, "Mac, you carry yourself as a man that has seen way too much in your life. I guess you never mentioned your full name last night. If you don't mind me asking, "Who are you?"

Walking over, I reached down and gingerly touched Keegan on her shoulder to wake her up and spoke to her. "Rise and shine little one. It would seem you got the day off from making breakfast. Our new friend Marty is an early riser and it smells like one hell of a cook."

Grabbing three plates, I handed one to Keegan and Marty and kept one for myself. Keegan was all smiles and full of good ole' mountain tales from the night before and happy that she was the one that did not have to rustle up the grub this morning. I started to pile up the eggs and bacon on Keegan's plate and mine. Taking a quick bite out of a piece of bacon, I sat down on a log facing Marty with Keegan sitting next to me intent on eating her breakfast and replied to his question. "My name is McCall Patton, but my friends call me Mac."

Marty almost dropped his spoonful of eggs he was heaping onto his plate and his eyes got a tad larger when he looked at me. "McCall Patton? The gray rider? The one some call Rebel Mac?"

Keegan sort of chuckled when Marty spoke and she then looked at me and said, "You seem to be a known man out here in the west, Mac. Not sure if that is a good thing or not."

Looking at Keegan with a smile, "I guess now I get to tell you to shush!"

Keegan laughed once again and started in on eating her breakfast as if there was no tomorrow.

Hugo was now fully awake and started into his morning routine of trying to chew a hole in the toe of my boot while I was wearing it. In between a couple of spoonful's of eggs and now turning towards Marty, I was able to mumble out a reply without having any of my scrambled eggs drop out of my mouth, "All true. One and the same."

A smile spread across Marty's face, and his eyes showed a sparkle of laughter. "I will be damned. It would seem the good ole' Lord works in mysterious ways and has delivered to Keegan and Hugo not only an angel of mercy, but an avenging angel as well."

After our tasteful and hearty breakfast, I asked Marty about the trail to Blackhawk to gather information on what to expect. He told me the quickest route would be to bypass Denver which was to the northwest ten or so miles and head straight west to the town of Englewood, which was by his recollection nine miles. Marty then suggested that we should veer northwest about three miles into the town of Sheridan. Then from Sheridan still following the trail more west than north, we would venture into the town of Morrison,

Colorado which by his reckoning was another eleven miles. From Morrison we were to head north nine miles to the mouth of Clear Creek Canyon and then follow upstream the flowing water of Clear Creek straight west twenty miles through the canyon to the gold camp of Black Hawk, which was one mile east of Central City along Gregory Gulch.

The town of Morrison, Marty went on to say, was at the bottom of the foothills and the gateway to the Rocky Mountain gold camps of Idaho Springs, Central City, Georgetown, Silver Plume, Nevadaville, Russell Gulch, Empire, and of course Blackhawk all of which were on the eastern side of the "Great Divide." Marty stopped, appearing to be deep in thought, pondering for a spell as if he was trying to gather some more information for me. He looked with those knowing old man's eyes of his and asked, "Have you ever heard of Lucas Eldridge the gunfighter? I met him once in a small town named Como, Colorado. He was a man much like yourself that was driven with a purpose."

Lucas Eldridge, as I recollect, was one of the most famous men in the Rocky Mountain frontier and as his story goes over a course of two years, he hunted and tracked down the Mexican bandit brothers named Juan and Jose Verdugo, which ended badly for the Mexican desperadoes. Eldridge was also linked with and maybe either kin or best friends with Chance Bondurant, another famous gunfighter and the famed mountain man Matt Lee. Even as far away as "Little Dixie," we had heard of Eldridge, Bondurant, and Lee. I could not recall any of the particulars why they were famous though.

Answering Marty, "Yes, even back east, where I am from we have heard of such men as Lucas Eldridge, Chance Bondurant, and of course the famous mountain man Matt Lee. Eldridge, as I recall, hunted and killed Juan and Jose Verdugo for the substantial bounty on their heads."

Marty Blake slowly shook his head "no" before he replied in a thoughtful and caring voice, "Lucas Eldridge at the end got the bounty on the Verdugo brothers, but that is not why he took two years to track those Mexican bandits down. It was because those murdering assholes killed his purpose in life when they butchered and took his wife from him. You see Mac Patton - Lucas Eldridge's purpose in life changed on the day his wife was killed.

Having a purpose in life is why we live. It's like having a ranch, starting a family, or being the best friend humanly possible; and from time to time in our lives that purpose may change as life and fate interfere with that purpose. Then it becomes something else. When that purpose is rude and swiftly taken from you, be it your own fault or someone else's, that purpose may become revengeful. You gather ice in your veins and blood in your eye, and that purpose turns into the hateful fire in your heart. You will never be whole or the same person again until you can put out that fire. I saw that blood in the eye of Lucas Eldridge so many years ago in the town of Como, Colorado and we now know how that story turned out. You McCall "Mac" Patton have the same look of blood in your eyes, and I can feel the chill of the ice in your veins. The difference my friend is the ending of your tale is yet to be told. Having said that, I would not want to be Captain Merna and his men with you on my trail with that hateful fire in your heart."

After hearing Marty speak his piece, I knew when I first met him that he had all knowing eyes and it would seem the old gold miner had an all knowing mind and heart as well. Rolling what he said around in my thinker some, I finally replied, "Well Mr. Blake I can hardly argue with what you just said. The only difference is that Keegan's and Hugo's safety are my first purpose, but once I see her safely to her Aunt Risa in Blackhawk, I will extinguish that hateful fire you spoke of with gunfire and lead."

CHAPTER 27

Keegan, Hugo, Sammy, Horse, and I got a slow start this morning not wanting to say goodbye to our new friend Marty. Marty and I shook hands and Keegan gave him a warm hug before we mounted the horses to continue down the Keegan Trail straight west toward the town of Englewood just as Marty had suggested.

Keegan and I both looked back over our shoulders one last time at the old gold miner, and he was still waving his hand smiling his almost toothless grin. Both of us realized this was probably the one and only time we would see the old man. When Keegan once again turned her head west, she said nothing at all, but her eyes told me her story as they were glistening with a tear or two. Not often do you run across someone with a true, genuine heart like Marty Blake. Looking at the young girl riding next to me to the left, I realized in a short time I had run across two such people with the same heart - Marty Blake and Keegan O'Rourke.

As we traveled the ten miles to Englewood, we crossed two large trails heading north toward the town of Denver. I was curious what the town was like, but it was not meant to be for me to know at this moment in time since I had more pressing matters to tend to.

It was an hour or so past midday when we entered the town of Englewood; it was a quaint little town with a couple of hotels and a few saloons. No one paid much attention to us as we stopped to water Sammy and Horse at a watering trough in the center of town. I remembered Marty had said the town was founded about twenty years prior when gold had been found at a place called Little Creek.

There was a trail that took off toward the northwest that had a sign that was printed saying Sheridan, Colorado was three miles away. Keegan and I joked some about all these folks living in towns along the trail we had named "The Keegan Trail." I wanted to scribble on the road sign to Sheridan - "Follow the Keegan Trail to Sheridan, Colorado." Keegan liked my idea, but talked me out of it since she didn't want me to get into any kind of trouble. We both had a good laugh about that.

As soon as we made the town of Sheridan, I felt a kinship to the small town. I felt as if I had arrived back home in "Little Dixie," not because of its ties to the Confederacy because there were none, but because of its size and the people. The town was roughly the same as my hometown back in Missouri and the people seemed genuinely peaceful in going about their daily chores and tasks. Sheridan, by Marty Blake's account, was also founded roughly twenty years prior by a man named John McBroom and originally named Petersburg. Since Colorado had recently become a state, the town of Petersburg was renamed Sheridan after the Union army general Phil Sheridan. It would seem that the North in their victory over the South had to keep reminding me, so they seemed to name all these little towns after their war heroes. Not like I needed constant reminding that they had won the war. Sheridan, known as "Fighting Phil," was a man I knew by reputation only and had never run across him or his troops in battle even though he was the Quartermaster General of Southwest Missouri when I was battling along the Kansas and Missouri border against the Redlegs. Petersburg, now Sheridan, was founded not because of gold, but of the rich farm ground from the banks of Bear Creek to the South Platte River and provided much needed farm goods for the much larger town of Denver to the north.

Since it was getting late in the day, I decided it would be a nice change of pace for Keegan to sleep in a real bed in a hotel here in Sheridan and then we both could take a much needed warm bath in a cast iron tub.

We found a suitable stable in the middle of town ran by a likable middle-aged short haired blonde headed fellow named Brett Hooper, who would feed and care for both Sammy and Horse for two bits. I threw in an extra two bits for some extra loving care, and Brett seemed pleased to get it and I had no doubt he would take extra good care of Sammy and Horse.

After renting a room at the Sheridan Inn with a double bed for me and an extra day bed for Keegan, we both took turns taking a warm bath with the hotel staff supplying the buckets of heated water to get rid of the weeks of trail dust that we had been living in. After getting cleaned up, Keegan and I felt like completely different folks. Keegan even gave Hugo a bath in the cast iron tub which he seemed to enjoy almost as much as the both of us.

After our baths Keegan, Hugo, and I walked the half a block down the boardwalk to Monaghan's, a saloon that doubled as an eatery. Hungry for something other than our own cooking, Keegan and I both decided on having a beef steak if that was on the menu. Of course after a short discussion, we both were hoping that there was some sort of pie for the offering - apple would have been both of our first choice.

The sun was setting slowly in the west behind the tall mountains that we had no trouble seeing now since we were so close. Keegan, Hugo, and I had stepped out into the street to see past the buildings to watch the glory of a Rocky Mountain orange and blue sunset to bring an end to this very late summer cloudless day. I had always enjoyed sunrise and sunsets, but here in Colorado and if what Marty Blake had told us was correct - we were now standing a mile above sea level - and somehow it seemed to make this everyday event seem more spectacular.

Before entering Monaghan's, I slipped the rawhide thong off the hammer of my Colt that held it in place from falling out while riding the trail. I did it more out of habit than anything else since I was not expecting any type of trouble in this small burg of a town. I felt at ease walking the streets of Sheridan, something I had not felt in what seemed a long, long time. Keegan has always been a joy to have by my side, but today she seemed happier than she had been since I had found her under the floor of her folk's farm house outside of Dighton. It was good to see her this way; it brought a smile to my face.

Through the bat wing doors that were on the southeast corner of the wooden building, we found that Monaghan's was a small saloon with about a half-dozen tables and a fancy wooden bar enriched with wood carvings of the mountains, trees, and such. At the foot of the bar was a shiny polished brass foot rest that ran the whole length of the bar for folks to rest their feet on rather they be standing or sitting while enjoying their daily whiskey. Behind the bar and mounted above a painting of a scantily clad woman was a sign proudly proclaiming Monaghan's as the "Oldest Liquor License in the State of Colorado." That sign made me almost laugh since Colorado had just become a new state, and I was not sure that being the oldest liquor license in the state was much of a boast, but these folks sure as hell seemed right proud of that fact.

Standing behind the bar was a man and a woman who were busy taking inventory and cleaning behind the bar. One man stood alone at the bar and I studied him for a moment. He was young, maybe in his late teens, but he was carrying a tied down Colt with the grip facing backwards for a standard draw. He looked at us for only a second and when his curiosity was satisfied, he turned his attention back to the shot of whiskey in front of him. A young couple with two daughters dressed in their best clothes were just finishing up their meal, and I spied a half-eaten piece of apple pie on their table. Tapping Keegan on her shoulder and with a nod of my head, I indicated the pie, which brought an ear-to-ear grin on the young Irish girl's face.

Hugo saw the young girls seated with their folks and he made a beeline in that direction, abandoning Keegan and myself to make himself acquainted. With their folks' permission and a nod from me indicating it was all right, the girls got down on the floor and started loving on the man killing pup. Shaking my head with a smile, I thought, "What a traitor that little shit was."

Keegan and I found a suitable table in the back so I could have my back to the wall and I could see the entire saloon while sitting. As soon as we got set, the middle-aged woman that was almost as tall as I was with dark brown hair with a beautiful gray streak from behind the bar approached us and with a gracious smile she said, "Glad to see some new faces in Monaghan's. My name is Shirley and that is my husband Joe behind the bar, and we own this fine establishment. My husband has sort of a grumpy exterior, so I wait on the newcomers so as not to scare them off."

Shirley had finished her statement with a slight chuckle and I liked her from the get go. Trying to keep the banter friendly, I asked, "I take it you folks are Irish since the name of your saloon is Monaghan's?"

Shirley chuckled at first and then it turned into an almost full belly laugh as she replied, "Oh hell no, our last name is Minter and we are English. We just bought the saloon from a fellow named Ivy Monaghan, and Joe decided we would keep the name since we all know no one can drink like the Irish can. My husband is always the thinker. And truth be known he would like nothing better than to take money and gold from the Irish. I hope I had not offended you if you are Irish."

Keegan and I both smiled as Shirley added the last sentence, "I am not offended Shirley since I am not Irish, but you might have to ask Keegan, for her name is Keegan Doreen O'Rourke which is about as Irish as it gets."

Keegan laughed out loud and then replied, "I am not offended Mrs. Minter, for my Pa would have said, "There is truth in them *thar* words!""

After the laughter and introductions were made, we ordered the only thing on the menu tonight and that was beef steak, fried taters, and cucumbers from Mrs. Minter's garden and of course a piece of fresh apple pie just out of the oven. As it turned out, Keegan and I were having a grand day.

After Shirley left to prepare our supper, her husband Joe, who was roughly the same age of his wife with the lean hips of a boxer and a full head of hair and a beard that was dark and peppered with gray, came over and introduced himself and I liked him from the get go as well. His exterior may have looked grumpy, but he was all smiles as he entertained Keegan and myself while we were waiting with a story from yesterday when his daughter Marilyn had purchased a new horse and had ridden it through the bat wing doors to show her Pa on a dare from her four sisters. The story Joe told was pleasant and funny up until she rode the horse back out and caught and broke her foot on the frame of the bat wing doors. Joe told us with a hearty laugh that she would recover, but the story would live on forever.

Half way through our supper, the young cowboy had paid for his drink and left as did the family with the two young girls. Hugo was a tad dismayed when his new friends left, but I fed him some steak, which made him quickly forget about the two girls.

After supper Keegan and I both stretched back in our chairs, and I thumped my belly like a ripe watermelon and the solid thump, thump sound brought a round of giggles from Keegan. As I watched her sitting there with Hugo now on her lap and full of smiles, the thought crossed my mind once again how blessed I was to have crossed trails with this young Irish girl.

Just as I was getting content and thinking that life in general was not all that bad is when the bat wing doors swung open and the one and only Allen Wells walked in - the same Redleg that rode with Captain John Merna and had been present when poor ole' Sandy was killed - the same son of a bitch that helped kill Keegan's folks and tried to kill me.

CHAPTER 28

A llen Wells's stride into Monaghan's showed his foolish arrogance in that he looked right at me for a second but never took the extra second to really get a good look at me to realize who I was. Of course Wells would have thought I had burned up and was sure enough dead back there outside of Dighton, Kansas in the house he helped set afire. It could also be that Keegan and I were sitting far enough in the shadows that he could not get a good enough look at me.

Keegan of course would never have seen Wells nor the rest of the Redlegs' faces since she had been in hiding in the crawl space under the house, so she was still happy as a lark with a full tummy and loving up on Hugo.

Wells marched right up and ordered a bottle of whiskey with one glass which meant he would not be expecting any of the others that I was hunting. For a few minutes I studied my adversary without his knowledge.

Wells was, as I remembered him, a skinny no-good, and no-account that carried two Colt pistols and fancied himself as a quick draw. He carried his pistols with the grips pointed forward. His blonde hair was a lot longer than I remembered, but he still had that short blond beard. His shirt was dark colored with a thick layer of trail dust on it. And his white Stetson cattleman crested hat that rode his head was almost yellow stained with sweat and dust.

Of course Wells was wearing those damn red leggings which gave these Jayhawkers their nickname over his rawhide pants from the top of his dusty boots to just below his knee. Folks here in Sheridan or for that matter anywhere in Colorado might not know the significance of those red wrappings on their legs, but for me they were a sign of hatred for all those folks and things that I loved back home. Up until the end of the Civil War, it was my pleasure and sworn duty to kill those sporting those red leggings. Up until what happened to Sandy back in Western Kansas, I thought those days were long gone. It would seem that not only in my dreams of those long dead but also even now when wide awake, I am haunted by my past. I could almost feel the ghost of my dead partner Sandy standing quietly at the bar observing what was about to happen.

Joe and Shirley Minter were going about their tasks as usual serving Wells his whiskey and tidying up their place of business. I did not want to confront Wells here in Monaghan's where there were such nice folks, but I sure as hell was not going to let Wells walk out of here on his own two feet. The time for Alan Wells's reckoning was now at hand.

My mind focused in on Wells and everything else in Monaghan's all at the same time as if I had a couple of extra sets of eyes and ears. I could smell the apple pie each and every time Mrs. Minter walked through the kitchen door. The tick tock of the clock above the door sounded like drums in my head. I could smell the tangy odor of the privy out back. Now that I had my mind set for the coming confrontation with Wells, I needed to get Keegan, Hugo, and the Minters some place safe so they would not catch a stray bullet.

Turning to Keegan and in a quiet but forceful tone so she would understand the seriousness of the situation, I said, "Keegan don't talk and just listen to me. Don't look at him, but the man standing at the bar is named Alan Wells and is one of those that killed your folks and my friend Sandy. I need you to take Hugo and walk over to Mrs. Minter and ask her if she would show you how to make apple pie. Then, once in the kitchen tell her about that man and that he had killed your parents. Tell her everything that has happened up until now. Then add that she needs to send her husband for the local law hereabouts. Do you understand?"

Keegan's eyes clouded over some once what I said had registered in her mind. I had to give her credit because she didn't say anything and she restrained herself from looking in Wells direction. She slowly nodded her head "yes" in understanding.

After a silent nod of my head to indicate she needed to get moving, Keegan got up slowly and told Hugo to follow her, making her way across the floor to the end of the bar where Mrs. Minter was writing something in a ledger book. Wells looked at her, but just more out of seeing movement than caring about what she was doing.

Keegan spoke just loud enough for Mrs. Minter to hear and Shirley replied with a smile, "Sure enough honey, follow me."

After what seemed like an eternity, but was only in reality five minutes or so, Mrs. Minter stuck her head out of the kitchen and looked at me for a moment and then motioned to her husband as she said, "Joe I need your help in the kitchen for a second."

Joe hesitated for a minute, but then he saw the look that only a wife can give her husband that he better jump quickly - which he did. If not for the circumstances, that look she gave him and his reaction would have made me laugh.

What Keegan and now the Minters did not know was that I was not going to wait for the law to show up. Allen Wells was my problem, and I was going to deal with it the only way McCall "Mac" Patton knew how.

Standing, but keeping an eye on Wells, I walked over to the bar and stood to Wells right about forty feet and placed my hands on the bar. I then slowly turned toward the Redleg with my right arm and hand falling loosely above my holster and Colt on my right hip, and then I spoke in a clear and confident voice, "You know Wells, you should really take those red leggings off because they mark you as the murdering scum that you are!"

I could see the redness of anger slowly flowing over Wells's face as he turned toward me and said, "Who the hell do you..."

Wells stopped speaking as it started to register in his pea brain who I was, and his face showed total bewilderment as he looked at me. I waited for his mind to catch up, for I wanted him to know the man who was going to kill him.

Wells's eyes showed recognition along with confusion when he finally was able to speak, "It is not possible! You're dead!"

Smiling slightly and still in a calm voice, "I believe those were Randy Vaughn's last words also after he told me of Merna's quest for the Reynolds' loot."

Wells still had confusion rolling like thunder in his mind and he was still trying to catch up with these turn of events. "Vaughn's dead? Did you kill him, Patton?"

Looking Wells straight in the eyes, I answered his questions, "Just like I am going to kill you, Wells!"

Wells was starting to gain his composure as his mind started to put two and two together, and he spread his legs so they were directly under his shoulders the way all gunfighters did before drawing their weapons. A small smile crept across his face as he was gaining confidence, and his mind was starting to clear in this confrontation. He felt assured in his ability to outdraw me and come out the victor. I knew better though, for my purpose, my retribution were a righteous cause and his was not. That alone gave me the edge. Justice and vengeance would be mine today. My gut told me that on this day I was unbeatable. Alan Wells just didn't know it yet.

Before I applied the justice this Redleg had coming, I needed to know if the others were here in Sheridan or elsewhere. My hope was I could end this whole bloody ordeal right here and right now. I took a deep breath and kept my focus on Wells waiting for the telling twitch of a finger or his eye that would telegraph his drawing of his Colts. I asked in a cool manner, "Where are Captain Merna, John Loveless, and LB? I am hoping once I have taken out the trash - namely you Wells - I can finish this right here in Sheridan."

Wells seemed willing to answer all of my questions, so he replied in a cold and deadly voice, "I never did believe that bullshit about the map showing the location of the Reynolds' treasure trove. The Captain would never show the rest of us the map and when I pressed him on that, he got red in the face and angry and told me just to follow orders like a good soldier. Hell Patton, the war ended a long time ago and I am through taking orders from that lunatic. I snuck out of camp a week or so ago the night before the Captain and the others headed to the South Park region on some foolish treasure hunt. I decided enough is enough and I am heading back home to eastern Kansas. And if you don't step aside Patton and let me do that, I am going to kill you - again!"

Shaking my head "no," slowly I replied, "Wells, you do not get a pass for killing my best friend. I am not stepping aside!"

I had my answer or at least a good clue on the whereabouts of Merna and the others, and Wells had his answer. I saw the sweat beading on Wells's forehead, and his right eye squinted slightly as he started for his right Colt first then his left Colt. I palmed my Colt with lightning speed.

He cleared leather with both of his six guns and actually got off a round from each, although the only thing that he was able to hit was the floor just in front of me as he started to buckle. My first round caught him off kilter somewhat and about two inches to the right of his heart. My second round caught him low in the throat as his knees bowed and he started to fall to the floor. His eyes first showed surprise followed by acceptance of knowing he was dying.

Wells was still alive and lying on the floor as his life blood seeped out of the two wounds that I had inflicted on him. I picked up his Colts and placed them on top of the bar out of his reach. Once that was done, I grabbed Wells by his hair with my left hand and lifted him just enough to force him to look me in the eye as I placed the barrel of my Colt against his temple with my right hand. I spoke slowly and clearly so there was no misunderstanding. "Sandy was a better man than any Redleg ever was. Just so you know, this last bullet is not for him, but for those poor Irish folks you helped to butcher outside of Dighton, Kansas."

I saw Wells's eyes clear for a moment as he remembered the O'Rourkes. Once I felt he knew the final coup de grâce was not for Sandy, but for the O'Rourkes, I pulled the trigger.

CHAPTER 29

Before standing, I wiped the blood that had splattered on my hand on Wells's shirt and looking about, I was pleased to see that the Minters, Keegan, or anyone else for that matter had not seen the final shot to put an end to Wells. I realized the final bullet was more brutal than most folks would have liked or cared for. It probably would have sickened some the manner of which I had applied his last and concluding justice. For me it was a suitable end to a man that deserved much worse for his actions in the war and since. I was not proud of what I had done, nor did it make me happy or ease my pain in the loss of my only true friend in the world. As I stood and looked down at the lifeless body of Alan Wells, it just seemed…fitting.

The smoke of the gunfight had not yet cleared before a man wearing a gold star slowly entered through the batwing doors and front entrance of Monaghan's with Joe Minter a step behind him. It would seem that Monaghan's had a rear exit for Joe to use to fetch the law because I had not seen him go through the front door.

The Sheridan sheriff was of Mexican descent and had his Colt 44 drawn and pointed in my direction which I did not care for at all. He was not a big man and was about 5'7" with a slender build, but had "the" look of a man who had confidence in his ability as a law officer. His hair was midnight black and short, and he was dressed plainly with a brown rawhide vest over a red and black flannel shirt, and his hat was a dusty black Bollman felt hat that had seen better days.

A few moments passed and the tension started to mount as a half dozen more men entered the saloon behind the sheriff. Keegan and Mrs. Minter also made themselves present after the shooting from the kitchen area behind the bar and stood behind me, but off to the right.

The sheriff of Sheridan spoke in a clear and unhurried voice, "My name is Daniel Basquez, and I am the law here in Sheridan and I would like you to hand over your weapon!"

I squared my feet underneath my shoulders since I had no idea how this confrontation was going to end, but I was sure as hell not going to turn my Colt over to this man or any man. Sheriff or not, my weapon stays with me. My Colt was an extension of my arm and I would not be without it… ever. In a calm voice, "Sheriff Basquez, I am no threat to you or anyone else in this saloon. The dead man was a Union Redleg soldier and recently was one of several that killed my friend Ron Sands and tried to kill me. These Redleg renegades are still under the command of Captain John Merna and have ventured out of eastern Kansas and are now present in Colorado, and along the trail they have left ex-Confederate soldiers dead, including a man and woman named O'Rourke just east of Dighton, Kansas. This man drew on me first and he paid the price. I have done nothing wrong except defend myself and right a wrong against me and others. So I will not hand over my weapon to you or anyone else!"

Sheriff Basquez was paying close attention to everything I had said and his face sort of went blank when I voiced my thought of not giving him my Colt. Still in a clear and level voice, "I recollect that is going to be a severe problem not handing over your weapon!"

I made no sudden movement to provoke a gun fight, for I did not want to kill this man for just doing his job. As the tension mounted, I once again replied in a calm voice, "There is no problem Sheriff; if you holster your weapon and you keep your Colt, I will keep mine."

Once again the Sheridan sheriff did not like my answer, and I saw a slight twitch in his eye that indicated this confrontation was now heading south to a possible bloody end.

Keegan must have also felt it as well, because she stepped in between the sheriff and myself and once she did that, Hugo felt empowered to attack my damn boot again wagging his tail in chewing pleasure.

Between Keegan and Hugo, I could see the eyes of Sheriff Basquez soften. Keegan and the man killing pup were natural tension relievers if they knew it or not. Keegan, facing down the sheriff, spoke in her almost angel voice, "My name is Keegan Doreen O'Rourke, and Sheriff Basquez what Mac says is true. The Redlegs killed his friend and killed my folks. Mac rescued me and Hugo and is taking me to my aunt who lives in Blackhawk."

Once again, Keegan demonstrated her bravery and kindness and she never ceased to amaze me what a true guardian angel she was. Never taking my eyes off of the sheriff's eyes, I saw them flicker and he believed her. With an almost silent sigh, he holstered his weapon. Once the sheriff settled his Colt in his holster, Keegan's face lit up with a smile from ear to ear and she turned to me and took a few steps and then hugged me.

Sheriff Basquez seemed relieved as well as he walked over closer to me and stuck out his hand in friendship. "I guess Mac, you did not mention your full name. I will need it for the report."

Not knowing when I did tell him my whole name if it would make a difference in how he would view me afterwards, I looked him once again in the eye and told him what he wanted to know as I grabbed his hand with a firm handshake. "McCall Patton, but you can call me Mac if you would like, Sheriff Basquez. All my friends do."

Sheriff Basquez's face showed recognition of my name and his hand instinctively dropped mine and touched the top of his holstered Colt as he spoke, "Am I going to regret not pulling this pistol?"

In a calm voice to reassure him, "No reason to pull your weapon. The men I seek wear red leggings and I see you have none."

Sheriff Basquez grinned and took my hand once again in friendship as he said, "Make no mistake "Rebel Mac" I don't even own a pair of red socks and sure as hell not going to buy any in the future."

After several hours of writing the report and giving a written description of what had happened in the gunfight and death of Alan Wells, it became a closed matter in the eyes of the law here in Sheridan.

Allen Wells had forty dollars in cash on his person which was more than enough to have him buried, and the rest went to the Minters for damages and cleanup. Joe and Shirley seemed to hold no grudge against me for killing Wells in their saloon, and Joe shook my hand and Shirley gave both Keegan and me a big hug and wished us safe travels as we left Monaghan's.

Sheriff Basquez was waiting for me outside and asked me how long I was going to be in town, and he seemed relieved when I said we were leaving at the break of dawn. He shook my hand one last time as Keegan and I walked the short distance to the hotel for a much needed night of sleep.

Once Keegan had lain her head down on a soft pillow, she fell asleep faster than I could blink, and Hugo had cuddled up to her side and was snoring softly as he also fell into a deep sleep.

Sleep tonight, I knew from past experience, would be hard to come by, for Allen Wells would now join those that haunted me in the dark of the night, and it would be forever now that his face would appear with all the others that I had put down and ended their lives. Those memories were impossible to suppress. Sandy sometimes said I was way too quick with my guns to have a conscience. It took me several years of nightly haunts to fully understand what he meant by that. Sandy had always been the thinker of the two of us.

Rolling onto my side, I looked at Keegan and Hugo as they peacefully slept and I tried to remember a time when I could sleep like that. I guess when I was young, maybe it was like that for me. Now with so many years of death and destruction before, during, and after the Civil War, it would seem I had forgotten the innocence of my childhood. Rolling onto my back, I turned my focus on those that needed my full attention and that would be Captain John Merna, John Loveless, and the man they called LB. Alan Wells, before his death, had given me another clue of the whereabouts of the remaining Redlegs, and it would seem from his tale they would be heading to a town called Fairplay, Colorado in the South Park region. It looked as if my trail of retribution would end in the mountain area known as South Park.

The night passed more quickly than I thought possible, and I only woke three times in a cold sweat as the dead faces of those that I had killed made themselves known to me in my dreams. Each time I was able to push each face far enough back into the shadows of my mind so that for a spell they did not haunt me, and then and only then would restless sleep overcome me again.

CHAPTER 30

After waking and settling our tab at the hotel, Keegan, Hugo and I had a breakfast of chicken eggs and beef steak at Monaghan's served once again by Shirley Minter. Hugo was strutting around as if he was something special because Mrs. Minter served up his breakfast on the floor on a plate just like Keegan's and mine. Hugo, I would have to admit, each day was becoming more and more of a fixture in my life. I even looked forward to his chewing on my boot each and every day. Mrs. Minter showed no resentment toward me in the aftermath of the shooting of Alan Wells and actually seemed pleased to see Keegan, Hugo and myself this morning.

After we finished up and paid for our meal, Mrs. Minter had a hug for all of us as she told us if we were ever in Sheridan again to feel free to stop by.

Sammy and Horse almost broke down the stall gate at the livery once they saw us. They were more than happy to be back on the trail and out in the fresh air. I could almost see the smiles on their long faces as we saddled them and got them ready for another day on the Keegan Trail.

As we started out more west than north on the trail, I pulled the reins slightly and brought Sammy to a halt just outside the town limits of Sheridan. Once Sammy stopped so did Horse, and Hugo firmly planted his butt just behind the saddle horn and with his tongue hanging out looked forward toward the west. Keegan and I both were wide-eyed as we marveled at the Rocky Mountains due west of us. They seemed from this distance to be a solid mass of rock and trees with no passage through them. And if I had not known better, it would have been intimidating.

The sun was directly on our backs and created long shadows of the horses and ourselves that sprawled out before us as if they somehow indicated the direction we should travel. There was no wind this morning, but the air was chilled as the autumn months were just around the corner. There were a few peaceful clouds that floated lazily in the sky above our heads, which told me that today's travels would be a pleasant undertaking.

Just ahead and to my right was a hand painted sign saying that Morrison, Colorado was eleven miles to the northwest on what we called the Keegan Trail.

Morrison was a town located just at the foothills of the Rockies on the banks of Bear Creek and was the gateway to the gold and silver camps of Blackhawk, Georgetown, Central City, Silver Plume, Idaho Springs, and Empire further north and west according to Marty Blake, the old gold miner. The area around Morrison was also the beginning of the saga of Lucas Eldridge in his own Rocky Mountain reckoning. If I ever have more time, I would like to hear or read up more on the righteous gunfighter Lucas Eldridge. Also, according to Marty, Eldridge was owner or part owner of a couple of successful gold mines in or around Central City called the Bondurant and Coeur d' Alene mines. This Lucas Eldridge must be an interesting man for sure.

This part of our Keegan Trail followed along the north bank of Bear Creek. After a couple of miles, we let Sammy and Horse get their fill of some cool creek water as it flowed eastward as we rode westward. Keegan seemed to be enjoying the quiet of the morning and asked me, "I wonder why it is called Bear Creek?"

Of course I had to stifle a laugh before I replied, "Well, Miss Keegan Doreen O'Rourke one can only assume it is because bears live along the banks of this here creek."

Keegan's eyes got big as she realized that was probably how the creek got its name and she started to laugh, "Guess that was sort of a dumb question!"

No longer able to stifle my laugh it finally comes out, "Well, I guess we make a grand pair of travelers since I have been known to think of some dumb questions; just with age you learn never to ask them."

Keegan was chuckling so hard now she almost fell out of her saddle, and after she finally gained enough control she said, "Guess I can't wait until I get to that age, Mac."

When the horses had enough to drink and in good spirits, we pushed on toward the town of Morrison.

We had no need to stop in Morrison and it was still early in the day, so we kept moving northwest and were surprised within a half of a mile outside of Morrison when we spotted slabs of rocks that looked as if the earth had rejected them and pushed them skyward. I had never seen mountains or rocks for that matter that looked as if they had just received a coat of red paint. I now remembered vaguely Marty Blake speaking of the "Garden of the Angels" that were painted with the blood of Christ near Morrison. He also said the locals just called them by the obvious name of Red Rocks. Whatever the name of these rock formations to the west, they were something to behold in all of their grandeur and brought forth that our lives here and now were just a speck and one tick of time in the Lord's grand scheme of things. These Red Rocks were obviously older than man himself.

As we rode through the Red Rocks, we came across a natural bowl that I could only imagine the ancient Ute Indians claimed as their own at one time using it as a meeting place to speak to their Gods and Spirits. I could see it in my mind as their chief and their holy men spoke from the bottom of the bowl to those seated on the hillside to the west. We stopped for a spell for some venison jerky and a couple of slices of apple pie Mrs. Minter had sent along for our noon day meal. Keegan, Hugo and I ate in almost total silence. It was like we did not want to disturb the sanctuary of this Ute Indian holy land. Surrounded by the towering Red Rocks, I know I felt at peace here. There was something beyond majestic about the Red Rocks. I almost didn't want to leave, but Keegan needed to be safe with family and I needed to settle a score with Captain Merna, John Loveless and LB, so we mounted the horses and moved on.

After our detour to visit the Red Rocks, we continued north and followed the outline of the eastern side of the foothills for about nine miles until we reached the mouth of Clear Creek Canyon, which had been cut down through the ages with the easterly flowing water of Clear Creek. We would follow between the banks of the north side of Clear Creek and the Colorado Central Railroad narrow gauge railroad tracks that headed due west through the canyon toward the gold camps of Central City and Black Hawk, Colorado.

Once we were on the banks of Clear Creek, the day was just about over and I decided to pitch a camp for the night close to fresh water for the horses and plenty of trees to shield us from the wind if it decided to kick up during the night. I knew to the east just a couple of miles was the town of Golden which used to serve as the capital of the Colorado Territory until Colorado became a state. Once statehood had been reached for reasons unknown to me, they moved the capital eastward and made the town of Denver the capital of the state. I almost laughed out loud as I thought of this, because I really had not been paying much attention when Marty Blake was giving us the history lesson of Colorado. Guess I was paying more attention than I thought I was.

Before unsaddling Sammy and Horse, I gathered enough stones and firewood for a cook fire tonight. Once I had the makings for the fire and had it ready, Keegan went about without asking and started our supper for the night.

After leaving the Red Rocks, I was able to shoot a couple of jack rabbits for our meal tonight and along with some fried beans and wild onions that Keegan had scrounged up, we would have a hearty, warm meal.

As Keegan set about doing the camp chores, I unpacked the horses and gave them a brushing down and used the curry comb on their manes and tails. Sammy and Horse were grateful as they always were for a treat of sugar this evening. After the horses were taken care of, my mind drifted to our next stop and I was suddenly saddened.

The next stop was straight west through Clear Creek Canyon about nineteen or twenty miles to the town of Blackhawk and hopefully the home of Larisa Devin O'Rourke - Keegan's Aunt. I had been so busy doing the day-to-day things about keeping Keegan and Hugo safe on the trail I had not given much thought to the time when she would no longer need me. In so many ways Keegan had replaced Sandy as my traveling partner, and she was tough as nails and it hit me like a ton of bricks I was going to miss her and the man killing mutt Hugo.

CHAPTER 31

The sun rose in the east and the sky was a light blue with an orange haze, but the warmth could not reach into the camp that I had chosen because of the trees. The long shadows of the trees were without emotions as they reached out and touched the chilled water of Clear Creek as it flowed easterly. Autumn comes earlier to these mountains than it did in "Little Dixie," and I could see my breath this morning.

About half of the trees that surrounded our campsite were aspens and during the night numerous leaves at the top had turned golden readying themselves for the onslaught of the winter months that lay ahead. Keegan and Hugo were still sleeping, so I sat up and watched the clouds that were building in the sky that were white and fluffy with not the look of rain or thunder. It would seem the day would be a good day to continue the trail toward Blackhawk.

Before I woke up Keegan, a red tailed hawk made three circles overhead and landed in an aspen tree not more than thirty feet away and seemed to study me. I watched his eyes and the hawk seemed smarter than most - hell he looked smarter than me. After I looked eye-to-eye with the hawk for a full minute or more, his curiosity in me must have been satisfied as he flapped his wings twice and took to the air, heading westward in the canyon. I watched the hawk until I could no longer see him. Red tailed hawks, owls, eagles and other birds of prey have always triggered my thoughts. As a kid, I always wanted to soar on the wind and could only imagine the freedom of what that would feel like.

Reaching down I softly shook Keegan's shoulder to wake her. "Wake up little one. The air is chilled this morning so stay bundled until I get a fire going."

Keegan's bright brown eyes opened and she exhaled and saw her breath, and a smile came across her face. "I love chilly mornings, Mac."

With a small laugh, "That is a good thing because probably from here on out until spring you will have chilly and icy mornings each and every day as we get deeper into the mountains."

I stirred the red hot orange embers left over from last night's fire until there was enough air to restart the flames. Once I had a small fire, I slowly added wood until the flames reached the point of a good warming cook fire. Once that was done Keegan joined in and we warmed up the remaining rabbit, beans, and some more wild onions for our breakfast. Of course Hugo wasn't happy until he started chewing on my boot again as was the little shit's routine. Once again, I was saddened realizing I was going to miss that damn dog. Once he had learned to find his balance riding with me on Sammy, he was no trouble at all.

While eating my breakfast, I thought about the gold camps of Blackhawk and its sister camp of Central City that lay westward. It was obvious that the railroad station ticket seller was mistaken back in Scott City, Kansas when he said trains do not travel to Blackhawk because the tracks of the Colorado Central Railroad were just fifty yards to the north and brought much needed supplies to the gold camps at the end of Clear Creek Canyon. Even if I had known the train traveled to Blackhawk, I think my decision to bring Keegan here myself would have remained the same.

According to what I had learned from Marty Blake the old gold prospector, Blackhawk and Central City were within a mile of each other. Both camps came to be after a man named John H. Gregory discovered gold in a gulch that now bears his name.

Somehow Keegan's Aunt Larisa Devin O'Rourke ended up in the rough and tumble gold camps. As of this moment I was still not sure if Aunt Risa was still there or even alive or if she was alive for that matter even wanted to care for the young Irish girl. Actually, until this moment I had not even considered if Aunt Risa wanted to care for Keegan and Hugo or not. I sure as hell was not going to leave Keegan and the man killing mutt with someone that did not want them. A frown crossed my face as I pondered that, knowing full well I would have to cross that bridge once I got to Blackhawk.

Once Sammy and Horse were saddled and packed, I gave Sammy some rein and a slight jab of my right spur and once again started westward with Keegan and Horse right behind as I took point. As a former soldier, riding through the bottom of a canyon was not my ideal way of traveling. During the war I would have been as nervous as a long tailed cat in a room full of rocking chairs from all the possible ambush points. It would take some getting used to riding the trails in the high mountains.

At mid-morning we came to a "Y" in the canyon where a smaller stream flowed into the much larger Clear Creek. There was a hand painted sign that the Argo gold mine and the camp of Idaho Springs were to the southwest part of the "Y" and a sign indicating that Blackhawk and Central City were still on the northwestern side of the "Y." After letting the horses get a drink from Clear Creek and to give Hugo a much needed stop for some outhouse duties, we continued on toward the northwest.

By midday we started to see more and more gold prospectors working the creek with their gold pans. Others had built small sluices and rocker boxes to help in the quest for the elusive gold nuggets and gold flakes. We saw several families with young kids wearing nothing but rags for clothes as they worked the creek together. Many of those we saw would gain nothing but despair and sickness as they searched for their fortunes and their dreams became broken. A few might strike it rich, but most would not. Gold and the wealth that came with it was what dreams were made of. In my mind you were never poor as long as you still had your dreams. Sandy used to quote a poem about broken dreams written by a German fellow named Reifschneider. It was a poem that touched me in many ways and could be applied to anyone's life. Remembering the words of the tale and story poem that Sandy used to recite of one man's broken dream and his search for hope, I spoke them out loud,

"Down through my life cemented in my past,
Broken dreams scattered, pieces of shattered glass.
Some dreams were never truly meant to be,
Some broken dreams were meant to set me free.
Cannot break me, a lifetime of broken dreams,
I am willing and stronger than most or so it seems.
From my past - broken dreams that cannot break me,
Not jaded, and daring to dream again is the key.
My broken dreams are not the end of the road,
For another dream comes along - waiting to be saddled and rode.
Broken dreams can mean life has a new direction,
For a new acquired dream for my reflection."

Keegan listened to my rendition of the poem, but said nothing. I could tell just as I was, she was deep into her own thoughts.

I thought of Sandy once again and with the thoughts of not having Keegan and Hugo with me after tomorrow drove home the fact that I would be all alone with my own thoughts. This probably was not a good thing.

Keegan and I rode in silence the rest of the day not wanting to look at each other - let alone talk to each other. I could not speak for her of course, but my gut feeling was she was also sad of our upcoming parting of the ways in Blackhawk. Since Dighton we had seen death, sickness, hailstorms, and tornadoes; we had bonded into a family so to speak. She had become my partner on the trail - our Keegan Trail. I was going to miss her something fierce. It was a feeling I have only felt once before and that was when Sandy had been killed by Captain John Merna and his men.

Toward the end of the day, I deciphered we were only a couple of miles short of Blackhawk and thought it would be best to try and find Aunt Risa in the morning, so we found a suitable spot to camp for the night after asking a couple of gold prospectors if it would be okay to spend the night on their claim. They happily accepted since they had not had any company in a long while. I was not in a jovial mood and declined their invitation to cook us our supper for the evening.

After seeing to the horses, I caught three rainbow trout in the stream that ran alongside the trail and we still had some wild onions for our supper this evening. Once again while eating our evening meal, Keegan and my conversation was lacking and we said only what was needed - keeping our thoughts about tomorrow to ourselves. Hugo even seemed distraught since he probably could feel the sadness that Keegan and I both felt.

After lying down to sleep, I was not haunted by those that had fallen under my guns as most nights before. No, this evening only two things floated around my thinker - the thoughts and ponderings of the young Irish girl and her man killing mutt.

CHAPTER 32

Waking at dawn, I saw that Clear Creek Canyon was still in the shadows of the mountains on each side. The air was crisp with a slight cool breeze of autumn. I looked to the aspens lining the creek, and even more leaves had found their golden hue during the night at the top. The stars from last night had been replaced with a never ending blue sky with nary a cloud. It would seem summer had departed the Rocky Mountains and the start of autumn had come to roost.

Since we were so close to Blackhawk, I decided to forego making breakfast so we could eat someone else's cooking in the gold camp. Keegan with a half-hearted smile agreed that was a worthy idea.

Hugo seemed almost attached to the end of my boot as he tried once again to chew a hole in it while I got Sammy and Horse ready for the trail. Knowing this probably was the last time Hugo would get the chance to chew on my boot, I reached down and picked him up and cuddled him to my chest while he was trying to lick my nose off. Thinking I should say my goodbyes to Hugo in private so

I didn't get all teary-eyed and look like a fool in front of others later, smiling I addressed Hugo, "Been a pleasure Mr. Hugo to share my saddle and the "Keegan Trail" with you. At first I reckoned you would be a pain in the ass, but you turned out to be a bigger pain in the ass than I thought. Guess in the Lord's scheme of things Hugo, you and Keegan were meant to be my traveling companions on this journey and adventure. No sir, I figure I would not have had it any different."

Squatting down, I gently set Hugo back on solid earth and he went to attacking my boot again. I watched him for a few minutes and then I looked up and Keegan was standing not ten feet away watching us. She must have been there a spell and heard everything as I spoke to Hugo because her eyes were full of tears. She quickly turned and walked away from me so I wouldn't think she was soft. Standing slowly, I wiped a tear that had formed in my eye and cleared my voice to say something, but I couldn't find any words. I had nothing to add that would make this day any better so I said nothing. Damn kid and that damn dog had wormed their way into my heart. I could almost feel the ghost of Sandy standing next to me with his hand on my shoulder for comfort. Slowly shaking my head, I thought, "Damn you too, Sandy!"

We were able to find a small saloon that served breakfast called the unlikely name of Crook's Palace in Blackhawk for some much needed food. I was also hoping to find some information and the whereabouts of Keegan's Aunt Risa as well.

Crook's Palace was built out of light sandy colored stone and had four very large broad glass windows that faced north. There were eight tables present with four chairs each. The bar itself was hand carved with dark wood, possibly walnut and very beautiful. Above the bar was not a painting of a scantily clothed woman as you see in most western saloons, but that of a painting of three hard rock miners applying their trade. Crook's Palace was a classier saloon than I would have expected in a gold mining town.

We were served by a young girl a little older than Keegan named Zane Deden who told us her aunt Natalie Arellano was the owner and operator of Crook's Palace. Zane was a pretty and slender girl with long brown hair with very stunning eyes that seemed to change from green to brown each time she blinked. Her personality was top notch, and Keegan and she within a minute of meeting each other seemed almost like best friends. Finding Zane, this young and pleasant girl, here was making me feel better about Keegan possibly living here in Blackhawk.

After Keegan introduced Hugo to Zane, she took our order of chicken eggs, pork, bacon and some fresh Dutch oven biscuits to mop up the egg yolk. As soon as she left the table, her aunt was making the rounds of all the tables now occupied asking if everything was okay and if anyone needed anything else.

Natalie Arellano was a long dark haired beauty with stunning eyes as well. She looked to be in her mid-thirties and was slender and looked to be about 5'6". There was no denying that Natalie and Zane were kin because of their eyes. And it appeared that Natalie was just as pleasant and helpful as Zane had been. After introductions, I asked her the big question that had brought Keegan and me here across two states and through all the hardships that we had encountered. "Miss Arellano, do you happen to know Larisa Devin O'Rourke? I was told she lived here in Blackhawk."

Natalie smiled and with an almost confused look spoke, "Larisa? Do you mean Risa? If it is Risa O'Rourke you are looking for, then of course everyone knows Risa."

My biggest fear of course in locating Aunt Risa was that I had never mentioned to Keegan that she might be doing what a lot of women had to do in these gold camps to survive and that she might be a soiled dove. I knew with what I had seen and done in my life that I was not one to pass judgment of these women since I did not walk in their shoes. If that was the case though, there was no way in hell I would leave Keegan here in Blackhawk. Keegan deserved more in life than that. I was almost scared to ask Natalie more about Risa O'Rourke, but of course I had to. "Does she live and or work around here? I need to get in touch with her over a personal matter."

Natalie stepped back and her face showed concern, taking a moment before she spoke again in a more serious tone, "I am not one for giving out that type of information without knowing why you are asking. Risa is one of my best friends so mister, I need to know your name and what dealings that you might have with her before telling you anymore. So let's start with an easy question. What is your name?"

It was obvious that Natalie was trying to protect her friend, so I took no offense to her new more serious tone. "My name is McCall Patton, but you can call me Mac."

Natalie's face went blank for a second as my name sunk in. "McCall Patton? The gunfighter? What the hell would Rebel Mac the gunfighter have to do with Risa O'Rourke?"

Well, Natalie's question had turned into several more and it was plain as day I was not making a very good impression on the owner of Crook's Palace. Trying to salvage this conversation once again, I spoke, "Yes, some call me Rebel Mac and some call me a gunfighter if I deserve that handle or not. I assure you Miss Arellano, it is not a reputation I wanted or needed. To make you feel more at ease, I have never met Miss O'Rourke nor do I intend to do her harm in any way. I have sent several telegrams to her since we have been on the trail from Dighton, Kansas with no answer back. I feared she no longer lived here or was possibly dead. It is important I speak to her because this young Irish girl here is her niece and her name is Keegan Doreen O'Rourke. Keegan's folks and Risa's brother Ardan and sister-in-law Bree were murdered at their farm just east of Dighton, Kansas by some Jayhawker Redleg scum led by a renegade named Captain John Merna. My mission for now is to see that Keegan and her pup Hugo are safe with family."

Natalie's serious tone turned more to a tone of compassion as she reached gingerly and touched Keegan's hand and spoke softly to her, "Oh my, I am so sorry to hear about your folks and Keegan you do have the look of the O'Rourkes in you and I should have known better."

Turning to me, Natalie spoke in a tone of forgiveness, "Mr. Patton, I apologize if I came off as harsh and I do recognize the sacrifice that you have made making sure Keegan was safe and bringing her here to be with family. And I assure you I meant no disrespect in using the term gunfighter, for I see now you are a man of honor and integrity. As for the telegrams you sent, I am sure Risa never got them nor any message that you were bringing Keegan to her. Our telegraph office burnt to the ground about four months ago and the owners have yet to rebuild it. The only things getting through to Blackhawk are letters sent by stage."

It was at that moment that Zane returned with our breakfast and set our food on the table, but I still did not know the whereabouts of Risa O'Rourke here in Blackhawk. Without trying to sound a bit perturbed, I asked once again, "Miss Arellano, I know you meant no disrespect and I appreciate your kind words. Could you please tell me where I can find Keegan's Aunt Risa?"

Natalie almost laughed before she replied, "Guess I got caught up in the moment after hearing your name Mr. Patton and it would seem I had forgot the question. Just follow the road uphill a quarter of a mile and on the north side you will find a rock building next to the Presbyterian Church that acts as the school house here in Blackhawk. Risa O'Rourke is the schoolmarm there.

CHAPTER 33

I almost laughed as my mind started spinning and my thought was, "Schoolmarm? Well, that's not so bad!" Unless she was like one that I had when I was a lad. Her name was Miss Masters, the meanest woman that ever held chalk in her hand. Not only could she screech the chalkboard with that chalk like no other but she also was like a sniper when throwing it at you. Under her skinny arms was some rock solid muscle so when she would whack one of her pieces of chalk off your noggin from across the room, it damn well hurt and left a bruise. Luckily, to the best of my knowledge, no kid had ever lost an eye to her deadly chalk walloping's. I hoped the good Lord had discarded that broken mold after he formed Miss Masters and used the good and caring mold for Risa Devin O'Rourke."

After finishing our breakfast and thanking Natalie and Zane, we located the school just as Miss Arellano had said. I never was able to keep track of the days very well, but it was the middle of the week, be it Tuesday or Wednesday, and the Blackhawk kids of age were attending school today.

Tying off Sammy and Horse next to three other mares that were hitched to a rail next to the side of the school house, I noticed a small house behind the school that I assumed was where the school teacher lived. The outside of the house was neat and tidy and had a vegetable garden and flower boxes adorning the exterior of the house. The vegetable and flower boxes were now empty due since it was past their growing season. I hoped that anyone that grew their own vegetables and had a hankering for flowers had a good soul. Keegan, Hugo and I approached the entrance to the school slowly and with reservations. I had no idea what type of person Aunt Risa was.

Keegan and I were both quiet and did not know what to expect since Aunt Risa as it turned out would have no prior knowledge of what had happened to her brother and wife and was not expecting a sudden visit from her niece and her dog, accompanied by a man she did not know that spoke with a slight Missouri accent. If anything at all, this meeting with Aunt Risa was going to be really interesting for sure.

The front door was open to let fresh air into the schoolhouse since the day was pleasant, and Keegan and Hugo walked in as if they owned the place and stopped just inside the door. I hung back some and stood behind the Irish lass and her man killing dog as I took in the surroundings of what was in front of me.

There were six kids and two dogs in attendance in the school today - three boys and three girls and a couple of sleepy mutts. The youngest was a boy, maybe six or so and the oldest was a girl that looked to be about Keegan's age or a shade older. One mutt kept sleeping even though it had woken up just long enough to notice that there were strangers present and even a strange dog, but even after seeing Hugo, it was not enough to entice the sleepy dog to come over for a sniff and tell. He promptly lay back on his side with a huge sigh and went right back to sleep. On the other hand, the other dog stood up with his tail wagging, and Hugo met him halfway across the room with his tail wagging as well, and they started the mutual sniffing of each other that dogs do.

All six kids turned to stare at Keegan and myself as their teacher had her back to us writing something on the chalkboard. Seeing the chalk in her hand almost made me laugh, bringing back thoughts of Miss Masters back in my youth. As soon as the teacher was finished with her task, she turned and a look of total confusion crossed her face as she noticed the strangers that were now blocking the warming sun in her doorway.

Seeing Larisa Devin O'Rourke for the first time was just as much of a surprise for me as it was for her. Aunt Risa it would seem was at least fifteen years older than her brother Ardan which made her only about five years younger than myself. She stood about 5'7" tall and carried a few extra pounds that was common for women of her age. She wore the clothing of a school teacher that consisted of a long dark dress that touched the floor with a small apron to carry her chalk and a pencil or two. On her feet she wore cowboy boots which somehow seemed more than fitting for such a woman. Her dark brown hair was long and tied into a pony tail that had a one inch streak of gray that added a wonderful highlight that spoke of a mature and gentle woman. Her eyes were stunning and the color of dark brown, and they also told a different story than her hair and that of a woman who might just have a bit of mystery in her past. I do not believe in my life prior that I had ever looked before upon a more beautiful woman than what now stood before me.

After a few seconds of looking at me, Miss O'Rourke spoke in a sing song voice, "Can I help you mister?"

Then Aunt Risa's eyes drifted down until they rested on Keegan, and then her face went blank for a tad. Then slowly by degree her beautiful face showed recognition. "Oh my God! Is that you Keegan Doreen O'Rourke? What on earth are you doing here?"

Aunt Risa had spoken in a loving manner, of course, but Keegan it would seem was at a loss for words as all the emotions that she had buried and concealed inside of her of what had happened to her folks and the danger, death, sickness, tornadoes, hailstorms, renegade Indians, renegade Jayhawker Redlegs, and all the other that she had to come to terms with on "The Keegan Trail" brought forth a flood of much needed tears. To add to the mix was that Keegan until this moment had not even had a clue if that her only living kin was even still alive. The question was still up in the air if everything that Keegan had endured would matter to her Aunt Risa. After even a few seconds, I knew in my heart that

Keegan now once again had a home that she could call her own even if Keegan was not quite so sure about it yet.

Risa O'Rourke burst into tears as well without knowing the full extent of the tragedy of where Keegan's tears flowed from, but nevertheless she started crying as well as she rushed forward to her young niece to comfort her as only a loving aunt could. There were several minutes of hugging tightly on to each other as the tears continued to flow. Keegan's waterworks were from the hurt and misery of what had happened to her folks and to herself, and Aunt Risa's tears flowed with the happiness of seeing her niece for the first time in many years. In Risa's singsong voice as she held her niece in a calming hug, "Oh Keegan sweetheart, it is so good to see you here. I never even dreamed I would see you again, let alone here in Blackhawk. Where are your folks, Keegan? Are they here in town as well? I can't wait to see them!"

Risa's question concerning the whereabouts of Ardan and Bree O'Rourke drove home the sadness of Keegan's tragedy to me like getting hit with a hammer, and I waited for a few minutes to see if Keegan could muster the words to tell her aunt what had befallen her folks.

I had to hand it to the little Irish lass, for she tried to speak to her aunt, but the words never came out and she was momentarily paralyzed. Aunt Risa knew from this reaction that something was dreadfully amiss and she stood up still holding Keegan tightly to her side, wiping a few tears from her eyes and clearing her voice as she faced her classroom. Every child there was taken in by the emotion of the moment and there was not a dry eye present - including mine.

Risa then glanced back at me and held my eyes for a moment as if she was searching for the obvious question of what happened to her brother and sister-in-law. After possibly seeing the answer there, she once again faced her class and in a quieter voice, "Kids, school is dismissed for the day."

I walked outside since I was blocking the doorway to give the kids the room as they slowly walked out. Even though none of the kids understood what was happening, each and every one of them felt the sadness that was in the new girl's heart.

Each child before they left gave Risa a hug and touched Keegan on her hand or shoulder. I was touched by their obvious sympathy for someone they did not know. Bless their hearts, each and every one of them.

Once the children were out of the building, Keegan and Risa had found a seat near the front door for the both of them, and Risa still had Keegan cuddled next to her. The teacher's eyes followed me as I took a seat across from them. Risa with eyes still watery and red finally spoke after clearing her voice, "I take it this is not a social visit, Mister?"

Shaking my head "no" as I locked eyes with the young girl I had learned to care so much for. Then looking up into Risa O'Rourke's eyes, I finally spoke, "Miss O'Rourke and no this is not a social visit and my name is McCall Patton. And you may have gathered by now your brother and his wife are both dead."

CHAPTER 34

O nce Risa heard the truth, she once again held Keegan tightly as they both grieved for their family. I felt like an intruder, and I excused myself and called for Hugo to follow which he did with his new buddy that he had just met. I reasoned that the O'Rourke girls needed some time to work through the initial shock of seeing each other again and the death of their loved ones.

Once outside Hugo and the other dog started to run and play with each other. It would seem that Hugo, just like Keegan, had found a forever home once again.

Thinking of Risa and Keegan and even Hugo and his new friend brought home the fact that I was alone in this world since Sandy had been killed. It never sank in until this moment that when the time came and I would die that no one would ever mourn my passing. I had no family that I knew of, and my only true friend in life was riding in my saddlebag as bone fragments and ashes. The only person that I truly cared about now was Keegan, and she was in the schoolhouse mourning with her kin. It was a sobering thought.

Not knowing how long I would be here and wanting to give Risa and Keegan all the time they needed, I kept busy unsaddling Sammy and Horse and proceeded to give them both a good currying and brushed out their manes and tails. Sammy seemed to sense my unease, and she snuggled up with her nose, and I returned the loving gesture in kind. After giving them both the last of the grain that I had and a taste of sugar, I went and found a shady spot under an evergreen tree to watch the comings and goings of the town of Blackhawk.

Pondering on the fact that Keegan was now safe with family, I started to focus on the next task at hand and that was trailing and dispatching of Captain Merna, John Loveless, and the gunfighter LB. Once again, I had to get in the mindset to go after and kill these men, and it would not be difficult since I had a sugar sack of Sandy's ashes as a reminder. Thinking it best to live in the morning at daybreak since my mission of getting Keegan to the safety of family had come to an end. I was going to miss that kid and Hugo as well.

Several hours passed, and I had fallen asleep under an evergreen tree and when Keegan woke me up, the sun told me it was mid-afternoon. Keegan seemed drained, but her eyes told me that she had found her forever home and I was happy for her. She grabbed my hand and pulled me up until I was standing next to her, and then she surprised me by giving me a hug, which at first was awkward until I hugged her back; all seemed right in the world at this very moment. Risa O'Rourke was standing behind me, and it sort of startled me when she spoke, "Mr. Patton, Keegan has told me everything that you have done for her since you rescued her from the crawl space under the house near Dighton. Keegan also spoke of your burying my brother and his wife and frankly, sir, I cannot find the words to thank you for everything that you have done. She also mentioned your quest for justice against those that have caused you and my family so much hurt. I was hoping you would stay for a few days so I could get to know the man named McCall Patton. I live in the house behind the school, but there is a spare room in the school that you can use to sleep and store your gear."

Keegan looked at me and held my eyes for a moment before she added her piece, "You have to say yes, Mac. I want you to stay."

Looking first at Keegan then at Risa, "Miss O'Rourke, I don't reckon the town folks would be happy to have me stay; it would seem my reputation preceded me here, and I recollect most folks hereabouts would have a problem with my staying even for a couple of days."

Risa's face sort of scrunched up before she spoke again, "Your reputation as a gunfighter? Yes, I knew who you were as soon as you told me your name. McCall Patton the gray rider known as Rebel Mac. I believe your heroics in saving my niece from thirst and starvation in a deep dark hole, or from renegade Indians, or from deadly tornadoes outranks your reputation as a gunfighter! If anyone has issues with that, they can speak directly to me. No, Mr. Patton, Keegan wants you to stay and so do I and the O'Rourke women do not take no for an answer so that will be the end of the discussion! So you need to store your belongings in the spare room in the school, and I need to get supper started so get a move on, Mister."

After saying what she needed to say, Risa turned to leave to presumably go start supper. Keegan hung back for a minute with that shit eating grin that she seemed to muster each and every time when I had been put into my place by either herself or now her aunt. Her eyes showed amusement and while looking at me, she shrugged her shoulders like "you better do as Aunt Risa said," which I guess I would. Then Keegan turned and followed her aunt. Hugo hung back with me for a spell not sure what the hell had just happened, and he kept looking at me and then at Keegan as she walked away with his tail wagging. He tried to decipher what to do as well. Pointing toward Keegan I said, "If you want your supper as well, I would follow Keegan; it would seem Hugo you have come home to roost."

Once said, Hugo decided his supper was in the direction of Keegan and he scurried after her to Aunt Risa's house.

The schoolhouse had its own outhouse, water well, and bucket so once I had stored my gear, I thought it best to clean up and put on some clean clothes for supper. It had been a long while since I had been invited to a sit down supper in someone's home.

My hand shook a little when I shaved and cut my own hair with my own bowie knife as I made myself less trail weary. It would seem that I was a bit nervous about the prospect of having to small talk after the eating of supper was over. I had no idea what to talk to Risa O'Rourke about, but one thing that I did know was that I wanted to talk to her.

Risa's home was neat and tidy on the inside as well, and she made me feel comfortable which was a surprise to me was since I had lived out of my saddle for most of my life. With Keegan, Hugo, and Risa, I did not feel as if the walls of the house were closing in on me as I felt most times when I spent more than an hour in someone's home. It was a pleasant feeling and it somewhat confused me.

Supper as it turned out was a grand affair with roasted beef, taters, onions, cucumbers, corn on the cob, fresh butter biscuits, and of course hot apple pie served up with a cool glass of cow's milk.

After supper, my worries about the small talk faded away as Keegan, Risa, and I spoke of many things other than my reputation as a gunfighter. Hugo, after finishing his supper, curled up and fell fast asleep next to the fire I started in the fireplace to ward off the chill of the night mountain air.

The evening passed quickly and I had lost track of time. It was close to midnight and I decided it was time to leave. Keegan of course gave me a long hug, which I returned in favor. Just as I was about to walk out the door, Risa surprised me with a hug as well and followed it up with a small and quick kiss on my right cheek. She must have thought I was addled because my face went blank and I slowly touched my cheek. Risa sort of giggled at that and then gently with her right hand shoved me out the door saying, "It has been a pleasure Mac to have you dine with Keegan and me, and we will see you in the morning."

While being pushed out the door, I could not remember my exact words that I had spoken, but it was something dimwitted like, "Yes, of course Risa. I am staying next door."

Shaking my head thinking, "Of course Risa knew I was staying next door." I stood for a full minute outside staring at the closed door behind me like some fool feeling the effects of good food, caring people, a happy dog, warm fire, and a very pleasant evening. The last image of Risa O'Rourke closing the door floated about in my mind. There was no doubt she was the most beautiful woman I had ever seen.

CHAPTER 35

The two days I meant to stay turned into ten, and I am here to tell you that those days spent with Risa, Keegan, and Hugo were the most wondrous days of my life. I was never much of a talker, but it would seem that I could always find something to jabber about with the ladies O'Rourke.

Keegan and Hugo of course started the next day attending the Blackhawk School and what I could gather with not having much schooling myself was that she was an apt student and it would seem that brains in O'Rourke women were passed out in ample quantities when they were born. During my stay while taking a break from doing chores and handyman work around the school and Risa's house, I would sit at a desk at the back of the school house and watch Risa teach and watch Keegan as her hand shot straight up in the air with the answer as if she had been hit by lightning, and it always put a smile on my face. I was proud of the young Irish girl, and I was also thankful that I had made the right choice to bring her here to Blackhawk instead of sticking her on a train.

Before and after school each day, I would spend every waking hour with Risa and Keegan doing mundane things such as eating meals and talking about all aspects of just living life. Pleasant topics were discussed as well as the everyday happenings in and around Blackhawk. If the townsfolk objected to my presence here, they kept it a secret and I was met with only friendly acknowledgment everywhere that I went.

Hugo adapted well to his new life in Blackhawk, and he became sleeping dog number three that attended school; he seemed to be very happy with this new life in the Colorado Mountains. Even in Hugo's new life, he never broke the routine of attacking my boot for a few minutes every time I saw him for the first time each day. At first Risa tried to scold Hugo when he did this, but Hugo never paid her much mind, and Risa finally accepted this as our normal behavior.

On the days that there was no school Risa, Keegan, and I explored the country and the surrounding gold camps of Central City, Nevadaville, and Russel Gulch. On these days Risa and Keegan would pack a picnic lunch or we would eat in an eatery in one of the gold camps.

On one such trip into Central City that was less than a mile to the southwest, Risa pointed out two men with a half wolf and half something else dog that were walking down the street in front of the Gilda Garter Saloon and told me that the half wolf was named Mutt and that the two men happened to be the most famous men in Colorado. After I watched Lucas Eldridge and Chance Bondurant for a minute, my gut instinct told me that these righteous gunfighters were no threat to me since it would seem they were men much like myself in the sense that their reputations were not something that they ever wanted or needed. It was fate, superior gun skills, and the idea of honor that separated men like Eldridge, Bondurant, and myself from other men.

Thinking of honor and what that word meant to me, and the fact that as happy as I was with Risa, Keegan, and Hugo, I must be pushing on since I had a quest to finish. Sandy's ashes and his memory needed to be avenged. I had stopped here in Blackhawk and felt the happiness and tender moments that we all craved and for a few days I forgot what made me the man that I am. It was in my nature to be a man that belonged to the trail. And these days in

Blackhawk almost made me forget those that had murdered Sandy and had tried to kill me. Almost forget, but not quite! There were three men that needed justice prevailed upon them, and I was the only one that was going to take care of the dirty work - there was no one else. These thoughts for reasons that escaped me soured my mood, and Risa noticed it but said nothing. She knew the type of man I was; there was no hiding it even if I wanted to.

The day before my departure, I had picked up a new clue about the whereabouts of those that needed my attention. A week old Denver newspaper that had made its way to Blackhawk on the stage had an article that told of several mystery deaths of some old Confederate soldiers in or around the mountains of South Park near Como and Fairplay, Colorado. The article did not mention names, for the authorities had none, but I knew in my gut that those responsible were the Redlegs Captain John Merna, John Loveless, and the gunfighter LB. The day of leaving Blackhawk and the quest for the reckoning of the murderers of Sandy was now upon me. I would have to set aside any feelings of happiness and tenderness that I was now experiencing here in Blackhawk. I needed my heart to be as cold as ice. I needed to be a killer once again and so it would be.

The night before I headed into the far mountains to the South Park region, sleeping was not to be had. I tossed and turned. It was not that I feared for my own well-being and safety in regard to the renegade Redlegs. Living at the edge of death was nothing new to me - it was living a normal life that made me lose sleep. For ten days my life had been normal and just like most men. I felt the joy of family and caring, and it was something at my age that I knew now I could grow to love.

Lying here awake most of the night before I was to leave, I knew that Keegan was where she should be and with kin that loved her. I had grown to love the young Irish girl while on the trail as if she had sprung from the well of Patton. I thought of Keegan as one of my own be it a daughter or granddaughter. Keegan, since I had rescued her, had become a fixture in my life, and I would take a bullet for her if it came down to her life or my own - this I had no doubt. When the day that death claims me, everything that I owned I wish it to be hers. What I owned now I could carry on a good pack horse and was little enough to just get me by. If the Lord seemed fit to help me make a better means and fortune in the gold fields, I would be doing so, not only for myself, but for Keegan Doreen O'Rourke as well. Telling Keegan the words "I Love You" was never in my nature and I struggled with the concept; this had proven to be bothersome.

Risa O'Rourke also played a role in my lack of sleep. She was a woman that a man could be proud to call his own. She was intelligent no doubt; she was pleasant, but with an ornery streak which I adored. It was evident she had gumption. For a woman to move away from family to a rugged and dangerous mining town took the courage of a higher order. In these few days that I had gotten to know her, I knew her to be a woman to ride the river with. She was tough as they came, and she had sand. From the first moment I saw her in the schoolhouse, I was drawn to her. It was more than her physical beauty which was plentiful, but her personality and how she dealt with the children in her charge in her school showed her true colors.

Even though I did not recollect ever saying the words "I Love You" to a woman - probably had a time or two - but those words never rang as true as when I looked into the eyes of Risa Devin O'Rourke. In these past few days I had fallen in love with the woman; this was the only thing in life that I was sure of. Tossing and turning in the night, I knew there would be no future for me with her and she deserved another - someone more prone to a life in a town; someone with a steady job who could provide for her and Keegan; someone that loved her close and not from afar. That man was not me. I wished it could be, but I had no future beyond tomorrow and the end of a Colt pistol. I had men to track and to kill down the line, and there was no backing up from that. Fate and destiny had dealt me a hand that I was stuck with. It was all in or nothing. Yes, my fate would be decided in or around the mountains and towns of South Park, Colorado. Risa Devin O'Rourke deserved better than me.

The night air had chilled and it made for better sleeping so with thoughts of Risa and Keegan making tracks in my mind, I finally fell asleep a couple of hours before dawn.

CHAPTER 36

Waking at dawn and feeling the effects of little sleep and sadness, I felt the front of my head pounding from a headache. The sun was up but had yet to bring the light of day into Gregory Gulch, where the mining camp of Blackhawk was located. The air was cold and I had to for the first time wear my winter coat. The aspens that were dotted along the tree line amongst the evergreens were now in their full autumn color of gold and if not for the unhappiness on this day of leaving Keegan, Risa, and Hugo behind, I would have rejoiced in their splendor.

Looking out of the window of the room I had used for sleeping, I could see the smoke coming from the chimney of Risa's house. Once again the sadness overwhelmed me because I had told both Keegan and Risa that I would leave at dawn and would not take breakfast with them. I had told them this as I left them last night only as I had walked out the door. I had no idea how to tell them both a proper goodbye. I thought it best for me to just be on the trail without seeing their faces before I left. Now looking at the smoke, I was not so sure that was a good idea and it might be something I would regret later.

After dressing quickly, I swung my holster and Colt into place and buckled and tied it down to my right leg. Sitting down on the cot once again, I felt miserable about not having the words for the appropriate goodbye to those I had grown to care for. Being hard headed as I was, there was no backing up on that and I would just saddle and pack Sammy and Horse and be on my way. Snapping on Keegan's Pa's hat and after squaring it on my noggin, I headed for the door and I opened it.

Standing outside and holding the reins to an already saddled and packed Sammy and Horse were both Keegan and Risa and once I had the door open wide enough, Hugo attacked my boot for one last chew.

The emotion of seeing Keegan and Risa almost buckled my knees, and more than a few tears formed in my eyes. Feeling like a fool, I tried to wipe them away as if dust had gotten into them. As soon as the tears had been wiped, a few more replaced them. Seeing my futile effort of not showing my emotions for all to see, Keegan burst into tears as well, and she rushed me with her arms wide open to give me one last loving embrace. I bent down and received her into my arms with all the love that this aging gray soldier could muster.

Once the initial hug was over, I held Keegan out and looked in her eyes and said with more than enough sorrow in my voice, "Be strong little one!"

Keegan through her tears finally found her voice and replied, "I will Mac! It is just I could not let you go without telling you the most important thing in the world and that is - I Love You!"

Well, damn it all - that kid really gets under my skin and now the tears started to flow even more. Keegan had found the words that I could not, and she had the mettle and strength to tell me how she felt knowing in my heart I felt the same about her. Pulling her back into my chest, I closed my eyes as if that would stop the water works - it did not. I finally found my voice, "I know you do little one, and Keegan make no mistake - I Love You As Well!"

Risa had hung back as Keegan and I had our moment of clarity on how it was to be between us from now on out and after a few minutes of Keegan and me wiping each other's tears away, I stood up and looked at Keegan's aunt and saw that she was not immune to the tears of heart wrenching goodbyes. Risa, with a sack full of food for the trail ahead clutched in her hands and hanging in front of her, also had the red rimmed eyes of tears as well.

Keegan slowly let go of me and was still watching my eyes and she spoke again, "Mac, you don't have to prove anything to us. You can stay here and we can be a family!"

My heart was breaking, and I almost told her I would, but then I glanced at my saddlebag carrying the ashes of Sandy and knew that if not now, it would be later that I would have to avenge the memory of my best friend. It was best to get on the trail even if it meant my death in the end. I had to do this since it was who I was. Reaching out gently, I touched Keegan's face to wipe the tears before I spoke, "I know I don't have to prove anything to you Keegan, but it is a matter of honor with me. I have to go."

Keegan's eyes started to flow tears again and she said in a forceful voice, "Screw your honor Mac!"

Having said that, she turned and ran toward the house. Hugo, who had sat back and watched Keegan and me, finally seemed confused and stood with no tail wag at all and looked at me and then at Keegan as she ran to the house then back to me. Knowing he was torn as well, I picked him up and hugged him and then gently set him back on the ground. "Hugo, you need to skedaddle after Keegan, for she needs you right now."

Hugo hesitated until I pointed in Keegan's direction and then he bolted as if his tail was set afire. He had finally realized Keegan needed him now in the worst way.

Once Keegan and Hugo had departed, Risa set the sack with the food on the ground and then stepped up so our chests were touching, and her eyes held mine as she gingerly reached up and touched my lips with her first two fingers on her right hand. "Now listen and do not talk McCall Patton, for I know you better than you know yourself. I know you have to do this and track down those responsible for your friend Sandy and my brother and sister-in-laws' deaths. I understand the honor and I want justice as well. You need to understand one thing Mac and that is when that is done and you are finished, you get on Sammy and you ride like hell back to Blackhawk and Keegan and me. Being O'Rourke women, we don't need you in our lives, but we want you in our lives. Mr. Patton, Keegan loves you as her kin and in the short time you have been here, I as well have fallen in love with you!"

Risa removed her fingers so I could speak, and I reached around her and pulled her tight still looking into those eyes of a woman I had grown to love. It was several moments before I spoke, "You are sort of direct and sassy don't you think for a schoolmarm? I want you to know I was not looking for a woman because the life I have led is anything but stable. I have no fortune or money to offer a woman and have ridden on the outside edge of death all my life and that is not something any woman should want. I have thought that I am not worthy of the love of a woman such as yourself. I need you to know that my time here and on the trail with Keegan and yourself has been the most wonderful thing that has ever happened in my life and please know that if in the end and justice has prevailed and I have lived to ride another day, I will make fast tracks back here to Blackhawk...back to Keegan and yourself. Risa Devin O'Rourke, on my part it was love at first sight; there was no "falling" in love with you. It was as if I was always in love with you; I just didn't know where you were. I do - Love You - with all my heart."

Our eyes still locked on one another as we moved slowly with fear and eagerness as our lips touched, and the love that I felt was finally shown toward the woman that I wanted more than anything. We lingered basking in our feelings and smell of each other for what seemed a brief time, but long enough to know that we were meant for each other. With more than enough tears to go around, we let go of one another, and I quickly stepped into the stirrup and squared myself into the saddle on Sammy as Risa packed away the food she had prepared in the pack now on Horse.

Reining Sammy around to get one last look at what I was leaving behind me, I saw Keegan and Hugo now standing up the hill and behind Risa at the front door of the house and Keegan shouted down to me, "I love you McCall Mac Patton!"

Damn kid got the tears flowing again as I replied in kind, "I love you Keegan Doreen O'Rourke!"

Risa reached out and touched my hand as I gave Sammy a slight jab of my spur and said, "Hurry back to us Mac! Hurry back!"

CHAPTER 37

After leaving Blackhawk riding Sammy and trailing Horse behind, I rode through the mining camp of Central City toward Russell Gulch, which was at the top of Virginia Canyon with the gold camp of Idaho Springs at the bottom of the steep and dangerous rift in the mountain. The journey down the canyon wall was slow and tedious, and the footing for the horses on the narrow trail was about as dangerous as it could get. According to Risa the locals had taken to calling the Virginia Canyon the "Oh My God Road," which obviously spoke of high adventure. It was about noon when on a narrow cliff that Sammy stumbled for the first time, and for a second I thought that I and the whole caboodle were going to take a tumble off a 400 foot drop. Once Sammy found her footing, she looked back at me and I swear I could read her thought of "Oh My God!" Of course that made me chuckle nervously as the local handle of the canyon seemed more than accurate.

Even though the high country autumn air was chilled under darkened skies, I sweated droplets from my forehead all the way down to just on the outskirts of the mining camp of Idaho Springs. One thing I knew for certain is that the good Lord did not make canyons such as this one back home in "Little Dixie' Missouri. I was starting to wonder how many more such trails and canyons I had to take to travel to the South Park region and Fairplay. It was plain to see that Sammy, Horse, and I had plenty to learn about mountain travel. I was going to have to recall most of what the old gold miner Marty Blake had told me of these mountains and try to apply it to our travels. I used to think I was too old to learn new things, but I was going to learn if I liked it or not.

When I stopped at the bottom of the canyon, the skies cleared and the heavens turned into an ever reaching blue as I ate two of the four roasted turkey and Dutch oven bread sandwiches for a quick noon time meal before venturing into Idaho Springs. Almost every business and rotgut saloon had the name Argo attached to it in some fashion or another after the largest gold mine on the north mountainside named the Argo Gold Mine. Riding through town, I decided not to stop, for it was a town full of hard rock miners, drifters, and what I could see walking the boardwalks a bunch of cutthroats and malcontents. It would not be wise for me to linger here in Idaho Springs. I had trouble waiting for me at the end of the trail in South Park; I did not need it here in this camp. So I slowly rode through southwest toward Georgetown, Colorado.

I followed on the banks of Clear Creek until about two hours before sunset when I found a suitable campsite for the night northeast of Georgetown that was close to the river but had a strong stand of trees that would block the wind if it picked up during the night.

Before taking care of the horses, I set out a couple of set lines baited with some Dutch oven bread that I had rolled into several hard balls. I hoped to catch a couple of trout that I had seen in the cool water of the creek that I had been viewing all day as they broke the surface, sucking up wayward flies and the such. Fresh trout would be a welcome supper for sure.

Once the set lines were baited and tied off to a fallen log, I unsaddled Sammy and Horse and gave them a good rub down and currying before letting them loose to graze on the long grass alongside the creek. Finding enough rocks of the right size, I ringed a spot and started my cook fire which I would also need for warmth tonight. Autumn and its aspen gold were here in full swing in the Rocky Mountains, and along with that cooler temperatures.

It was not long at all before I had caught, gutted, and fried a couple of three pound rainbow trout; they smelled wonderful and my gut was rumbling in anticipation.

After a supper of fish and a half of an apple pie that Risa had sent, I lay back on my bedroll and watched the end of a Colorado mountain day as the ever-growing long shadows of the night overtook my campsite as the sun dropped below the western horizon with the brightest blue and orange sky I had ever seen. Being new to the high mountains, I was amazed at each and every sunset and the colors within. They only thing I could decipher was being near the heavens brought about the bright colors. Whatever the reason, the sunset and sunrises were something to behold, and I don't think I would ever get used to them.

As the darkness crept in, Sammy and Horse instinctively moved closer to myself and the fire. They were just as new to the mountains as I was and I could only imagine the wild critters such as wolves, bears, and mountain lions that were just beyond the circle of light of the fire used the darkness looking for prey. I kept my Winchester close as well as my six shooter; it would not be a ride for justice if I fall prey to such creatures of the night.

I thought about what was ahead of me and hopefully the upcoming encounter with the Redlegs. Captain John Merna, John Loveless, and the gunfighter Larry Brown known as LB. They were of course hard and dangerous men and if what I thought was true about Captain John Merna, he was also touched in the head. It would seem that the Civil War was still replaying in his mind which made him very unpredictable as well as dangerous. This whole idea of his having in his possession the map indicating the whereabouts of the Reynolds' gold and loot intrigued me. Even if Vaughn and Wells never thought he had the map, I am now starting to believe that Captain Merna thinks he has the actual map to the loot. It was the only thing that made any sense at all in this mad dash to the Rocky Mountains on their part. Wouldn't that be something if Merna actually found the Reynolds' treasure trove before I found him? I still had the advantage in that Captain Merna had no idea I was trailing him and his cutthroats, for he thought me long dead. It was going to make my day when he saw me for the first time. Hell, he might just have a heart attack and drop dead and save me all the trouble of shooting him.

Risa luckily had been to Fairplay last summer and was able to hand draw me a map and spoke to me at length about the trail and what I should expect. Taking out the map, I studied it some more by the light of the campfire trying not to get too close and set it afire. It would seem I just follow Clear Creek upstream to the mining camps of Georgetown and Silver Plume which was just a mile west of Georgetown until I was at the trailhead of Loveland Pass. From my accounting of the map and what Risa had told me, I reckoned it was roughly seventeen miles from my campsite to the base of Loveland Pass. It should be an easy trail since all I had to do was follow the creek. Loveland Pass, of course, would be a whole different story since it went over the Great Divide.

This was a grand adventure, and I was saddened that Sandy was making it only as ashes and bone fragments in a sugar sack. Knowing Sandy the man, he would have done the same with my ashes if it had been me that had perished back there in Kansas instead of him. Others would not understand this unless they felt the brotherhood and bond that Sandy and I had known down through the years.

Watching the orange and fiery embers of the fire float and dance above the flames, I thought of these things and much more tonight. Even though I had not been gone for long, I longed for my girls. "My girls?" I smiled of course as it was set in my thoughts that Risa and Keegan of course were my girls. Then my smile vanished because I knew those thoughts of a normal life with Keegan and Risa back in Blackhawk would probably get me killed if I let them lollygag around in my thoughts and feelings. Men such as myself with a gunfighter reputation - deserved or not - could not afford to think as normal men. There were others out there that wanted that reputation that would not hesitate to shoot me down in cold blood just to be known as the man that killed the "Gray Rider Rebel Mac."

It was time to tune out any thoughts of a normal life with Keegan and Risa. I needed to track down and kill those responsible for Sandy, Ardan and Bree O'Rourke, and countless others deaths. To do so, I needed a cold and black heart and needed to bring forth the man that had faded into the background in Blackhawk in those ten days of happiness. That man that had faded into the background had the killer instinct needed to survive the upcoming battle with the Redlegs.

Pulling my flannel blanket up higher to ward off the night chill, I found an uneasy sleep.

CHAPTER 38

Waking at dawn, I ate the remaining two turkey sandwiches that Risa had packed, and I quickly readied Sammy and Horse and was back on the trail hours before the sun ever breached the autumn shadows from the mountainside as it rose in the eastern sky.

My day on the Keegan Trail was uneventful as I made my way southwesterly along the banks of Clear Creek through Clear Creek Canyon. I sort of chuckled to myself since I still thought of this new country and the trail ahead as the Keegan Trail even though Keegan was back in Blackhawk. I had no idea what the trail that lay ahead of me was called or even if it had a name, so in my thinker it was and always will be the Keegan Trail.

I quietly rode by the mining camp of Georgetown and remembered some of the history of the town told to me by Risa before I left. The town was discovered during the Pikes Peak gold rush but quickly become known for the silver mines that were found in the Argentine Pass area.

The day had all the makings of a beautiful day that promised for decent travel, for the sky was blue with just a few flat, white clouds overhead. Although the temperature was cool enough to break out my winter coat, it was not yet cold enough for any type of gloves or hat to cover my ears. The air was cool and crisp as I breathed it in, and it would seem I was getting adapted to the thinner air in the high mountains. On this day I felt strong and just as adventurous as any mountain man I could envision in my thoughts. Yes, indeed it was a glorious day to be alive.

Just a mile away, I rode by the mining camp of Silver Plume, and it was here not long ago that the Central City righteous gunfighter Lucas Eldridge ended the life of one Juan Verdugo in a gun battle that almost cost Lucas his life as well. Silver Plume was also another mining camp that came to be as a gold mining camp as well, but it was silver here that made it into the bustling town that it was now after it was discovered that the funny looking rock that folks were kicking around while looking for gold was in fact actually silver.

The end of the day brought me to the base of Loveland Pass and the first of two passes over the Great Divide I would have to travel on the trail to reach the South Park Region and the town of Fairplay that was roughly in the middle of the high mountain plateau.

Toward the end of the day, I located a campsite sheltered from the wind and close to the creek for water for the night. After taking care of Sammy and Horse and giving them some sweet sugar as a treat, I let them loose to graze as they may in mountain grass, and then I sat down at my campfire and ate the last of the remaining grub that Risa had packed for me. A small slab of roast beef, hard biscuits, and the last of the apple pie almost made my belly burst. It was some good eating that was for sure.

Loveland Pass was before me and in this light, I could still see all the way to the top and the snow that was shrouded over the high peaks…not new snow from this year, for winter was still several weeks away, but snow that never melted even during the warmest time of year during the summer months. It was hard for me to imagine snow that never melted. Hell, in "Little Dixie" it only snowed one time that I could remember and it didn't amount to much and melted within a few minutes after meeting the ground.

Looking at the high mountain pass with its forever snow at the top gave me a reluctant feeling maybe I should have stayed back home. Risa had told me that the pass that was looking so insurmountable in front of me topped out about two thousand feet above timberline where even the trees could not survive.

This country - this state of Colorado and the Rocky Mountains - were the most majestic countryside I had ever seen, but deadly of course. Within the mountains if it was not the wild critters that caused your death, it would be the snow, ice, and the bitter cold that brought about a quick death for those not tough enough or smart enough to survive these conditions. I was not a man born of the mountains, but I was smart enough to realize the dangers that lurked here in the high mountains. It was obvious to me you had to be a quick learner here, but I felt I was up to the challenge. Night comes quickly here, and the cool night air tonight made for good sleeping weather.

The following morning Sammy and Horse and I after a cold breakfast started up the steep incline that zigged and zagged back and forth from side to side, but always upwards. It was past mid-morning that we broke timberline; it was among the snowfields and tundra that trees never grew and it was country like I had never seen before. It was cold and barren and the air was so thin it made it difficult to breathe for not only myself but also for the horses. Risa had told me that six or seven months out of the year that this pass and other mountain passes just like this one could not be traveled, for the snow could reach up to forty or fifty feet deep. When Risa first told me how deep the snow could get here, it seemed unbelievable at the time, but now rising to the top of Loveland Pass, I no longer doubted it. This land above timberline was as about as hostile as it could be.

Around noon I reached the summit of the pass and was able to look eastward from the top, and I almost fell out of the saddle with what I could see before me. The sky above was blue with the hint of darkness above. I could see some clouds floating beneath me in spots as they rode the air like ghosts in the sky. Never in my life could I see as far as I could see today. There would be no way I could ever count the miles that lay before me in all of its splendid glory. I had read that the world was round and all the non-believers of that notion should be made to ride to this spot, and they would become believers, for you could see so far that you could see the curve of the world. It boggled my mind.

Dismounting, I wanted to sit and watch for a spell the world that stretched forever in front of me. My first thought was how Keegan would love this. If I was skilled and lucky enough to live through my confrontation with the Redlegs and somehow make it back to Blackhawk, the first thing when the weather would allow it was to bring Keegan here. How wonderful would it be to be with the young Irish girl for the first time she experienced this - this view of the world.

Not wanting to spend too much time here and get caught on the downside of the pass when darkness started to overtake the mountains, I remounted and reluctantly spurred Sammy downward still trailing Horse. I zigged and zagged in the same manner on the east side of Loveland Pass as I had on the west side. The horses and I were making good time and made the bottom of Loveland Pass an hour before dark.

Along a river that was not on Risa's map so I did not know the name, I found a location with good shelter and plenty of down evergreen tree limbs for a campfire to wait out the night. Sammy and Horse and I were getting back into the routine of the trail and after taking care of them, I started a fire and fried up some fatback bacon and beans for supper. After supper I took out Risa's map to study and in the morning I would skirt the west side of Grizzly Peak and Lenawee Mountain. Lenawee I assumed was a Ute Indian name since the Utes, before the whites ever ventured here in what is now Colorado, called these mountains their home. I would follow this trail until I reached Montezuma, Colorado.

The camp and booming town of Montezuma, for reasons unknown to Risa, was named after an Emperor of the Aztecs, which made absolutely no sense to me. Montezuma just like Georgetown was a mining camp founded on silver mining in or around the Argentine Pass area.

After folding and storing my map, I sat back warm and with a full belly under my flannel blanket, I looked heavenward. With not one cloud above my head, I watched the stars in the sky dance their nightly dance of light. The stars seemed brighter here in the mountains and the only explanation I could think of was because I was closer to them. The wind picked up slightly and dislodged some of the golden aspen leaves of autumn, and they joined the stars' dance as they floated gracefully and silently on the mountain wind. It would seem that nature was content for the evening. Trying to put thoughts of Keegan and Risa out of my mind proved an epic failure this evening and with thoughts of my girls, I fell asleep.

CHAPTER 39

The sound of a crow "cawing" woke me before dawn and even in the low light of the fading stars and the dying embers of the fire, I was able to see it in the shadows sitting on a branch of an evergreen not fifteen feet above and in front of me as it looked at me as if it was searching my soul for answers.

During my time at Blackhawk, I had made friends with an older Ute Indian and his wife that lived just outside of Central City on Bald Mountain who was a member of the Grand River Ute tribe. He had told me many things about the Utes and their way of life before and after the white man had come to the Rocky Mountains.

One of the old Utes' tales of days long gone was about the beliefs of the spirit animals. He spoke of the Utes' belief about crows and he went on at length talking about that. He said the Utes believed a crow held all the answers to the mystery of life and that sometimes foretold of the coming of death. I had not put much stock into what I thought was Indian nonsense. Now looking at the crow that had locked eyes with me, I now was becoming a believer.

The crow now before me seemed to have a higher intelligence than any other bird I had ever seen before. The crow watched me as if it was studying me and seemed to be not at all alarmed to be here in such close contact with me. The presence of this black as midnight crow sent a chill up my spine. The thoughts that were floating around in my brain pan were if the mysterious crow was trying to clue me into my life mystery or was it foretelling death. Possibly my own death? Though I had seen way too much death in my life and had lived a whole life until this moment living on the edge of death, watching this crow made me a tad nervy and fired up my gut instinct. The crow and I studied each other for a good ten minutes or more before it flapped its wings and took flight in the direction of Montezuma as if it knew the path of my life and it was showing it to me so I did not stray from that trail. The crow and the thoughts it had stirred in my soul confused the hell out of me.

After the departure of the crow, the sky started to lighten in the eastern horizon, but my campsite would be in the morning shadows of the mountains for a spell, which made for a chilly morning as I stirred the ashes to reawaken the fire. After coaxing the still hot embers of the night before, I was able to get a small trickle of flame and quickly added kindling before adding some larger wood. It was not long before I had a large enough fire to warm my hands and to fry up some bacon and beans for my breakfast.

Both of the horses, after being made ready for the trail, seemed eager as they pawed the ground and snorted more than a few times. Sammy and Horse had been my family for so long now I thought in the terms of three. They were an extension of my mind and soul and of course I loved them as if they were my kin and partner, which of course they were. Once squared in the saddle, I gave Sammy some rein and her head and with a slight jab of my spur, the three of us headed down the Keegan Trail toward the mining camp named after an Aztec emperor named Montezuma.

It was not until mid-morning that the sun was high enough above the eastern mountains to be able to rain down some of its warmth on me, and it felt good to have the morning chill leave the mountain air. Sammy and Horse did not seem to care one way or another; then of course their bones were not as old as mine.

At midday I skirted Montezuma seeing no reason at all to stop and kept on the trail toward Breckenridge and the Blue River.

As I rode on the eastern side of Keystone Mountain, I was once again amazed at the beauty of all that was before me with the aspens still in their final death song of the season as autumn here was now in full swing. The air was crisp and clear and each breath of mountain air was invigorating. The music of the mountains was at a full tilt this morning as the slight wind played the familiar song of the aspen. In the distance I heard the eerie bugle of an elk hidden by the trees. If I had not been on a ride to avenge the death of Sandy and the O'Rourkes, I would have stopped and made myself one with all that was around me, but I had more pressing matters. Looking back at the saddlebag carrying Sandy's ashes and bone fragments, I refocused my thinker.

As my ponderings came full circle, it was Captain John Merna, John Loveless and Larry Brown that my thoughts fixated on - not with hate, but resolution. This task...this manhunt...was all that mattered now. If somehow I survived the encounter, I could then think about a normal life back in Blackhawk with Keegan and Risa – but only then.

The day dwindled and the sun had already dropped behind the mountains to the west, taking its warmth once again with the mountain air chilling quickly. I deciphered it was roughly three miles from the mining camp of Breckenridge when I found a campsite with a small flowing brook and plenty of evergreens to shelter the horses and me from any night wind.

Once again, I woke at dawn, but my campsite once again was in the shadow of the mountains to the east, making it even colder than the day before. After a quick breakfast of a squirrel that I had shot the day before and some beans, I spent no time lollygagging and got Sammy and Horse ready for the trail.

Heading south, I came upon the Blue River and knew that if I followed its banks due east, I would run into the mining camp of Breckenridge which sat on the western side of Boreas Pass. According to the map that Risa had drawn for me, on the eastern side of Boreas was the high plains plateau of South Park and the trail to Fairplay, Colorado.

Recalling most of everything that Marty Blake and Risa told me about Breckenridge, I knew it to be a town and mining camp that was formed to supply the original placer gold miners when the elusive metal was found in and along the banks of the Blue River. Once the Blue and its banks had been picked clean, then the miners followed it upstream and were able to find numerous veins in the surrounding mountains, and then the hard rock miners took over.

Breckenridge, like most mining camps, was full of hard working, decent folks and more than a few hard cases looking to strike it rich. Most, of course, would fail. Moving along the trail that followed the Blue River, I passed several mining claims of those that worked those chilled mountain waters, and they did so with enthusiasm never knowing from one minute to the next if fate would make them rich.

With no need to stop in Breckenridge as well, I skirted once again on the outskirts as I headed to the western slope of Boreas Pass - another trail and pass over the Great Divide.

Boreas Pass, according to what I remembered from Risa, was not as tall as Loveland Pass, but still topped out at 1000 feet or more above the timber line. I had reached the base about midday and I debated about if I should continue on and try to make it over yet this day or wait until morning. Looking at the sun and the clouds, I thought it was a good enough autumn day for me to try and traverse the mountain before me.

After eating some venison jerky from the saddle and drinking a half of a canteen of cool river water for my noontime meal, I urged Sammy forward. I looked back at Horse, and she was trailing nicely as I started up the western slope of Boreas.

The trail was the same zigging and zagging manner that I had experienced on Loveland Pass, and the horses seemed to have gained experience from that and were having no difficulty in their task of getting my butt to the top and over.

From this vantage point I could not see the summit of Boreas, but I could only assume just like Loveland Pass, it had a substantial amount of snow above timberline where summer never reaches.

About half way up we spooked a bull elk that was standing in the middle of the trail. As he turned his massive head and antlers, I could see his eyes were glazed and he was maddened by being in the rut of the mating season. He was 750 pounds or possibly bigger, and his antlers raised a good four feet above his head with seven points on each side, making him from hoof to antler tip close to ten feet tall. He was the biggest elk I had ever seen and he did not look happy to see us on his mountain. Sammy and Horse seemed to sense that the bull elk was not the most peaceful critter at this moment in time Sammy started to snort and paw the ground; Horse was snorting a bit nervy; then they started to back up in a half ass panic. I started to scan the tree line looking for a possible escape route around the bull elk, and it would seem that fate had placed the monster elk in front of us at the worse possible place on the mountain since we were pinned in on both sides by a thick stand of evergreen trees. The bull elk had now made the complete turn and was now facing us; he lowered his antlers and snorted as if he was challenging us and was ready to charge.

CHAPTER 40

Sammy had backed up so much that she had now tangled the rope that was securing Horse to my saddle, because Horse was not as alarmed as Sammy; she was just hanging back flatfooted waiting for events to unfold. After about half a minute, I was finally able to get Sammy under control and stopped her from backing up anymore. The whole time while dealing with Sammy, I kept my eyes on the massive elk in front of me. Not wanting to shoot this grand looking creature, but fearing for my life and limbs, I slowly pulled my Winchester from its scabbard and pointed it at the head of the beast now blocking the trail in front of me.

The bull was only forty feet away and having seen elk run before, I knew it would just be a second or two that he could cover that distance if he wanted to take me and the horses on in battle. The elk had not advanced, but his stance with his antlers lowered into a fighting posture foretold of bad things that could happen. Today was not a good day to get gored. Using the lever action on the Winchester, I jacked a 44 shell into the chamber. Then I waited.

Time slowly moved forward as the standoff with the bull elk started reaching a crescendo. It was nerve wracking knowing even if I shot the beast that his headlong charge would still have a devastating ending for myself or Sammy in that the distance was too close to one or both not to get gored.

What happened next surprised the hell out of me. The bull elk must have decided, even though I was riding on top of Sammy, that I was way too small to challenge his authority and mastery over the elk women folk on Boreas Pass, and he lifted his head in a less threatening manner. Still not convinced and with still no place to move out of his way, I held my Winchester steady, keeping it pointed at his head.

The colossal beast before me slowly moved all his muscle and brawn and turned around facing the same direction I was and that was up the slope of Boreas. The bull elk was now facing away from me, so I lowered my Winchester onto the top of my saddle behind the horn. I was now content for the bull to take his sweet time getting out of my way. After about five minutes, the elk bugled his eerie mating call, and it almost made me pee my pants since I was not expecting that. Sandy would have loved that and my reaction and if he was still alive, I would never have heard the end of it. I chuckled at the thought of Sandy giving me shit.

What seemed an eternity, but I knew it was only about another five minutes, the gigantic elk slowly moved out and started moving away from me. Using the lever action, I jacked out the shell that had been in the firing chamber of my Winchester. I once again made it safe and then stored it back into its scabbard. I then untangled the lead rope and waited about twenty minutes, giving the elk a good head start up the trail. Once I thought enough time had passed, I gave Sammy some rein and her head and Sammy hesitantly moved forward.

The bull elk must have found himself a lady love elsewhere because I never came across him again. The bull elk left tracks in the snow as he ventured south of the tail that I was on, and I was thankful for that. A bull in rut is an unpredictable force of nature that I would rather not have to deal with. I tipped my hat in his direction bidding him farewell and good fortunes in his future endeavors in his romantic notions.

About three quarters of the way to the summit, it started to snow, not just a tad bit of snow, but a full-fledged snowstorm. The clouds moved in so fast that one moment it was a nice sunny autumn day, and then all of a sudden it was cloudy and snowing. Marty Blake had warned me of the weather at these lofty heights and told me that the weather was never your friend and always your foe. He said it was his thought that being so close to the sky that the weather could change in a heartbeat. This I had no doubt because it just did. With the snow the mountain air turned cold enough that I had to get my scarf and gloves out of the saddlebag. Now I thought I might have made a mistake in venturing onward and upward over Boreas so late in the day. The rutting elk had delayed me and now it was snowing.

Having no other choice now, I pressed on and within a half hour I reached the summit of Boreas. There was not a lot of new depths of snow on the ground, maybe two inches is all, but the wind had picked up and whirled the new snow of the day into a ground blizzard. What was strange to me was that I could look straight up and if I squinted my eyes just right, I could see the sky was blue not ten feet over my head and above the snow. It would seem that I was smack dab in the middle of a snow cloud. Folks back in "Little Dixie" would have thought this to be a tall tale if someone had said you could ride the world inside of a cloud. Hell, I was living and doing it and could hardly believe it myself.

Knowing I needed to keep moving to get myself out of the cloud and the snow, I started down the east side of Boreas Pass. I could not help but think of how back home in "Little Dixie" that autumn was just barely getting started and the days could still get hot as hell. Here in the high country of the Colorado Rocky Mountains, old man winter was already kicking down the door of autumn.

Because of the snow I could not relive the view from the top of the world as I had on top of Loveland Pass. That sort of saddened me because I had been looking forward to experiencing it once again. It was not long before I was below the cloud and snow, and the sky above me turned blue once again. Turning in my saddle and looking behind at my back trail and toward the summit once again, I was amazed at the quickness of the changing weather here above timberline. Within less than a minute, the cloud and the snow at the summit faded into the blue sky once again. The summit and the forever snow were now basking in the autumn sun. Shaking my head, I turned forward once again and gave Sammy a slight jab of my spur moving downward. My thought was there was still a hell of a lot I had to learn about the Rocky Mountains.

The sun had already set on the west side of Boreas Pass, and it was well past dark when I finally made the bottom of the pass on the eastern side. It had been a long and tiring day from the tension from the standoff with the bull elk and the ground blizzard on top of the summit. Both horses and I were exhausted from climbing Boreas Pass, and it was probably an hour or so before midnight before I had the horses unsaddled and curry combed. I spoke lovingly to both for their endless work of dragging my mangy butt up and over the mountain. I could not be more proud of Sammy and Horse as I was at this moment. They never once faltered on the steep incline in the darkness. I promised to never get them in that type of situation again as I fed them a treat of sugar.

Not wanting to take the time to start a fire, I ate a half a pound of venison jerky for my supper and laid out my bedroll for the night. I wanted to study Risa's map some more to see what was next on the Keegan Trail and how far it was to South Park and the town of Fairplay, but since I only had the light of the stars to work with, I decided the map reading would have to wait until morning.

After I got settled under my flannel blanket for the night, I began to reflect on the difficulties of my man hunt for Captain Merna, John Loveless, and Larry Brown the gunfighter. South Park and Fairplay, Colorado were just going to be the starting point of my Redleg manhunt. It was highly doubtful that the Redlegs would still be there and if by chance that they actually had located Reynolds' confederate treasure trove, they would probably already be headed back to eastern Kansas and home. This task of hunting down Sandy's and the O'Rourkes' murderers could take months, and possibly even years.

My mind started to drift toward Keegan and Risa back in Blackhawk, and I was starting to think it was foolish on my part to even dream of a normal life with them. I knew full well that I was a man that could not quit on this quest to serve well deserved justice on Captain Merna and his men and was just going to have to let any life I could have had back in Blackhawk drift away. The task before me was too great and time consuming. Hell, I will probably get killed anyway. Family life was not meant to be for a man like myself, and the only thing I should expect out of this life that fate had thrown my way was a bullet from the end of a Colt pistol from some wannabe famous young gunfighter.

Rolling on my side, I tried to block out any and all thoughts of Keegan and Risa. The problem with that was that Keegan, Hugo, and Risa kept finding a back door into my thoughts.

CHAPTER 41

I awoke in a foul mood at dawn and it just so happened it matched the weather of the morning. The skies had clouded over and the wind had picked up during the night. The dead and dying aspen leaves were riding the chilled autumn wind with several leaves landing on my face only to be gusted away with another swirl of wind. I was hungry and my bones ached and I was cold. Sandy of course would have told me to quit my belly aching and get my ass up, which brought a smile to me thinking of my dead partner. I sure did miss him and all the good natured ribbing we used to give each other.

The venison jerky that I ate last night had not filled the void in my stomach, and I was feeling the need to make a warm breakfast. After checking on the horses, I gathered enough stones to make a ring for my campfire. After gathering some kindling and down tree limbs in just a short time, I had a warming fire that doubled as a cook fire.

I looked into my grub sack, and it seemed I was going to have to fry up the remaining bacon and beans since that was all I had. I remembered there was a town not far from here and I would have to make a stop and replenish my supplies before I hit the trail to Fairplay.

Looking to the east, I saw a stand of mountains about twenty or thirty miles away, but between here and there it was as flat as the plains in western Kansas and eastern Colorado. So this is what they called South Park, Colorado.

Marty Blake and Risa both spoke about South Park as well as Middle Park and North Park. All three were grassland flats formed within a basin that covered roughly 1000 square miles each and were surrounded by the Rocky Mountains in central Colorado. Snickering to myself, I thought that some "genius" came up with the names since North Park was the farthest north, Middle Park was in the center, and South Park which I was sitting on the far western edge was the furthest one south.

South Park, from what I could see on Risa's map I just unfolded, was in between the Mosquito Mountains and the Park Mountain Ranges and was home to the headwaters of the South Platte River that flowed all the way to Denver and beyond.

I studied the map and it showed that the town of Como was only two or three miles to the south of my campsite. I didn't want to stop, but I needed some supplies for myself and grain and sugar for Sammy and Horse. I hoped that Como was not full of hard cases and was a peaceful town and that no one there had ever heard the name of McCall "Mac" Patton the gray rider.

After putting out the fire and burying it, I made Sammy and Horse ready for the trail to Como. As I did this, I tried to remember everything that Marty and Risa had said about the small mountain town. It was believed that the town was named by miners from Como, Italy, who worked the coal fields in and around Como. Marty could not remember, but he believed that they were still in the planning stages of building a railroad over Boreas Pass to connect Como to Breckenridge and Leadville. That of course explained some of the odd markings and strips of red cloth I had seen on trees that I had run across on both sides of the pass. I must have passed some of the proposed railroad beds. Seemed sort of foolish to me to build a track over a pass that could get thirty to forty feet of snow, but what the hell did I know?

Between my last campsite and Como was the Como cemetery, which was on the west side of the trail and a burial was being conducted with about a half dozen mourners and some sort of padre saying kind words over the deceased. I stopped and watched for several minutes even though I was far enough away that I could not hear the words being said. This reminded me once again how alone I truly was in the world. If I would die today or tomorrow, there would be no one that cared about me that would bury my body and say kind words over my grave. Looking back at the saddlebag with the sugar sack carrying my friend's ashes, I decided soon I needed to bury him as well and say the right things that came from my heart before it was too late.

Looking to the south, I could see the outskirts of Como and the smoke rising from the fireplace chimneys of the camp. Taking out my binoculars, I studied the town for a spell and decided it was no different than any other such town in the Rocky Mountain frontier, and I gave Sammy some rein and she started toward the edge of Como.

As we rode down the main street, there were numerous tents many of them saloons set with a couple of whiskey barrels and a plank in between them to be used as a bar. I also saw a hand painted sign that read "Lee Saunders, Doctor of People and Horses." It would seem that the small camp had at least one educated fellow in it. There was a wooden two story hotel named the South Park Hotel with a huge banner proclaiming it was now open and next to it was a general store called Boone's General Store. Tying Sammy and Horse to the hitching rail out in front of Boone's, I took the rawhide thong off the hammer of my Colt and stepped up on the boardwalk.

Stopping for a minute before opening the door to Boone's, I surveyed the townsfolk and everyone seemed to be going about their daily chores and business with no one taking an interest in the new stranger in town - which was to my liking.

Once I was satisfied that no one seemed to care about me, I proceeded into Boone's. Once inside I was able to purchase the much needed supplies from a likable young man named Glen Boone.

After packing and storing my supplies, I looked across the street and saw another hand painted sign stating that the tent beneath it was Peg's Dining Emporium. Even though it was not quite midday yet, I thought I would treat myself to some cooking other than my own and headed in that direction. Once inside of Peg's I saw that out of the twelve tables there was only one open, and it was to my liking because I could sit with my back against the exterior of the tent and I could face the door to be able to see everyone that walked in. This was an old habit of mine and on more than one occasion it had saved my life and Sandy's.

The short and older woman with long gray hair in a ponytail that waited on me happened to be the owner herself Peg. She was helpful and pleasant and not too nosey, and I liked her right off the bat. Peg told me in the most pleasant sounding voice that there was only one thing on the menu today and that was the special which was beef steak and eggs with butter biscuits. Peg also stated for an extra two bits she would save me a slice of apple pie that was baked just this morning. Having no choice, I ordered the special and the apple pie. Thinking about the fresh apple pie made my mood swing a tad toward the happier side.

The steak was rare just as I liked it, and the butter biscuits were the best I had ever had including my Ma's. And of course the apple pie was just about the best I had ever had next to my granny in Little Dixie. After my meal I unfolded the map that Risa had drawn for me again, and it would seem Fairplay was almost due south of Como about eleven miles.

Not sure what I would do when I got to Fairplay, but it was the only clue I had of the whereabouts of Captain Merna and the other two Redlegs John Loveless and Larry Brown. So it would seem Fairplay would be my starting point. Once I got there, I thought the best course of action was going to the local law office there to ask some questions. Maybe some unexplained deaths had occurred regarding former soldiers of the Confederacy or maybe they might actually know Captain John Merna. As much as I hated to admit it, if the murdering Redlegs kept leaving dead ex-gray soldiers everywhere they went, it could only help in my tracking them down and bringing an end to their renegade ways. The more I thought about Merna and the others, I could not help but ponder the loot that they were after - the Reynolds' gang's ill-gotten gains. Wouldn't that be something if they actually found it after all these years? Those that had been robbed so many years ago would now be scattered to the wind and or dead. Nobody was missing that money any longer and most thought it was just a tall tale as well except for Marty Blake the old gold prospector of course; he had experienced it first hand and had been robbed of $300 of his hard earned money.

Folding up the map once again, I put it back into my shirt pocket and then placed one dollar in paper money on the table for a tip to Miss Peg. As I was just getting ready to stand up, the door opened to Peg's Dining Emporium and a man walked in who was about 5'10" and weighed in about a buck eighty, clean-shaven with dark brown hair. He also wore red leggings.

I could hardly believe my eyes, and I had to take a second look, because I was not expecting to see Larry Brown the gunfighter here in Como of all places.

CHAPTER 42

L arry Brown looked right at me and then glanced away as if he never saw me or at least it did not register who I was. It must be because when folks thought you dead, they simply erased any thought of you as a living person and at a glance it did not register in their thinkers that you might be still alive. I might as well have been a ghost; to LB it would at least seem that way.

It would seem I might not have to make the trip to Fairplay to find the men that I was hunting or at least in this case, it was true of the man that was called LB. LB stood at the door for a minute waiting for a table to clear so I got a good look at the gunfighter and how he was armed. His well-cared for and shiny Colt pistol was tied down to his right leg with the grip pointing backwards for a standard draw. LB also had a foot long bowie knife hanging on his left side in a sheath adorned with beads and rawhide. He looked comfortable with each weapon and if the rumors were true, he was skilled in causing the death of others with both.

Once a table on the other side of the tent was cleared and wiped down, the owner and waitress Peg pointed to LB and then the table for LB to take a seat, which he did. There were three empty chairs sitting at the table, so I waited to see if the other Redlegs Merna and Loveless might show up as well.

I focused on everything around me and there was so much I had yet to know in the coming confrontation with LB. Was LB alone in Como? If so, where were Merna and Loveless? There was only one thing I was certain of at this moment and that was that LB would order beef steak and eggs with butter biscuits, because it was his only choice. Peg's Dining Emporium was packed with folks that had their feed bag on, and it was not a place to press matters with LB. I would have to postpone my introduction until he was outside in the street, so I ordered a cup of coffee and another piece of apple pie while I waited.

After eating and paying for his meal, LB walked outside and I was just a few steps behind him. He seemed he was in some sort of hurry and was making tracks across the main street of Como in record time when I spoke to him, "LB when you kill a man you damn well better check to see if he is actually dead!"

The Redleg gunfighter stopped in the middle of the road with his back to me. I kept an eye on him as I made my way to the middle of the road about forty-five feet to the west of him.

Larry Brown slowly turned to face me, and his jaw dropped open in disbelief. I waited until his eyes caught up with his thoughts floating around in his mind. By instinct the gunfighter known as LB made ready his stance with his boots directly under his shoulders.

As LB was putting two and two together, I noticed that LB's red leggings were dirty and dusty from the trail and looked as if they had never been washed. Knowing the outcome of what was to come already in my mind, I started to focus on all things that could affect the outcome of what was just about to happen here on the streets of Como. The air had a slight autumn chill to it, and the wind was a mere trickle out of the north and barely enough to move an out of place hair on my forehead. The sky was blue with no clouds that could hide the sun that was directly overhead, giving neither LB nor myself an advantage. The boardwalks were full of people who had turned to look when I had spoken out loud to LB.

The townsfolk did not bother me since I needed them to witness this gunfight for it to be judged legal and fair. None of these folks of Como would know what had led up to this moment or that it was justified on my part. This gunfight had to be viewed as self-defense by these people.

The mind of the man known as LB had finally caught up, and he blinked his eyes several times before a slight smile crept across his face before he spoke, "I will be damned if it isn't McCall Patton the gray rider! I thought we killed you back in Kansas!"

I overheard a man on the boardwalk exclaim, "I will be a son of a bitch! That's Rebel Mac - McCall Patton the gunfighter!"

The stance of LB told me he was as ready as he was ever going to be to bring this gunfight to a conclusion, but I needed to know a few things first. "Where are Merna and Loveless? Did you find what you were looking for here in South Park?"

LB was confident in his ability with his weapon and he sort of laughed when he spoke again, "Merna and Loveless? They are both here in town someplace. As for finding what we were looking for, we did and it was more than we could have dreamed of, Mac! How did you know about that anyway?"

Both Merna and Loveless were here in Como which was good news and bad news. The good news was I didn't have to ride another mile to find them. Bad news was I had no idea where in town they were, and they could be standing in the crowd waiting to gun me down. Focusing on Larry Brown, I could not afford taking a chance to look at the townsfolk hoping to catch a glimpse of Merna and Loveless. Fate and destiny were now in control of what was about to happen, and the outcome was yet to be determined. Speaking in a clear and confident voice, "Randy Vaughn told me in Dighton, Kansas and Alan Wells confirmed it in the small burg of Sheridan, Colorado right before I killed each of them. It would seem LB that the Redlegs of Kansas are a vanishing breed. You and the others need to pay the ultimate price for trying to murder me and for murdering my only true friend in the world Sandy."

Speaking louder so all those on the boardwalk could hear me, "This man is named Larry Brown also known as LB the gunfighter. He is a Kansas Redleg and along with his Captain John Merna and another man known as John Loveless, they have been murdering ex-confederate soldiers from Missouri to the Rocky

Mountains in some sort of twisted revenge for the Civil War! They also butchered a family named O'Rourke just outside of Dighton, Kansas! He and the others killed my best friend in Kansas and they tried to kill me. On this day I, McCall Patton will have my justice!"

LB's face showed bitterness and anger as I spoke to the crowd and he had enough of my speech to the crowd and with lightning speed, he drew his firearm. Larry Brown was the fastest gun I had ever seen as he had matched my own speed with my Colt. We both fired at the same time. Sometimes you live to fight another day not by skill, but by being luckier. I was luckier on this day. His bullet caught me low and far to the right piercing my side through and through. None of my vitals were hit. My first bullet caught him in the middle of his chest, stopping his heart at once. As Larry Brown was falling and dying is when my second bullet caught him in his disbelieving right eye, creating a red mist of blood that hung in the air for several seconds. The gunfighter known as LB was surely enough dead when he collapsed into the dirt and dust on the streets of Como.

As soon as I realized LB was down for good is when I could feel the pain of being shot. Reaching with my left hand, I gingerly touched my wound and I could feel the moistness of my blood. Knowing I was not out of danger, since according to what Larry Brown had said both Captain Merna and John Loveless were in town, I put my pain and the wound I had received in the back of my mind. I quickly reloaded two shells into my pistol and started looking into the crowd on both sides of the street for the telltale sign of the red leggings of my enemy. I heard him first as he bolted for his horse, and then I saw the red leggings and the scabbard at his side carrying his saber. Captain John Merna looked the same with his short dark brown hair, and his beard of the same color had a couple of weeks' worth of growth. Seeing the outlaw Redleg Captain as he was fleeing from me told me he was in truth a coward of the highest order, and I spun and ran to the hitching post for Sammy.

The crowd of onlookers were confused as hell as they started to realize the gunfight that they had just watched did not end in the death of Larry Brown and was far from being over as they also realized that John Merna and I were heading for our horses on opposite sides of town.

As fast as it was possible, I untied Sammy from the hitching post and then without any care for my wound, I stepped into the stirrup and planted my butt hard in the saddle pulling Sammy firmly around into the same direction of the fleeing Redleg.

Just as I had gotten Sammy pointed in the right direction to chase after Merna, he had reached his horse as well. His mare was startled by the gunshots and the fast changing events of the day and went to bucking as Merna grabbed her reins and tried to get control of her to no avail. Holstering my Colt as fast as I could and pulling my Winchester with almost the same motion from the scabbard on the side of Sammy, I levered a shell into the firing chamber. Taking aim, I held my finger until Captain Merna's horse stopped bucking, for I wanted the best possible shot at the murderer of Sandy and the O'Rourkes.

In the excitement of the gunfight and of seeing Merna flee from the fight, I had forgotten all about the other renegade Redleg John Loveless. Out of the corner of my eye, I saw a pair of red leggings step up to the front edge of the boardwalk on my right and I glanced that way. The man wearing those red leggings was a man older than Captain Merna with shoulder length white as snow hair that matched his goatee and weighed about 150 pounds. John Loveless was known for his sharpshooting ability in the Civil War, and he had his Winchester pointed in my direction.

His first shot missed by a hair and skidded along the left side of my noggin leaving a nasty quarter inch furrow. His second shot followed so close to the first one that both shots sounded as one hit me high on the meaty part above my left shoulder.

Sammy reared up in panic as I was being shot to pieces on top of her which saved my life for the moment, but not hers. Loveless' next two shots hit my beloved horse solidly on the right side of her neck. My only thought at that moment was the bastard shot my horse.

What happened next I will always say was guided by the ghost of Sandy. Sandy had always been the marksman when it came to rifles - but me not so much. As Sammy was buckling on her way down to meet the ground, I was able to get one shot off in the direction of the Redleg Loveless. The only explanation I have is that Sandy somehow aimed and pulled the trigger because the bullet was true to its course and without hitting anyone else standing in the crowd behind or next to him hit Loveless in the throat killing him where he stood.

After the shot that killed Loveless, Sammy had fallen in such a manner that my left leg that was still in the stirrup was caught underneath her and I was pinned to the ground where we had both fallen. My Winchester during the fall had been pitched even further left and out of my reach.

I tried to comfort Sammy by stroking her neck as she tried to look at me, not with panic, but with the acceptance of her own impending death. We both knew at that moment Sammy was not just my horse - she was more kin to me than those back home. I loved her and if she could have seen me she would have seen that there was love in the tears in my eyes. Sammy's breathing became more labored and she shuddered twice before she breathed her last breath and died.

The shooting scrape with Loveless and the death of Sammy happened so quickly I could not deal with the leader of the Redlegs Captain John Merna, but I had not forgotten him and it would seem he had not forgotten me. I was still pinned under Sammy, and Merna had obviously gotten control of his horse and was now sitting in the saddle on top of her not more than forty feet away, looking at me with all the hatred he could muster that he had in his black heart. Reaching out, I tried to grab my Winchester, but it was a good four feet beyond where I could reach. Merna, realizing I was still trapped under the weight of Sammy, slowly dismounted and pulled his saber almost silently from its scabbard.

As I was still struggling to free myself, Captain John Merna was enjoying this moment and he was going to savor it for as long as he could. He brought his saber up to his face as if he wanted to admire the glint from its metal or the sharpness of his blade. And he spoke in a clear unhurried voice, "I have to say Patton, you are one hard man to kill. I don't even care how you survived our last encounter. The only thing I care about is how it is going to feel when I look into your eyes when I run my cold steel through your body!"

Captain John Merna, outlaw Redleg, could not put the Civil War behind him and the butcher of so many people, including Keegan's folks and my best friend Sandy, took three steps closer as he raised his saber as I lay pinned under Sammy on my left side. I stopped him cold in his tracks with what I said, "Hey dumbass! You forgot one small detail! I still have my Colt!"

Pulling my Colt from my holster on my right side was awkward and slower than I wanted since I was pinned to the ground, but it didn't matter much since Captain Merna had brought a saber to a gunfight.

EPILOGUE

The next six months after my showdown with Captain John Merna, John Loveless, and the gunfighter Larry Brown in Como went by in a whirlwind fashion. The Sheriff in Como contacted the Lewis brothers the law in Dighton, Kansas as well as their counterpart Sheriff Daniel Basquez in Sheridan, Colorado who all vouched that my part of the story was true. Also, with all the statements from the townsfolk that had witnessed the whole deadly affair - in the eyes of the law, it was decided that the deaths of the outlaw Redlegs were justifiable and righteous and no charges were filed.

My encounter with Merna and the others was the biggest gun battle in some time in Colorado on par with some other famous Colorado gunfighters' battles such as those of Lucas Eldridge, Chance Bondurant, and Matt Lee. Every newspaper in the country tried to track me down for an interview that I was not willing to give. My reputation as a gunfighter was something I never wanted nor needed. Most of the newspapers wrote their stories anyway without any quotes from me. And so on this date I have yet to read any of their accounts of what happened in Como - nor do I care to do so.

The town of Como sold the horses and saddles of Merna, Loveless, and Brown to pay for their burial at the Como Cemetery, the very same graveyard I passed as I rode into town the morning of the shootout. When I left Como, I rode out to the cemetery and after speaking to the man tending to the grounds there, it would seem that the graves of Merna, Loveless, and Brown would forever go unmarked, which seemed fitting to me.

My wounds, although severe, were not life threatening and after about a week after I was cleared of all charges, I headed back over Boreas Pass, Loveland Pass, and ventured back up the "Oh My God" road to be home with Keegan, Risa, and Hugo. I wish you could have seen the tears and smiles the day I got back. It feels good to love and be wanted and it is good to love as well. Not a day goes by that I do not tell the girls in my life how much they mean to me and how much I love them. I think that is important. Risa and I have planned our wedding next autumn which is both of our favorite time of year. Keegan is excelling in her school work and doing well.

Horse returned safely back to Blackhawk with me and in time overcame her grief in losing her friend Sammy. After purchasing a new horse, I gave Horse to Keegan. Keegan and Horse are now inseparable.

A week after my return to Blackhawk and my new family, Hugo the man killer mutt finally was able to get that hole chewed all the way through the end of my boot so it is now leaking water. Hugo now has a used set of boots sitting on the front porch for him to chew whenever he has an inkling to do so.

Sandy's ashes and bones were laid to rest in a quiet ceremony at the Central City cemetery a mile from Risa, Keegan, Hugo, and my home in Blackhawk. I thought about taking his remains back to Little Dixie, but discarded that idea since in truth, I was his only family and I would have missed not visiting his grave. Before we buried what was left of my best friend, I pondered for a spell what to have written on his tombstone and after the debate with myself, it ended up being a simple affair that stated,

Ron "Sandy" Sands

THE KEEGAN TRAIL

A Simple Man
He Was My Friend
I Will Miss Him
I loved Him

I assume you are wondering about the loot from the Reynolds' gang. Even though John Merna was a cutthroat murdering bastard, he was anything but stupid. He and the others had found the hiding place where the Reynolds' gang had stashed their loot when so many others down through the years could not. Where was it hidden? I have not a clue since I killed all those that had known. Where is the treasure now? That is the ironic thing about this story; after the folks in Como sold off the horses and saddles of Merna, Loveless, and Brown so they could pay for their burials and any expenses that the town had incurred, they gave me the rest of their belongings to use or sell to help offset any wrong done to me or those that I loved. In those belongings was a very heavy duffel bag that contained another bag wrapped in oilskin. Underneath that oilskin was $32,000 of currency and gold dust and nuggets. How is it ironic you might ask? That money was stolen to help fund the Confederacy in the quest to secede from the Union. After being hidden it was finally found by a man who fought for the Union and hated anything that was gray that reminded him of the Confederacy. I find it ironic it ended up with a former Confederate soldier.

During this story of everything that made up the telling of the tale of "The Keegan Trail," there was only one who survived that even knew about the Reynolds' gang's loot - and that was me. I take that back; there was another who might have guessed and that would be the old prospector named Marty Blake, who was so helpful to Keegan and myself while on the trail. Marty was the only person that I knew that suffered any loss to the Reynolds' gang so many years ago when they robbed him of $300 in gold dust. Knowing this I set up a bank account in Blackhawk and deposited $5000 in his name and then sent telegrams all over Colorado to every mining town I could think of in hopes of reaching him to tell him about the money set aside for him. I did this all anonymously of course. I am happy to report as of yesterday, Marty came to Blackhawk and picked up his money.

You might also ask, "Do I feel guilty in keeping the remaining $27,000 for myself and my family?" The answer to that is - not one damn bit!

AUTHOR'S NOTE

If you, the reader, has made it this far, that means you have finished reading my book "The Keegan Trail," and I would just like to take a line or two to thank you for purchasing my work, and I hope you enjoyed the adventures of Mac and Keegan.

It is my hope you have found Kansas and Colorado to be full of living and breathing characters such as McCall, Keegan, Hugo, and Risa. I love Colorado and Kansas and everything they have to offer.

I also wanted to assure you that the Kansas and Colorado geography, along the path my heroes McCall "Mac" Patton and Keegan Doreen O'Rourke traveled through the plains of Kansas and Colorado as well as the Rocky Mountains, does in fact exist - every mountain, mountain range, mountain pass, mining camp, river, creek, and all the towns in Kansas and Colorado.

I took some liberty in using the modern names in some cases or the more historical names if I thought it fit the story better. I wanted folks who were locals or familiar with these Colorado and Kansas areas mentioned in the book to be able to follow along on Mac's and Keegan's adventure more easily in their mind and to be able to travel if they wanted to on horseback, foot, or even by car or 4 wheel drive the same path of Mac in his quest for justice for his friend Sandy.

ABOUT THE AUTHOR

Kurt James was born and raised in the foothills of the Colorado Rocky Mountains. With family roots in western Kansas and having lived in South Dakota for 20 years, Kurt James naturally has become an old western and nature enthusiast. Over the years Kurt James has become one of Colorado's prominent nature photographers through his brand name of Midnight Wind Photography. Along with being a member of Western Writers of America, his poetry has been featured in the Denver Post, PM Magazine and on 9NEWS in Denver, Colorado. Kurt James' poetry is also featured at Creative Exiles, a collection of some of the finest poets on the web. Kurt James Reifschneider is also a feature writer for Hubpages with the articles focused on Colorado history, ghost towns, outlaws, and poetry. Inspired at a young age by writers such as Jack London, Louis L'amour and Max Brand, Kurt has formed his natural ability as a story teller. "The Keegan Trail" is Kurt James fourth novel, but not the last novel of the western frontier of the wild and dangerous Colorado Rocky Mountains. Kurt James is currently working on his next Rocky Mountain adventure called "The Daunting" set in the year 1976.

Follow Kurt James on Facebook, Twitter, and his author page on Amazon.

www.ingramcontent.com/pod-product-compliance
Lightning Source LLC
Chambersburg PA
CBHW060211180626
46813CB00007B/2778